TIME

JIM ABLE OFFWORLD
BOOK 3

ED CHARLTON

Jim Able Offworld: Time

Originally published in four episodes: *Sonloi, Shed, Sea, and Shock*

Revised and updated 2025

ISBN: 978-1-935751-65-6

Ebook 978-1-935751-72-4

Subscribe to Ed's monthly newsletter!
edcharlton.com
Free eBook for new subscribers.

Books in the **Jim Able Offworld** trilogy

Beauty Rising, Larc Ascending, Time

Books in the **Assassin** trilogy

Book One, Book Two, Book Three

Books in **The Aleronde Trilogy**

The Problem with Uncle Teddy's Memoir, Saint John's Ambulatory, Aleronde the Great

and

Hoyle Station

CONTENTS

PREVIOUSLY

Previously in Jim Able Offworld

Jim, with his chameleon-skinned boss Tella, has completed a mission to the planets of the Tanna system, successfully preventing an interplanetary war.

The intelligence needed for the mission came from the galaxy's premier spacecraft manufacturer, the Praestans Rapax. In gratitude for Jim's work, they have presented him with a custom-built spacecraft for his personal use.

Knowing that keeping such a gift would cause trouble in the ultraparanoid world of the External Intelligence Agency, Jim has arranged with his brother Matt to berth the ship at Europa Biological Monitoring Station, a space station where Matt has complete control.

Meanwhile, elsewhere...

JIM ABLE OFFWORLD

ED CHARLTON

AUTHOR OF "THE ALERONDE TRILOGY"

01 ALFIE

All called her "The Artist." Her apartment on station Sonloi-AC smelled of paint. As she walked calmly down the utilitarian pastel corridors, her long brightly stained smock gave off a hint of strong chemicals, history, and anarchy. Her hair, itself of several striking colors, was almost to her waist. Her face was never painted. Her smile was natural, as were the wrinkles framing the sparkle in her welcoming eyes.

Her name was Alpha, though few knew it. All called her "The Artist," but she was addressed as Alfie.

"So, Alfie, darling! How are you this morning?"

Alfie looked sideways at her companion. "Oh, for a morning to be something in, Jayde!"

Jayde laughed, "Sorry! I've been down there for three months. You soon slip into it again."

Alfie shook her head and poured coffee from a carafe.

The table in the café boasted one of the finest views on Sonloi-AC. The planet Sonloi—or Pec Sonloi, to be precise—shone in full sunlight, filling the window.

Alfie sipped her drink and said, "It's funny, I've always thought of it as 'over there,' you know? 'Across,' perhaps. Not really up or down."

"They think of us as 'up there.' Jayde said. "And"—she paused—"that's what we need to talk about."

Alfie frowned. "Oh dear, that sounds ominous. You mean we have to 'talk about' something? I thought we were getting together to chat."

Jayde, sitting up straighter, whispered, "Sorry!" and drank some coffee.

Alfie asked, "How is young Yarl doing? Settling in?"

Jayde nodded. "Yes, very easily. You were right; he has a great attitude. I suspect he listens a little too well and is picking up on things he maybe shouldn't, but his work is impeccable."

Alfie smiled. "I am glad. I really wasn't sure where he was headed." Her gaze drifted out to the planet. "I painted him, you know." Jayde nodded, watching her friend's face. "And I worried when he disappeared off on his second walkabout."

"It doesn't seem to have done him any harm. Not particularly uncommon for them, is it? I think it's nice that young Meoena are given the room to go and find themselves."

Alfie nodded and replied wistfully, "I wish my kids would. Probably too late now!"

They both laughed and continued chatting until Alfie finally said, "Alright, Station Administrator, about what must we talk?"

Jayde sighed. "How much do you follow Meoenan politics?"

"Not at all."

"You might need to."

"Ugh!"

"There's a new face. A bit of a rabble-rouser. Lert Carn."

Alfie nodded. "Heard the name."

"He's coming up here. Somehow he's got permission to run an office with staff and to use the station's facilities."

Alfie paused, looked Jayde in the eye, and suggested, "Use them to rouse his rabble?"

"That's our fear. It's all been done with the proper paperwork and made to seem entirely reasonable. But I, for one, don't trust him."

"What harm do you think he can do?"

"He and his friends want Meoena to"—Jayde raised her hands, making air quotes—"'do more for themselves,' to 'realize their full potential,' to be 'free of foreign influences.'"

"Oh shit!" said Alfie quietly.

"Yeah, where have we heard all that before?"

Alfie shook her head. "They don't want to do more for themselves! It's not their way. Their culture has completely embraced employing aliens."

"But Lert preaches they are being oppressed by aliens. He has the whole victim mentality down pat. And he wants the kids taught practical skills instead of philosophy, so they can industrialize and build a shiny new...something."

Alfie nodded. "That's how they always dress it up. First, make them feel aggrieved, then stop teaching them how to think. Finally, stop teaching them how politics and government work. Keep them ignorant, poor, and docile."

"He wants your apartment."

Alfie put down her cup with a thud.

Jayde continued, "Sorry. I'll do my best."

"I was given use of the rooms in perpetuity after Lem's death! Can they undo that?"

"He's trying."

Alfie reached out; her pale hand, stained with blue and green paint, touched Jayde's brown arm. "Okay, Jayde. I officially don't like him."

Jayde laughed lightly. "Agreed. The arrangement for your rooms came out of deep appreciation from the Meoena to both The Caretaker and The Artist. That appreciation he can't unmake. But he can promote the idea that aliens like us are lording it over them, that we're taking what's theirs and keeping secrets from them for our own gain."

Alfie snorted.

Jayde continued, "You know there are those who will fall for it."

Alfie was silent, staring at the bright white, blue, green, brown wonder of the planet. Finally, she said, "If you can't stop him, what will happen?"

"Different rooms...I hope."

"I have a pipeline of portraits. They keep coming over to sit and get their souvenirs."

"Alfie, do not dismiss your work that way. No Meoenan I've ever spoken to thinks of your portraits as souvenirs. They treat them very seriously. And your portraits are wonderful!"

Alfie nodded but didn't reply.

Jayde continued, "Worst case scenario: we're all out of here, and the Meoena take over all admin and maintenance."

Alfie shook her head. "If he had one, Lem would be turning in his grave. It'd be a disaster!"

"Agreed. I'm doing my best to avoid it."

Alfie joined her palms together and bowed to her companion. "Thanks for letting me know."

Jayde frowned. "Of course! You and your family are part of this station. I'm just a newcomer here. And he's got the fight of his life on his hands...He just doesn't know it yet."

As Jayde started to get up, Alfie said, "Perhaps I should try and get him to sit for a painting? I could get to see what kind of Meoenan he is."

Jayde stood and put her hand lightly on Alfie's shoulder. "If there's any poking bears with sticks—or brushes—to be done, let me do it. Keep your head down and stay out of trouble."

Alfie looked up and smiled. "Since when?"

▭

Station Sonloi-AC had no fixed morning or evening. Internally, its inhabitants and visitors moved from shift to shift. Externally, the whole station moved slowly through its own cycles. It danced around the planet, the three moons, and the other—newer—stations. For much of the Sonloi year, it graced the planet's night sky and then passed into months of watching the daylight. Year by year, it partnered with the other dancers but—like its artist resident—always keeping its own schedule, hearing its own music, and marking its own time.

Humans built it. The Meoena of Pec Sonloi were Earth's first contact with an interplanetary peer, forever the first alien race to make serious and lasting mutual contact with Earth. The station—a symbol of harmonious partnership and trust between two species—became the springboard for many other collaborations.

One of the chief engineers in the construction, Alfie's husband Lemuel, stayed on through the early trials, the opening, and the first few years of operation. To his recurrent surprise, he and his wife never left. In the Meoenan Melu dialect, "Lem" meant janitor, or custodian, or caretaker. And so, he became the institution and the local legend known as The Caretaker.

The Meoena, generally, thought of the humans as clever engineers, makers of tools, and deliverers of projects both within budget and on time.

Humans, generally, thought of the Meoena as odd: presenting a quiet, philosophical demeanor; talking long and eloquently of what they wanted to achieve; and ultimately doing very little. They had modest industry, no space fleet, only a minimum of economic structures. What they boasted of most were their culture and things they had engaged others to do for them.

Meoena and humans, generally, got on well.

▭

Half a year came and went after Jayde told The Artist the news. Nothing had happened. Nothing had come of Lert Carn's office. The Artist was still in residence.

Her current subject was a young Meoenan named Huilend Girr and known as Huil. She guessed he was past his adolescence and perhaps had already gone on some kind of walkabout or spiritual search. But she could also tell his search remained unfinished.

The Artist talked as she sketched and talked as she painted. She also talked as she thought. Not all her subjects appreciated her consistency. Huil was worse than most, answering in monosyllables of Standard mixed with muttering in his own tongue.

"So, Huil," she asked as she drew his left eye again, out on its own, in the corner of her board, "Do you know much about Lert Carn? I hear he's a popular figure nowadays."

Huil fixed his otherwise wandering gaze on her face. Her pencil flew in tight stabs against the board as he answered.

"We know of him, yes. I have not met him...nor wish to." He looked away.

"Look up, look up!" she encouraged.

"I hope he has not disturbed you in your life here."

Her hand stopped. "Well, no. I am...undisturbed. Thank you."

Huil nodded—a gesture all Meoena learned to make when addressing humans.

She finished sketching his eye and smiled to herself. The Meoenan eye, twice as large as a human's, caught reflections in its semitransparent fluids that fascinated her. There was a hint of relentlessness in their looking. She wished she were more skilled in capturing that outward search, the inner search, the unexpressed longing she saw again and again within those eyes.

She straightened up and firmly said, "How do you know about all that? The business with Carn."

Huil's pale blue face flushed with traces of green, and his eyes once more fixated on the floor.

"Simple enough question, dear," she prompted.

Huil said slowly, "I don't think I should talk of it. You are a proud person. You have your ways and do your work yourself, not asking others for help. Meoena prefer to ask. We prefer our work to be together. But we respect your...space."

"Me? Proud?"

Huil nodded deliberately. "Yes, and rightly so!"

She pulled her smock around her and brought a small stool to seat herself in front of the youth.

"Huil, I don't understand. Thank you for the compliment, but I don't understand how what you say connects with Lert Carn. Please, explain it to me."

She found his expression fascinating to watch; he seemed quite lost for words. "Is it a secret?" she asked quietly.

Huil nodded carefully.

"Well, that's nice. If I promise not to tell anyone else, will that help?"

He nodded again.

"I promise. Now tell me."

Huil reached out tentatively and took her hands in his. The light blue Meoenan skin always felt warmer than a human's. Huil's hands were hot.

"You are The Artist. We come to have you paint us. Your skill is beyond anything we can do ourselves. Your art is so precious to us. You show us...ourselves."

"Yes, dear."

"When word came that someone might make your life other than it is or that perhaps we may not come to sit here with you as I am fortunate to do, we decided."

"You decided what?"

"We...intervened."

Alfie blinked. "Who is 'we'?"

Huil looked at her face and then looked away. "Those who care for you. Those who appreciate what you do, those who remember you and The Caretaker from the time of the station's construction."

"Oh!" Alfie felt a small tear forming. "I see. Thank you."

"I have spoken of things I should not."

Alfie shook her head. "No! It's okay. To know that I have friends is good news to hear. Thank you, dear. It's quite...wonderful actually! Very nice to know."

They looked directly at each other, and Alfie smiled again to encourage him. "Now, I have finished my preliminary sketches. I don't need you to come back for...perhaps two days. Will you return home or will you stay on station?"

"I must stay. I will find friends to spend the time with."

"Very good!"

As Huil was almost out of the apartment door, Alfie was struck by a thought. "Huil? When you say you 'intervened,' I hope you didn't put yourselves in any danger."

Again, his eyes were everywhere but on her. "I think you know we are careful in all we do. There is much in Meoenan philosophy that shields us from performing actions that might be rash or precipitate an unexpected consequence."

Alfie replied, "Ah...I see. Then continue to be careful, please. You are all precious to me as well. That I have a home here, among you, is a wonderful blessing I am constantly grateful for."

Huil nodded and backed out of the apartment.

02 JIM

Jim Able sat alone in his ship's command seat. All was quiet. He sighed and said aloud, "Raeda! Call Tella."

His ship replied, "Calling Tella. Please wait."

All was quiet again.

The ship said, "Your call cannot be placed at this time."

"Hmm. Call Matt."

"Calling Dr. Matthew Able. Please wait."

Soon the ship said, "Dr. Able is not taking calls. His calendar shows him attending a biological sciences conference on Harsak Station. Do you wish to contact the conference administrators?"

"No. No need."

Jim sighed. He looked down the central corridor to the airlock that had led for the last few weeks—and for the foreseeable future—to his brother's domain, The Europa Biological Monitoring Station. Matt had recently renewed his prohibition on Jim entering it.

"Raeda! I'm going to take a nap. Call me if anything happens."

"Acknowledged."

Jim walked up the ramp to the right of the corridor to the upper level of his ship and into his personal module. Looking at the mess around him, Jim sighed.

I should clear up one day.

Unable to nap, Jim wondered again what he was doing with his life. *Working for EIA isn't going to be a career. Tella got me out of a jam, but it's only a step up.*

The reality of his situation weighed upon him. *Income is good. I can't do anything to jeopardize it.*

The ship interrupted. "Incoming message from the Office of External Affairs, Sol Earth Luna."

"What? Who?"

"Captain Anne Brewer of the OEA. Tactical Response Unit."

Blinking and fully awake, Jim jumped up. With a smile he said, "I'll take it at the seat."

"Jim! Good to see you!"

"Anne-with-an-E! Wonderful to see you! It's been a while. How are you? How are things?"

She laughed. "Fine, Jim, just fine."

Anne's face filled the screen. Her smile and laugh were just as Jim remembered. "Where are you, Jim? Is that some kind of ship?"

"Home! Do you like it?" He gestured to encompass the ship. "I've acquired mobile lodgings."

"Congratulations! That command seat suits you! Does that explain why I couldn't find you at the Office of External Affairs?"

"Ah...yes. I had to move on. I'm officially EIA now."

Anne swore. "Really? What the hell are you doing with them? I thought that was the last place you'd go!"

Jim nodded. "Yeah, well. I got fired. Finally broke free from all the crap with Liz."

Anne shook her head. "So, maybe I can't talk to you then."

"This isn't just social?" Jim shrugged. "I don't see why we can't talk. What have you got?"

"I was hoping to have an excuse to call you before, but now something's come up, and I thought..."

"What 'something'?"

"Jack Katrigg."

Jim started to reply but stopped.

"See what I mean?" she asked. "Is he still of any interest to you, now you've become a super spy?"

Jim pursed his lips and thought of how to reply. "Well, I haven't forgotten him. I don't have any instructions not to talk about him. Is he back?"

"Popped up at a hotel in Hon Hen Flereat. Ever been?"

Jim shook his head. "Er, no. Not my thing."

"Right. He was arrested for causing trouble in the foyer of The Golden Lasso Hotel. It's one of the cheap ones."

"Okay." Jim frowned. "Two things. What sort of trouble? Why was he there?"

"I'll send the hotel camera footage. My guess is bad recreational substances. He's totally out of it."

Jim shook his head. "No. Not him. Too professional for that."

"He was arrested, sobered up, and released. As to question two...That's all I've got."

"After all this time. I thought you'd do better than that." He smiled.

"Up yours! I've been keeping an eye open for you in case he showed up. Sorry this isn't any more useful."

Jim said, "No, it's useful. Thanks! I go through phases of resigning myself to his trail having gone cold. And then he lurches out of the mist again. Raeda, receive data transmission from this source and store with my confidential files."

"Acknowledged."

Anne snorted. "A voice activation system, Jim? Really?"

"It's a pain in the ass, but it gives me someone to talk to. Any luck with the mines Katrigg left in orbit when he left Ch'Garratt?"

"Ah...well, yes. But if you're not OEA. anymore, I'll be hung out to dry sending that as well, wouldn't I?"

"Shit! We'll have to get together somewhere we can talk privately."

She smiled. "Looking forward to it. Transmission's complete."

The ship intoned, "Data received and stored as specified."

"It really is great to see you!" Jim said. "How did you find me?"

"EBMS has a record of you. I called the admin office. It wasn't hard."

"Great! My boss hasn't managed to contact me recently."

"Who is that now? Anyone I know?"

"Tella, the Neraffan. I'd worked with him before. He found a place for me."

"Nice."

Jim could see her working out what to say next.

"Better go, Jim. We'll talk again soon."

"Sure. Thanks for the tip. Looks like I'll hold my nose and go to Flereat."

With a mischievous smile, she said, "Enjoy!" and ended the call.

"Shit!" Jim said.

The ship said, "Please restate query."

"Shut up."

03 ALFIE

The Institute for Art had never invited her before. Yet, in her hand, she held a paper with a formal seal and signed by the commissioner.

The Institute for Art,
its staff, and patrons
request the presence of
The Artist of Sonloi-AC
at a dinner in her honor.

Well, I'm not going.

▭

In the café, Jayde sighed. "Don't cause me another—unnecessary—headache. Go! Have fun. At least the food will be good."
Alfie shook her head.
"For goodness' sake! Why the hell not?"
"Because."

"Alfie...?"

The Artist said quietly, "It doesn't seem right."

"What do you mean? It's about damn time they honored you properly!"

She nodded. "True as that may be, why now?" She turned her face to her friend's and repeated, "Why now?"

"I—I don't know...specifically."

Alfie shook her head again. "Not right. I'm old, yes. I'm cranky, yes. I'm suspicious...but that doesn't mean I'm wrong. There's something fishy."

"Perhaps it's your friends who are behind it?"

Alfie shook her head once more. "I asked. They are surprised too."

"Ah," Jayde said, frowning and placing both hands carefully on the table. "I didn't know that. That makes a difference."

"So where is it coming from?"

Jayde grinned. "Only one way to find out!"

▭

The shuttle from Sonloi-AC was small but well apportioned. The uniformed crew was quiet and courteous, like all Meoenan officials.

Jayde, having both promised to come along and dressed to kill, had been called away at the last moment.

I knew it. This is such a setup, Alfie thought. *Oh, well...*

The Artist had also dressed for the occasion. She wore a black trouser suit with a wide scarlet waistband. She had dyed her hair afresh: Meoenan pale blue on the left, Earth green on the right, scarlet through the middle.

To Alfie, Sonloi barely changed as her shuttle flew across toward it. But, slowly, the nightside of the planet disappeared into the blackness until the sweeping view of the lights of Tuanomena, the capital, became all she could see.

She knew where the Institute for Art was, but the shuttle landed in a large empty area. One smart black unmarked vehicle waited for its passenger.

"Is that the commissioner come to greet me?" Alfie asked aloud.

"No, Madam. The driver will take you to your destination."

"Well...I'm sure that'll be nice."

After many minutes, the vehicle stopped in an alleyway.

"Where are we?" she asked the driver.

"Meeting another passenger, Madam," he replied.

The Meoenan was breathing hard as she climbed through the door. "Sorry, Madam. So sorry!"

"What is your name and about what are you sorry?"

"I am a doctor, Madam. I am here to anesthetize you, but I'm afraid my experience with humans is somewhat limited."

Alfie smiled sweetly and said, "At least you're honest about it."

The doctor held up a small spray bottle and squirted Alfie in the face.

Alfie rolled her eyes and looked down her nose at the doctor.

They both waited.

"Well," said Alfie, "that didn't..."

04 JIM AND DAVEY

Tella still couldn't be reached. Jim was beginning to worry. He was supposed to report to the office sometime, but Tella hadn't said when. He was supposed to be working, but Tella hadn't come up with a new assignment. Jim hoped some salary was still coming in.

Suddenly, to Jim's surprise, a noise broke the silence.

His ship was docked at a little-used port at the far end of the medical module of EBMS. The docking hatch connected to the airlock at the rear of Jim's craft. The ship's main corridor ran straight from the airlock to the flight room and the front windows.

The sound he heard was a knock on the door—the outer airlock door. It boomed in the corridor. Someone from the station was knocking.

Jim unsealed the airlock and looked through the roundel to the docking area. There was no one to be seen.

The knock came again. He opened the hatch.

A stocky teenage boy stood off to one side of the door. He glanced from the docking area to Jim and nodded to indicate the inside of the ship.

Jim silently held the door open.

The boy was dressed in loose black exercise clothes. His T-shirt showed a vaguely ghoulish design. The boy's hair, Jim noticed, was black and unruly. It was all Jim needed to see.

As he closed the hatch behind his guest, Jim said, "You're Davey?"

The boy nodded. "You Uncle Jim?"

Jim nodded. "Nice to see you again. You've grown some."

The boy grunted and nodded.

Jim smiled and said, "Welcome aboard!" He waved Davey down the corridor. "Come in! I presume your father doesn't know you're here."

"Hell no! I'd catch it!"

Jim nodded and said, "Yeah, well...families are complicated, aren't they?"

"Did the Rapaxans really build this?" Davey asked as he took in all he could see of the ship.

"They did. It's something of a one-off, I think."

"Bloody ugly from the outside! Nice inside though."

Jim smiled quizzically. "Thanks...I think. Can I offer you anything to eat or drink?"

"You aren't allowed on station. Where do get your food from?"

His nephew's bluntness caught Jim a little off guard. "I stocked up at Yugel Wolt Sixty-three last time I was out. Is there a problem with that?"

Davey shook his head. "Mom was asking. No one seemed to know."

"Well, tell her I said 'hello,' and she's welcome to come and ask for herself, if she'd like."

"She can't come. Dad won't let her."

Jim smiled again. "And he won't let you. So, I appreciate your coming.

"Sure."

"How's your brother?"

Davey grunted. "Don't see him much."

"Oh, I thought—"

"Wow!" Davey shouted. "What a great setup! It's so minimal!"

He walked quickly to the main control panels and fell into the command seat. "What kind of armaments do you have?"

Jim laughed. "I'm not entirely sure. But I wouldn't tell you anyway."

"Why not? I won't fire anything."

"That's not the point. How old are you, Davey? I've forgotten."

"Sixteen."

"It's been that long? Yeah, that's why not."

"I couldn't believe it when Dad said we couldn't see you."

"Drink?"

Davey shook his head. "No thanks. Does it have voice command functions? I've heard a lot of PR ships do. I'd love to, like, sit in the bath and fly a ship at the same time!"

Jim stood behind the seat and said, "See how this seat is rock solid, like it's made to be part of the floor?"

"Yeah, it doesn't move at all."

"That's so you don't tip out of it when something goes peculiar. It's also specifically designed to make the pilot look impressive. It's *my* seat. Stand up, Davey. Sit over there."

Davey grunted as he pulled himself up.

Jim noted the effort Davey put into moving and commented, "You don't get to work out a lot living on EBMS, I guess."

Davey shrugged. "Mom says I like food too much. Dad says I'm big-boned. Clo—that's my girlfriend—says I'm just fat." He shrugged again. "Who cares?"

Jim shrugged and held up his hands as if to say "Not me."

"Can I ask you a question?"

Jim nodded. "Sure, whatever you like."

"Your friend, the Neraffan. Is it as creepy up close as it is on the security archives?"

Jim sat back and looked Davey up and down without answering. Davey settled himself into a chair at the nearest set of controls.

"Okay, nephew, two questions. One, if your dad didn't let you near enough to see Tella in person, did he really let you watch the security records? Two, why would you think any alien 'creepy'? They are what they are! You get tentacles, slime, eyes on stalks. Sometimes there's more than two legs or two arms. There's beards and bad breath more often than you'd think. So what? Some of the things I've seen up close and personal look like they got assembled in a shipwreck, but they're not creepy! Different, for sure. But your folks like you the way you are. Tella's parents thought it was a beautiful baby too."

Davey looked uncomfortable and glanced around. "But it disappears."

"Yep. Isn't that cool? I ask him to...We recently had to interview a policeman who'd gone rogue, you know what I mean?"

"What'd he do?" Davey interrupted, his eyes flashing.

Jim waved the question away, "Just selling stuff...armaments and so on. Anyway, we had to interview him, so I had Tella strip off and stand by the wall; the guy couldn't see Tella at all. I had the chance to ask the questions and Tella could study the guy's body language, his breathing, where his eyes went. It was brilliant. He had no idea Tella was in the room!"

Davey grunted and said, "Wow! That is...like, neat, I guess..."

"Tell you what," said Jim, smiling, "next time it's here, I'll ask Tella to sneak into your room and surprise you."

A look of horror froze Davey's face.

Jim laughed. "Just kidding, Davey! I wouldn't do that to you...or Tella."

Davey shook his head, smiling reluctantly.

"But now tell me about the records you saw. Have you gotten yourself access to some good stuff?"

Davey hesitated. "Kind of..."

Jim waved him to continue. "Me, you can tell. Your dad isn't someone I'm going to be reporting back to."

"Nothing much, just some of the security feeds. I found them when I was looking into the bio-data from the ocean. They've got the science stuff locked up tight. Took me forever to crack them. But the security feeds are easy. Knuckleheads don't know what they're doing." Davey's eyes wandered around the flight room.

Jim smiled. "Funny that, isn't it? The people who should know better often get lazy when it's their own data."

"You done any hacking, Uncle Jim?"

Jim nodded. "Built my early career on it."

Davey's eyes focused on Jim's face, and he said, "Wow!" quietly.

Jim watched him and said, "But you're wasting your time hacking human systems. The real fun is with the alien ones."

"What do you mean?"

"Look, the same way the differences aren't in what an alien looks like...Well, think of it this way—they all use computers too. Their computers have to talk to ours somehow. All the functions that we expect our machines to perform, theirs have to as well. The fun part is working out what that looks like on their side. What does an 'open *file*' command look like in their code? What does an 'open *fire*' command look like?"

"I never thought of that..."

"And, in most cases, they use code languages that have elements like their spoken languages, but without the redundancies and the emotions...or the humor. Now for that, you need to find comments embedded in the code. Once you know what the function of a system is, then you can go further and get to see something of the mind behind it. Even if you can't always read the notes of its creator, you might see what they name things, where they store information..."

"I thought hacking was just about getting into the actual data, not about, like, how they put it there."

"Pull your chair over, young man." Jim smiled. "Suppose a hotel guest stayed at, say, The Golden Lasso on Hon Hen Flereat. How would you go about interfacing with their systems? The whole resort's run by people from Urgan Trin. They speak a language called Trin-agol, but on most of their computers, you'll see Standard. So what do you do first?"

Davey's eyes widened. "Umm..."

05 TELLA

Tella did not see the call request come in from Jim. The Neraffan was standing motionless against a wall, its skin featureless and the same color as the paint. It watched three EIA agents carefully combing through drawers and cupboards, books and magazines. Each object they picked up, they put back exactly as they found it. They were thorough and professional. Tella was impressed.

The apartment was large enough to allow the team to creep around without bumping into the tall alien, though if they walked by too quickly, they might cause a draft and move the leaves of the nearby houseplant. Tella feared green edges appearing on its skin.

The apartment's absent occupant was Jim Able.

Tella had overheard another agent mention the operation, but not the reason, to search Jim's home. Everyone in the office knew Jim was staying with his brother on EBMS. They would have all the time they wanted.

It had waited, naked of course, outside the apartment and followed the team in. They were nearly finished, and it still had no idea why they were there.

Near the end of the search, an agent pulled a rucksack from beneath an easy chair. He emptied the contents onto a low table and fingered his way through the pile of small items.

Tella saw several devices it did not recognize. One, it thought, was of Rapaxan design.

It let out an involuntary sigh when it saw a red and black commercial data storage capsule. A sigh that almost revealed his presence.

The agent spoke without looking up. "What did you say, Ron?"

Ron replied from the bedroom doorway, "Didn't say anything."

The agent grunted and placed most of the pile back into the pack. He plugged the storage device into a small tablet and watched images play across the screen.

Tella stretched its neck to see them.

Another agent came and looked over the man's shoulder. "Anything?"

"Nope. Vacation pictures, I guess."

"Which planet?"

"No idea. Just this ruin, over and over again."

"Put it back. It's not what we're after."

Tella calmed its breath and waited.

Time dragged for the Neraffan until the search was over—and apparently unsuccessful. It leaned away from the living room wall, stretching away the stiffness from its transparent limbs.

It brought out the backpack once more, retrieved the data capsule, dropped the backpack on the floor, and immediately left Jim's apartment.

06 ALFIE IN PRISON

Alfie woke up on a bed under a blanket, still dressed in her black suit. A small light shone over her head.

She sat up. Three sides of the room were made from thin vertical bars. Outside was darkness.

"Oh dear."

She looked around. The furniture included a large wing chair, a table with a stool beneath it, and drink-making equipment. There was also a toilet, a sink, and an open shower area.

"Well," she said, "I will not be using that! Who went to all this trouble but left the facilities on full display?"

A voice from the darkness outside replied, "I'm sorry. We did our best. Your comfort is a concern for us."

"Well, you should have thought at least to put a screen around the toilet! Really!"

"Again, I'm sorry, but you must be visible at all times."

Alfie sighed to herself and said, "But when you've got to go, you've got to go."

She tossed the blanket up to drape it over her head and body.

When she finished, she washed her hands at the sink, sniffed the soap several times, then turned and stood at the bars.

"Now, Mr. Voyeur, tell me your name and your business."

"My name is of no use to you. My business is to acquire you, keep you safe and unharmed, and—at present—deny you liberty to leave."

"I see. You are my jailer but not my captor. When do I meet your boss?"

"My client will join you shortly. When the time is right."

"Food?"

"As you require it."

"Information?"

"I can provide very little of that."

"I'm sure." She walked to one end of the cage and back to the other. "There's another cage."

"There is."

"For whom?"

No answer came.

"You are Meoenan."

Again, no answer came.

"By your voice, I can tell you're middle-aged and slightly overweight. Your family has done well, and you were taught Standard by good teachers. It's a long while since your walkabout. I'm sorry you have so obviously lost your way."

"If you would prefer to have another watch you, that can be arranged."

"That's interesting."

She looked around at the table and the desk. "I would like a mirror to do my hair."

"I will request it, though I fear it must be a small one."

"I have a lot of hair and it requires looking after."

"Of course."

"Like the soul. Let it go too far and you get into the most dreadful tangles, don't you?"

The voice was silent.

.   .   .

Alfie sat for a while in the wing chair and thought. She assembled what she knew.

The pilot, driver, and doctor are independent actors, working under someone else's direction. This jailer, if he's to be believed, is the same. Hired guns. Whoever provided the soap works—or worked—on station. A lightweight, utilitarian brand, easily transported into orbit but not favored on Sonloi itself. This is a well-planned, probably expensive operation. Not many could put up the money for this.

She called, "Tell me the name of the person behind all this."

"When, or if, my client wishes to be identified, it is not for me to say."

"Very good, not saying male or female. Did I ever paint you?"

She thought she heard a slight gasp but wasn't sure. She received no verbal answer.

Many hours later she asked, "Are we on board a ship?"

"We are."

"Going where?"

Her jailer didn't reply.

She asked, "How long will I be in here?"

"That is uncertain at present."

"Why? What does it depend on?"

"I cannot say."

"Well, then, I shall do my best to make this as dull and irritating for you as it is for me. Bring food."

"Of course."

"I'm vegetarian. I will get deadly sick if you feed me anything from Sonloi's oceans. I'll tell you the rest of my restrictions as we go along. Now run along and cook me large amounts of food. I'm very hungry."

"One hour."

Alfie smiled and sat at the desk to examine and inventory the pencils and paper provided.

07 THE KIDS AND MATT

Clo and Davey huddled in a corner of the station's small library.

"He didn't!" she whispered.

"He did! He downloaded the whole thing to this capsule!"

"Wow! I mean, can you understand it?"

Davey shook his head and glanced nervously around. "Course not! Not yet. But...he said...how he does things. Like, it all seemed to make sense. I've no idea really."

"How can we work on this without your dad getting in the way?"

"Well, he doesn't watch you as closely as he does me. You can go see Uncle Jim more easily than I can."

"Is your uncle...alright? I mean..."

"Yeah, yeah. Totally."

"I'd prefer if you were there though. I always do." She squeezed his arm.

Davey whispered, "Yeah, I know..." and kissed her.

The next day, Jim opened the door to the two of them.

"Aren't you two in school or something?"

"Not now. Not really," Davey said.

"Don't stay so long that you get me into trouble!"

"Promise." Davey nodded vigorously.

"Pleased to meet you." Clo held out her hand.

"And you, Clo. Welcome aboard. Has Davey told you about our little project?"

She nodded. "A little. I don't see how we're going to help if we can't speak Trin-agol or whatever language they speak. I mean, when they are writing in Standard or something, that's easy. But we don't have a manual for how the hotel's system is configured or anything. It's not like we've got a lot to go on. Maybe you can tell us more about it, or can get us access to a test version of the system maybe? Oh, sorry...Am I talking too much?"

Jim blinked. "No, you're fine. Let's start at the beginning with what we've got and then work out what else we might need."

Clo nodded, suddenly shy about saying anything else.

They worked, leaning over printed pages and squinting at screens, for about an hour before another knock came at the airlock.

Jim frowned. "I'm not expecting anyone."

Both teens looked scared.

Jim stood and walked a few steps down the corridor. He gestured to them. "You two, upstairs! Second module on the right. Close the door. Quietly!"

They held hands and hurried up the right-hand slope to the upper level.

Jim opened the airlock door.

"Jim."

"Matt? Good to see you."

"Can I come in?"

Jim smiled. "Of course. Whenever you like."

Matt muttered something Jim didn't catch as he began to walk down the corridor to the front.

"What can I do for you, brother?"

"You've been docked for a while. Just wondering when you're off next."

"You need the berth?"

"No. No, I suppose not. I—I'm used to knowing what's happening on my station, Jim. That's all. Just like to be kept informed."

Jim shrugged. "Not much I can tell you. EIA business is largely secret, and my missions are generally not for public consumption."

"You've been sitting here scratching your backside for fifteen days. I've been to a conference and back again. You haven't moved!"

Jim shook his head.

"Why?" Matt continued, "What the hell are you doing in here?"

Jim started to smile but stopped. "You really want to know?" he said, raising his voice.

Matt glared back at Jim, his face reddening at Jim's tone. "Wouldn't be asking if I didn't!"

"My boss isn't accepting calls. I don't have a mission. I can't find out even if I'm being paid for my downtime. Happy?"

Matt's face softened with surprise.

Jim continued, "You have a nice job here, get paid a salary, and I'm sure it's a whopper. And you're in no danger..."

"What? What are you saying?"

"Nothing. There are dangers in my job that you have no concept of."

"Oh, but wait,"—Matt looked horrified—"if you are in danger, don't go bringing trouble to this station! It was bad enough when that drone showed up. You take your problems elsewhere, hear me?"

Jim bit his tongue and nodded. Then he said, "That's the idea. I work out there, not here. This is a hidey-hole, nothing more. I certainly don't want anyone changing that any more than you do."

Matt struggled to put his thoughts into words. Instead, he sighed and said, "Well. Okay. I'll see you later."

Jim nodded. "Sure, Matt. Anytime."

As his brother turned to leave, Jim glanced up to the upper level checking there was no movement.

"Hey, Matt!"

"Jim?"

"I understand the bit about you not wanting me to disrupt your—and your family's—routines, but I still resent that you don't want me seeing my nephews. Anyway, since you don't want me coming onto the station, can you have the stores send someone to get orders from me and deliver stuff to the door?"

Matt shrugged. "I guess."

"Thanks."

Matt left, and Jim sighed deeply.

He returned to the seat and said quietly, "Raeda! Open the door to module three."

"Module door opening."

Jim called over his shoulder, "He's gone. Time to go, you two!"

After a minute, Davey and Clo ran down the ramp to the lower level.

"Um...everything okay?" Davey asked, a little breathless.

"Sure. Just me and your dad being...us."

"Um...see you later!" Clo mumbled, avoiding eye contact.

Jim escorted them down the corridor, waiting until they were in the airlock before saying, "Get your clothes straight before you go out there."

Without waiting to see how embarrassed they looked, he turned and went back to the flight room.

08 JAYDE

"This is Station Administrator Jayde Duke. I wish to speak to Chief Solma Fiet Recan."

The assistant's voice came over Jayde's desk speakers. "May I ask the topic you wish to address?"

"You know damn well what it's about. I've been given the runaround by your organization for three days. He will speak to me now or the lights are going off up here! Do you understand?"

The assistant did not reply immediately. "Station Administrator, I'm not sure I understand your tone. You seem determined that this call should be some sort of confrontation between yourself and either myself or our chief of police. I am perhaps misinterpreting you. I'm sorry if my fluency with human speech is not meeting the standard required for this occasion."

Jayde laughed coldly, "Ghui, your fluency and your experience in human-Meoenan dialogue is unsurpassed. We both know it. Damn, that's why Solma is making *you* take my calls." She paused. "This station has weathered many problems. There have been true misunderstandings between us in the past. I am telling you this is not like those times. Never before has a dear member of our community been kidnapped by members of yours. This will not stand. Nor will Solma's silence on the matter."

She waited for the reply.

"Perhaps you underestimate how much personal effort our chief is putting into this investigation. I'm sure he does not want to provide you with anything less than definitive information. I urge you to continue to be patient while he works—"

"Are you familiar with a creature from Earth called a 'horse'? I think we have some pictures of them up here."

"No, Madam Administrator, I am not."

"They are legendary because of the volumes of shit they produce. Are you personally in competition with a horse, Ghui? It sure as hell smells like it from where I'm standing."

"That is quite offensive."

"I know. My own fluency with Meoenan dialogue is undergoing an urgent upgrade. I understand well how my insults will embarrass you and your boss when I make them publicly. I want the truth out of you and Solma, not more platitudes. I will not be patient. The Artist could be dead or dying in an alley somewhere while you—and your boss—sit in your offices masturbating." She didn't let him reply. "Let me ask you, Ghui. How bad do you want this to get?"

"I must protest at this! This is unheard of language from our human friends! Why are you treating us in this way?"

"Ghui! Shut up! You are not the victims here. Don't pretend to me that you are. But you do have a crisis on your hands. Solma will speak to me. He will include us in the investigation, and he will do so today!"

"Madam Admin—"

She cut him off.

Sighing, she turned to the three others in her office. The two humans looked red in the face and worried. Yarl, the only Meoenan present, looked implacable and unmoved.

"Well?" she asked.

Phil, her right-hand man, answered, "You did what you said you would. I'm concerned now as to what they will do in return."

Barbara, her office manager, said, "I think you were quite clear."

"Yarl? What did you hear in his voice?" she asked.

The Meoenan closed his eyes, stretched his long blue fingers and relaxed them again. "Fear."

09 JIM

The kids had chosen two entry points into the hotel's systems. They found a guest database with data names they thought might be words.

In the quiet of his ship, Jim said, "Raeda! Cross-reference this list of data names with the language dictionaries. Identify the language. List the possible meanings."

"Acknowledged."

Jim went to take a nap. He was thinking ahead to how he would approach Jack Katrigg—once he found him, of course. How would he make the courier face his crimes?

How well will I have to arm myself?

He was awoken by the ship. "Request completed."

"Show me."

On the main screen in the flight room, Jim read, "Baar."

"Where is the Baar language used?"

"Baar is a common sublanguage related to Standard, Meln-coersal, and Fitt. Its use extends to one-hundred twenty-five trading-related systems."

"Great. Still a haystack."

"Please restate query."

"No, cancel query."

So the hotel is run by someone who speaks Baar rather than Trin-agol. Can't wait for the kids.

Jim studied the hotel's registration system and easily found his way into the guest records. He saw Jack Katrigg's check-in and checkout details.

He ran the video Anne had sent, and the dates matched. He was reluctant to watch the images of Katrigg behaving erratically. Jim didn't want to trigger the memories of Ch'Garratt and the horrors of their previous encounter. Katrigg had been calm and businesslike then—just before he destroyed a space terminal in an attempt to kill Jim.

"Raeda, link to the EIA information system."

"Access codes are required. Please enter the codes at your terminal."

Jim sat and entered his ID and password.

For the next hour, he was completely absorbed trying to persuade the EIA system to let him see the data he wanted.

Eventually, he stopped and stretched. He had no idea of the time of day, no idea if the folks of EBMS were asleep or awake, no idea where the sun was shining on Earth. He felt alone.

However, the EIA had given him a thin thread to pull.

At the time Jim was working for the Office of External Affairs and traveling, for the second time, to Turcanis Major, a small data breach was reported to the EIA by someone in Jim's office.

The intruder hadn't compromised any systems but had accessed a few confidential areas. The investigation had shown no results, except revealing that the originating computer system was a public terminal located at The Golden Lasso Hotel, Flereat.

The date of the hacking attempt matched up with a previous stay at the hotel by Jack Katrigg.

Has he been stalking me, just like I'm trying to follow him? If this hotel is a favorite haunt of his, who are his friends there?

Well, I'm not going. At least, not on my own. He sighed in the stillness of the ship. *Though if Tella's not around, maybe I'll have to.*

Jim wondered for a moment about taking Clo and Davey along just to upset Matt—but only for a moment.

Jim sent a message to Tella, saying what he had found and why he was going. There was no acknowledgment.

━━

Jim spent some time building the flight map to Flereat.

He thought of his contact on Turcanis Major V-I, Madhar Nect. She hadn't believed him when he told her how ships navigate through the galaxy. The workings of the D-switch were still a mystery. Devised by a species with whom contact was difficult, the switches had the capability of transferring a ship from one location to another without any passage of time. Only as he tried to explain it to Madhar did Jim realize how much he took it for granted. D-switches were there before he was born. They had always been there. Without them, the distance between planets would have made the galactic trading culture impossible and his life far duller. As he described to Madhar, "It's the galaxy's dark little secret. No one knows how it works."

The flight plan consisted of a long list of coordinates, separated by the distance his sensors could scan to ensure he would safely appear in empty space. Short hops took no time, but in between each jump, the navigation system loaded the next coordinates. That activity—only a fraction of a second for each jump—mounted up on long trips.

The journey may have taken a day and a half, but Jim wasn't counting. The time passed quietly, much as it did while docked at EBMS.

━━

While he waited for local traffic to clear, Jim got his first sight of Flereat.

Jim was well aware of the place by reputation. Properly called Hon Hen Flereat, it ranked at the lower end of galactic culture. Its entertainment verged on the crude. Its many vendors specialized in the gross, the tacky, or both.

"Station" was too small a word for what he saw. A central ring and dome, though fashionable for trading stations long ago, would not suffice for "The Galaxy's Favorite Destination." It boasted twenty-five domes with seven more under construction. Each dome flashed with neon signs, bright beacons, and the hint of vast crowds moving inside. Huge lengths of cargo-tubing flexed between each habitation area and the next, shooting tourists at dangerously high speeds to their next piece of expensive entertainment.

Below the bustle of the station hung the planet Hen—empty save for algae flats, floating on toxic oceans, awaiting better days. The distant star, Hon, cast a golden Machiavellian glow upon planet and station alike.

The main traffic approached the enormous facility from only one direction. Jim was approaching from another, his flight being "business" not "pleasure."

The original domes had been completed many years before, with new ones being built retro style to match. Beneath the domes, out of sight of the habitation windows, modern enameled boxes, built to interlock, encrusted the station's nether regions. Waves of construction had covered the surfaces. Then, these had been subsumed by subsequent encroaching modules until all were part of a lopsided, anarchic conglomeration that Jim found endearingly impractical. He thought he'd seen more orderly garbage dumps.

He changed into a nondescript flight suit; he could pass for a technician or a pilot for hire.

Eventually, Traffic Control sent his instructions. Being a low-priority visitor, he was forced to dock at the end of a long and partly finished stalk of cargo bays, workshops, and empty bays still waiting for their occupants to attach their generic modules to the skeletal frameworks.

The walk was long and, in parts, dangerous. Near one of the empty bays, Jim could feel that the air pressure was lower than it had been in the previous section.

Is that a leak? No, just imagination. They would've fixed an actual leak, wouldn't they?

He called the ship. "Raeda! If I don't come back within two days, undock and return to EBMS under emergency protocols."

In The Golden Lasso, he found the public terminal used to hack the OEA inside a café and bar area. The bar boasted "The Best Earth Beer on Flereat!" Jim was curious.

He watched the other people in the bar while he tested the bar's claim. He saw a variety of species coming and going. Few, though, used the public terminals.

He asked a fellow drinker, "Those terminals there, are they safe to use?"

The stranger, short, fat, and ape-like, shook his head. "More viruses than the whores." He laughed, a little too loud for Jim's liking.

"Guessed as much."

The alien looked him over, put down his half-finished drink, and left.

"Something I said?"

Several drinks later, Jim walked through a shopping alley leading to the Dome of the People, the iconic tourist site. Behind the curtains and flags, he could see the structure of the white enameled boxes brought into the dome to provide cheap and easily rearranged infrastructure. The facades were different, but the shops—and, in large part, the merchandise—were all the same. The roof of the alley, he guessed, mirrored the floors of another such alley above. Below his feet, perhaps the same.

He sighed and wondered what souvenirs he might get from a place like this.

A salesman accosted him. "Human, I know your kind! You want to buy your Chin-Chin here! Nowhere is better. Best price! Best quality! Your wives will thank you."

Jim smiled, shook his head, and walked on.

"Chin-Chin" was the personification of Flereat. In comics, cartoons, and movies, he was the sharp-nosed possum-like star and protagonist. On his drooping shoulders the employment of millions rested. He wore jewels, glitter, and loud colors. He carried his penis coiled over his shoulder. Near the end of every cartoon adventure, he would use it to lasso his female counterpart.

Meko—his equally sharp-nosed, demure, and constantly pregnant wife—gave birth to several new, glittery, multicolored offspring every season, just in time for the toy shops to swell with their plush, gaudy bodies.

The Chin-Chin family appeared not only in countless films, comics, and books but also in live theater. The extravagant productions played exclusively at Flereat.

The marketing department of Flereat was an unstoppable force in the galaxy. Every species could relate to an icon of fertility. Most males, whatever the species, quietly enjoyed the hierarchical nature of the couple's relationship. The unrelenting marketing primed every child to collect each member of the bizarre, enormous, and ever-growing Chin-Chin family.

The Flereat operation was a rare marketing trifecta: characters who belonged to no particular planet, stories with universal resonance, and an audience held captive on the rambling station. It was the perfect combination for the extraction of money from all types of visitor.

As Jim walked, his plan became firmer. He would make inquiries, posing as someone who needed to do some hacking. Once he assessed who at the hotel knew about such matters, he could start asking about Jack Katrigg.

"Able?"

The comfortable buzz from the beers instantly left Jim.

"Who's asking?" he said as he turned around.

A large dog-like creature loomed over him. A great clawed paw reached to grab his throat. Jim swung backward, but the claws still caught his fight suit. He was lifted off his feet.

The alley whirled around him, and his head struck the floor.

. . .

Jim's eyes opened to a long snout sniffing at him.

"Back off!" Jim growled.

"Ha! He wakes."

Jim was sitting at a table. He tried to stand, but his knees had no room to move. The table stopped him from rising—as did a moment of dizziness. He sat back.

"Why are you here, monkey? Is this place work for you?"

"Who the hell are you?"

The canid snorted.

Jim shook his head to get his eyes to focus on the creature opposite him.

The canid was tall, even when seated. He wore a crimson cloak over a suit of yellow and orange. A hoop of bright gold dangled from his right ear.

His fur was black, though gray in places, and small bald patches betrayed the presence of old scars. His claws stretched out on the tabletop.

Jim's mind went back to his recent encounter with canids from Tanna Gul. "Marhan? Are you Marhan?"

"Of course! I am Ernot Dirl Marhan, and you..." He paused to spit sideways. "You will answer my questions! The first time we met, I had to answer to you. Now things stand differently between us."

Jim shook his head. "Are you insane? Why did you attack me?"

Marhan lunged across the table. Jim could see the blood pulsing in the veins around his eyelids.

"Too much of my time has been wasted by you. I will not permit it again!"

Jim now saw they were seated in the corner of another bar. But he doubted any of the other drinkers would come to his aid. Flereat really wasn't that kind of place.

"Calm down!" Jim urged, "I'm in no position to go anywhere, am I?"

"Are you hurt?"

Jim shook his head. "No. No thanks to you."

Marhan turned his head and observed Jim with one eye. "Do you need beer to loosen your tongue?"

Jim nodded, hoping to buy enough time to understand what had happened and what was happening.

Marhan said, "They have beer here—sour and hot, as it should be."

Jim coughed and muttered, "Ugh. Sure. Whatever."

At Marhan's order, a waiter brought two drinks, both slightly steaming: one in a tall bowl for the canid, one in an opaque glass for the primate.

10 TELLA ON ITS OWN

The head office of the EIA held many secrets of course. One enduring secret involved how office space was allocated to its many teams and individuals. If there were a plan, or even overall coordination, the minds behind it were malign or incompetent—or some dire combination of the two—so it seemed to Tella and others.

Tella was assigned desk U3-B2, which it found on one of the basement floors. The room had three desks, and all were already occupied.

Tella looked at each occupant in turn. None looked up or acknowledged the Neraffan.

"Humans!" it said quietly to itself and left.

In the agency car outside, Tella came to a decision.

"Driver! A friend of mine wants some warehouse space. Do you know of anywhere?"

"Not really," the driver replied, not looking back.

"Hmm," Tella said, "He can pay for it. And I can pay for the introduction."

The driver glanced back smiling. "How quickly?"

"Now would be good."
The driver nodded.

Mist hung across the empty floor of the warehouse; the temperature was lower than in the center of Unity City. Out here, the sea breezes chilled the air but couldn't quite clear it. Tella could smell rat urine.

James Able would not like this place. It's ideal.

Tella asked the broker, "What was this place before?"

"Not sure. I think they stored a dirigible in it at one point. Open the end doors there, and you have a clear path to the sea."

Tella looked down at its hand, watching the black and red from the data capsule cast streams of color across its skin.

"Ideal," Tella said.

11 MARHAN

"Okay, Marhan, take a breath," Jim began, hoping to regain some control. "Start at the beginning. The last time we met..."

"You came, you found me, you were quick with pretty words. I did not trust you then, and I do not now."

"I rescued you! The Rapaxans would have left you there—"

"Don't even speak of those liars to me!"

"I got you out, and I set you free to go home."

Marhan nodded. "And in return, you asked me to do you a favor. You sent me on a walk into the wilderness. You lied to me. You made a fool of me."

Jim thought but didn't say, *making a fool of a jumped-up idiot like you is no difficult task.* Instead, he said, "That's right. I asked you, since you were going to be near there anyway, to check on Darl. He helped me and Tamric...before Tamric was murdered by your people."

Marhan snapped his jaws at Jim and growled. "Darl! What kind of game do you play? Why do you make up these stories, monkey? Does it amuse you so much?"

"What do you mean? I told you what happened. Darl helped us

after I got attacked by some kind of beast on the trail. He was living alone in a hut."

Marhan moved his head from side to side, his eyes locked with Jim's. "Lies!" He drew a long scratch in the tabletop with a single claw.

Jim sat back. He disliked Marhan in a way he disliked few people, but the huge bony dog seemed to be genuine in his irritation and his conviction. "Tell me," Jim said, "What did you see there?"

Marhan waited and then relaxed. "Buy me more beer."

Jim sighed and waved at the waiter. He held up two fingers, though he had no intention of finishing the first appalling drink on the table before him.

Marhan began, for once talking quietly and occasionally glancing around at the other customers.

"I followed the old path beside the river. I found the tracks. I found your tracks, you and the Rapaxan monk's."

Jim nodded. "I thought you'd be able to. There's not much traffic through there."

"I found a hut. A sad, lonely hut. Dust and decay! It dates from long before the building of the base, before the wars, before I was born."

"Did you see Darl?"

"No one. No one lives there, monkey. No one has, not since before. It stands just as it was with no one to disturb it, sheltered from the world, inch by inch filling with dust."

"I...don't understand."

"Do you still say you saw this Darl?"

"No, I didn't. Tamric spoke to him. I was unconscious. When I came round, Darl had gone off."

Marhan began to laugh.

"What?"

"Did you leave anything in the hut, monkey?"

Jim shook his head. "No, I don't think so. We probably should have—to tell Darl thank you. Wait! Yes, we did. I remember arguing with Tamric about leaving some of our food—protein bars, I think. I took a couple out of my backpack."

Marhan slapped his paw down hard on the table; Jim's heart missed a beat.

On the table he saw two protein bars, their wrappers dirty and unopened.

Jim was silent as he looked up at Marhan, who said nothing. He took a long swig of foul beer and didn't notice the taste.

The Gul's snout came closer, making Jim more uncomfortable. Marhan spoke in a whisper. "There was no Darl. The monk lied. That a Rapaxan lies is no surprise to me. Is it to you? If the monk lied about this, what else did it lie about, monkey? How much of a fool did it make of you?"

"That monk," Jim said, through gritted teeth, "saved my life!"

Marhan's eyes narrowed. "Perhaps. But to what end?"

Jim got a face full of hot, acrid breath as the Gul snorted.

Marhan continued, "You were injured? Unconscious? What wounds did you have?"

"Um, I...I had some cuts, bruises. I got a nasty infection."

"How thoroughly did your doctors examine you?"

Jim was taken aback. "Well enough!"

Marhan sat silent, waiting, his eyes not moving from Jim's face.

Speaking slowly, Jim said, "I was treated on Tanna Jorr. But they'd never seen a human before. And then I stayed on my brother's station. That's where they dealt with the infection. And they damn well kept me in quarantine for far longer than they needed to!"

Jim watched Marhan quickly slurp the remains of one drink and start on the next.

"You asked me a question, James Able. And now I will answer it."

Jim nodded.

"I see a dumb monkey walking in the wastes of Tanna Gul. Behind him is a Rapaxan monk, cunning and well trained, young and fit, fulfilling a mission, following his overlord's instructions. I see him attack the monkey and yet still pretend to be his friend."

Jim shook his head. "You're crazy! Tamric wouldn't do something like that. Why? Why would Tamric do something like that?"

Ignoring the question, Marhan continued, "I see the monk overcome you. Perhaps you fought well and that is why you were hurt? Perhaps you fainted and he hurt you deliberately? I see the boy monk make up a story to cover the fact of your injuries. Remember, I have seen the Rapaxans at work. I know their treachery all too well. I know the scent of their lies. You are a fool, monkey—the Rapaxans' fool."

Jim again shook his head. "I said you were crazy. I'm sorry. That's way too mild a word for your insanity. I worked with Tamric. I knew Tamric." Jim almost shouted, "You never even met him."

"Nor did I meet the Rapaxan scribblers who drew the blueprints of their craft, yet I found out their lies. I did not meet their operatives who worked on Tanna Jorr, but I saw their deceits. I did not meet this Tamric, but I saw his path: doubt, lies, and injury following in his wake."

Marhan picked up one of the protein bars, ripped open the wrapper, and put the whole bar in his mouth.

Jim looked the Gul up and down as he chewed the bar noisily. Jim picked up his beer and put it down again. "You can't be right."

"Don't allow yourself the luxury of only believing the words of your friends, James Able. You do not like me, and I do not care, but I tell the truth. Which do you prefer, monkey, falsehood or truth?"

"Fuck you."

Marhan laughed loudly, turned to catch the waiter's eye, and shouted, "Earth beer for the Earth monkey! He has more sorrows to drown!"

12 JAYDE

Jayde was silent for most of the journey in the shuttle. She felt cold at the thought that she might never return to Sonloi-AC.

Before leaving the station, she had asked Phil, "Do you think I've overplayed my hand?".

"Maybe. It's uncharted territory. But that's true for both sides."

Now, she and Yarl watched the planet swing slowly before them as they made a turn toward the dawn over Tuanomena.

The staff at the police department's entrance had been briefed on her arrival, though Yarl's presence seemed to confuse them.

They waited in the corridor outside Chief Solma's suite of offices.

Jayde said softly, "I'll do the talking. Let's get Solma to repeat things. We'll intimidate him with the possibility of his words coming back to bite him. Best of all, let's see if we can catch where his information is coming from."

Yarl answered cautiously, "They are Meoena. It will be challenging."

"I know." Jayde nodded.

The double doors opened toward them. Ghui bowed and invited them in.

She whispered, "Showtime."

The scene in Solma's office was not what they had anticipated.

Solma sat behind a long table set horizontally across the middle of the room. With him were several Meoenan politicians, an army general, and a stenographer. The arriving pair were offered no chairs.

Ghui bowed again and walked over to stand at one end of the long table.

Solma nodded to the stenographer and began, "This meeting is called to address the sad downturn in relations between the current human staff serving on our old, but still functional, space station known to date as Sonloi-AC. Note the attendees."

Jayde held her gaze on Solma, hoping to show neither surprise nor any hint of being intimidated.

Solma asked, "You are Yarl Breen. What is your purpose here?" The stenographer clattered at her machine.

Yarl stepped forward and made a gesture Jayde had seen before but did not understand. "I am Yarl Breen. My family is of Gertuoker. I am employed by the current human staff serving on our old, but still functional, space station known to date as Sonloi-AC."

Jayde smiled as Yarl mimicked the tone and delivery of each word.

Yarl then nodded—the human gesture—and added, "I am employed by the humans to whom we owe so much and in whom our people have placed their trust again and again."

One of the politicians muttered in Melu, "Watch your tongue, boy! Or you'll not find employment anywhere else."

Yarl nodded again and replied, "Thank you, sir, for your warning." He then translated into Standard what had been said for Jayde's benefit.

Jayde asked quietly, "Where is The Artist?"

Solma rolled his large eyes and said, "Please do not try to change the subject. The small but inconvenient case of one missing human must take a second place to the future of our relations with each other as peoples, don't you think?"

Jayde waited. Solma waited.

Jayde asked, "Will you answer my question, Chief Solma?"

"In due course. Other matters have preeminence."

Jayde turned her head right and swept her hands left, in the Meoenan gesture to say "No."

She turned and headed to the door. Two armed guards blocked her way.

Yarl was at her side in an instant. "Please open the door. The Administrator wishes to leave."

One of the guards looked over their shoulders toward the table for an order.

"Please do not leave. For the sake of our relationship," called Solma.

"Is The Artist being held in this room?" Jayde called back without turning round.

A murmur of voices rose from the table. Solma laughed and said, "Of course she is not here!"

"Then we will go to where she is. Open the door."

Neither guard moved, both looking in vain for a clear instruction.

Yarl opened the door. Jayde led him out.

"Where now?" Yarl asked.

Jayde answered quietly, "The Institute for Art. I want to interview the person who sent Alfie the invitation, and I want to do it before they realize what we're up to."

13 MARHAN

Jim realized he was drunk. Marhan was still buying, and the so-called Earth beer was starting to taste better.

"This is bad," he muttered to himself. *How many times have I been here before?*

Marhan was silent, staring at Jim across the table.

At least it's not just me alone with the beer this time.

"What," Jim asked a little too loudly, "are you dressed like that for?"

The canid looked puzzled. "Like what?"

Jim waved his hand vaguely at Marhan's crimson cloak and orange and yellow suit. "That getup. It's loud! Where did you get it?"

"Here! I came here to celebrate, and I will continue the party once I have sent you on your way."

"Celebrate what exactly? I thought you were part of a failed coup?"

"Ha! It is true. Thanks to the Rapaxans, I was too late to help in the resolution of Tanna Gul's problems. The Raeff is dead. You were there?"

Jim nodded.

"The Raeff's brother rules as regent while the Luminants assess his son."

Jim nodded again.

"The Luminants jockey for power with the generals. Neither wants the son to rule"—Jim waited, watching Marhan's face suddenly become thoughtful—"Dol, the Regent, bought me off. He suspected I would cause trouble if he kept me around." A smile rippled along Marhan's long lips. "I am rich, monkey! Far richer than I ever dreamed to be."

"But you came here?"

"Where else? This place is famous: the Domes of Chin-Chin! Anyone who celebrates comes here."

Jim shook his head. "Not really."

"What? Is it too expensive for Earth monkeys?"

Jim snorted and smiled. "It's tacky, Marhan! It's cheap and bawdy. I can name you ten places better than this without thinking."

"Ah! Even in my choice of recreation, the monkey mocks me!" Marhan stood suddenly and ripped away the table between them. He pulled Jim up by the shoulders. "Better places even than this? Show me!"

As their glasses and bowls rolled on the floor, Jim stared up Marhan's snout. *You stupid ass!* With a clenched jaw, he said, "Your ship or mine?"

14 MATT

Matt Able sat at his desk. An EIA agent sat opposite. All that worried Matt, so far, was the lack of eye contact.

She was young—a lot younger than Matt. She was pretty in a way that the scientists on EBMS rarely were. She was someone who looked, to him, as if she had been hired specifically to do public relations.

"Dr. Able, I've been sent on a somewhat sensitive inquiry. I hope I won't cause any alarm or...personal trouble," she said.

"Agent Brown, get to the point. I'm busy. You have my undivided attention—but not for long. I presume you want to ask about my brother?"

Ah, eye contact! And, oh—only one of them is real. That's a letdown.

"That's very perceptive of you, Dr. Able."

"An inspired guess. What about him?"

"Well," she almost giggled, "I thought you would be a good place to start. You see, it's actually less him, more the Neraffan called Tella."

"Neither are here. Anything else?"

"When was the Neraffan last on station?"

"When the drone incident happened. Your people were here too."

Agent Brown nodded. "Are you sure not since?"

"Yes."

"Could you tell me, how long has Agent Able been staying here?"

"He hasn't."

Agent Brown blinked with both her natural and artificial eyes.

"That's not what I understood. I thought—"

"He may have docked here on occasions, but I don't let him on station."

Agent Brown's face wore a puzzled frown, a pert smile still on her lips.

Matt thought *Cute!* but continued, "Don't you know this? I thought you people knew everything?"

"Well, that is a little...As a confidential matter—not to be repeated to anyone please—one thing we don't know is where the Neraffan has gone. We were hoping you had seen it departing with Agent Able."

"You've tried looking for it?" Matt laughed. "Oh, wait, it can be invisible, can't it?"

"Dr. Able, this is no laughing matter."

"It is for me. I don't employ aliens. I don't even have any visiting. I don't have the problems that the EIA apparently has."

"I was assured of your cooperation on this." Her smile was gone.

Matt looked at his wristwatch. "You've already had quite a lot of it. How much longer do you need?"

Agent Brown stiffened in her chair. "Will you supply your brother's flight plans and other activities, please? Will you also let me have copies of all security feeds of the Neraffan when it was here?"

Matt nodded. "The feeds? You can ask Hal Trubeck. Flight plans? No. We don't do those. Jim comes and goes from an otherwise empty berth at his own discretion. This is a courtesy I have been offering to my friends at the EIA"—Receiving nothing but a puzzled stare, he added—"You're welcome. Anything else?"

"Well, perhaps you could let us know when Agent Able returns."

"He's your employee. Doesn't he have a supervisor? Don't you pay that supervisor to keep track of him? Don't ask me to do the job you are already paying someone else to do."

"Dr. Able—"

Matt stood up and pointed at his visitor "Stop right there! I have been polite and even helpful, but I won't be pushed and prodded. If Jim and the Neraffan are a problem, they are not my problem. I will not let you make them my problem. You have resources at your disposal that I can only dream of. Go and see Hal Trubeck. We're done."

Agent Brown stood and held out her hand, her face red.

Matt sat down again and picked up a small tablet from his desk. She withdrew her hand and said, "Thank you for your time, Dr. Able."

Once he was alone, Matt made a call. "Trubeck! Give the EIA agent whatever she wants about the Neraffan and nothing else. You hear me? Nothing else! And make sure you monitor that girl's every move. I want to know where she goes before she gets there! While you're at it, try and tap into the feed from her eye. That's no device for a human."

15 JAYDE

Outside the Institute for Art, Jayde looked at Yarl.

He said, "She was already well prepared for your questions. She spoke the words provided to her—without conviction."

Jayde nodded. "I thought so too. Thank you. I'm glad you are here."

Yarl nodded. "I believe she will now report everything to the chief of police."

Jayde grimaced. "I'm open to ideas."

Yarl asked quietly, "Would The Artist have allowed her abduction to proceed without offering resistance?"

Jayde laughed. "It depends. I would've left a trail of bodies had it been me. Alfie is more subtle perhaps. I doubt she would have let them push her around much."

Yarl suggested, "Then, perhaps, she was incapacitated, drugged, or otherwise rendered unable to defend herself?"

"Who would know how to knock out an adult female human?"

"This is the question I think we should now ask," Yarl said.

"Doctors," Jayde said. "We'll have records of all Meoenan doctors who have had human medical training."

She placed a quick call to the station. "Phil, get the librarians onto the doctors' records. Any local doctor with training with humans."

Yarl led her into a crowded covered market. He asked quietly, "Would you allow me to take you to the temple?"

"What temple?"

"The Temple of Tuanomena, after whom the city is named."

"Is it far?"

Yarl smiled. "It is not far, though it may not be visited quickly. Time spent there will be something unexpected. And it will worry our adversaries."

"Sure. Let's do it!"

━━

Through the centuries, the buildings in Tuanomena City had lost their color, bleaching white in the light of Pec. The newer the building, the fresher and brighter the decoration. The older facades were once covered with panels of now faded flowers and leaves. Newer fronts sported more geometric designs and bolder colors, perhaps hinting of encounters with other planets.

The market opened to the modern street where they had entered and, at its other end, to an older street. From there, Yarl led Jayde through increasingly ancient streets and alleys until they were suddenly in the wide square before the temple.

The temple had many levels, all of bleached, white stone.

━━

Yarl spoke as they approached the pale steps of the enormous ziggurat. "The stairs remove the temple from the dirt of everyday business. Each level we will enter is raised up from the concerns of those below it. We see it as shedding the worries we carry, removing the distractions, becoming spiritually naked."

"So there's a lot of climbing?" she asked.

"Yes."

They ascended to the first entrance to be met by several robed officials.

"What's this?" Jayde asked under her breath.

Yarl ushered the officials to one side and spoke to them for several minutes before returning. "I have corrected them in a misunderstanding about our intent."

Jayde asked, "What does that mean?"

"They were told we had come to cause an incident and were prepared to refuse us entry."

"But you persuaded them?"

"I have corrected their error."

"Again, I'm glad you are here. How much trouble are you getting into?" Jayde asked him.

"How much of the dirt of everyday business have we shed on our way to this door?" Yarl asked.

He turned and led her through a cool stone tunnel, decorated with a mural of clouds and Sonloi vines, into the warmth of a sunlit courtyard. The light fell in sharp rectangles through high shafts in the walls and in one central circle of bright light.

At once, she felt transported, breathing the warm air of the courtyard with relief. She smiled. "Oh, this is quite lovely, isn't it? It reminds me of quiet summer afternoons at my uncle's farm when the stone walls of the yard caught the sun."

Several arches and tunnels led from the central courtyard into the darker parts of the first story.

"Here are the tourist shops and booksellers," Yarl said.

"It's a big attraction?" Jayde asked.

"It is. Before the modern expansion, it was the center of the city and the center of our faith. And still, all come here eventually."

Taking a wide staircase to the next level, they passed by groups of silent, but curious, pilgrims. Jayde asked, "Is the temple dedicated to any particular deity, Yarl?"

"Yes."

His lack of further response had her biting her tongue until he sighed and said, "But perhaps not a deity in the sense a human might understand it."

At the next landing, they walked into a bare room fitted with seats for a lecture and flooded with sunlight from a small high window.

Yarl continued his thought, his eyes searching the dust of the floor. He spoke softly so that his voice would not carry beyond the room. "The temple is here because of someone, or something, that was here. But even that is misleading. We, over the centuries, have encountered Tuanomena—which is but one of the many names. We come to seek contact, to refresh contact, to..." Yarl looked to her face.

Jayde encouraged him, "Go on. I know this sort of thing is difficult to translate in Standard."

Yarl turned his head right and his hands left. "It is difficult to put into speech."

She asked, "Is Tuanomena 'God'?"

Again, Yarl gestured. He smiled and said, "As in The Creator and Determiner of All? No, not at all. Someone, or something other. Other than us. Other than God. A mystery, shall we say." He led Jayde back out of the room. "I hope you will find what we share." He smiled. "And I hope you will share what you find."

As they went through a dim corridor, Yarl continued, "This second level is reserved for the theologians and philosophers. A great library occupies the many rooms here. Tourists are not permitted any higher. The next level has accommodations for the pilgrims who come on retreat. But please don't return to this level without me.

"Sounds ominous."

"I hear rumors of complications with the retreatants. I'm sure everything will be fine. Access to the upper levels can only be gained by much study. There are many obstacles to advancement. But let us continue."

Each level of the temple had courtyards and rooms. From some rooms came singing. From others, they heard voices raised in prayer or preaching. Pilgrims in the courtyards remained respectfully quiet but watched with some wonder as the human passed.

Up more staircases and through several more tunnels, through the stacked levels of the temple—each one smaller than the last—and through what Jayde found narrow and claustrophobic corridors, they came, at last, to a courtyard containing a small pool.

"I am sorry to lead you here so quickly and without all the necessary liturgies."

"I doubt I would have understood them," she said, "but is it okay for us to be here? You said tourists can't come up this high."

Yarl nodded. "It would be difficult for me to translate the liturgies, so many words, so many difficult concepts. Is it proper for you to come so far and unprepared? I have taken that responsibility upon myself."

Jayde frowned and said, "I don't want you getting into trouble. Though, I realize I may have done that already."

They paused while a pilgrim came to the pool and washed her feet and hands.

Yarl nodded. "I have a special role here. I was in residence some time ago. And my father is a leader of the monastic community."

She looked surprised and asked, "You were a monk or something?"

Yarl nodded deliberately. "No. More 'something.'"

Jayde said, "But your father's a monk?"

"Of a sort. There will be time to explain more later." Yarl pointed to the pool. "Please wash your hands and feet in the pool. Put your shoes along the wall. We will then go through to The Walk." Yarl smiled and said, "And my first warning to you: in our language 'walk' is also 'circle' or 'cycle.' It will be...complicated."

Jayde shrugged. "I trust you."

The pool had a low edge, only a few inches above the floor. They rinsed their hands. She, rather more clumsily than he, dipped her feet in the pool's warm water. They toweled down their feet and lined up their shoes with the others.

Through a low arch, they came to a wide sunlit corridor. Two sounds filled the air: the soft patter of bare feet on sand and the low hum of quiet conversations.

She stood behind Yarl and watched as groups of pilgrims walked, quite leisurely, from Yarl's right to his left.

Yarl half turned and whispered, "We will travel The Walk once in silence. All walk in this direction only. Do not turn around. When we return here, I will explain more."

She nodded, and they stepped out into a gap between a couple of Meoenan females in flowing robes and four similarly dressed Meoenan males, walking side by side, heads bowed, holding hands.

The corridor was wide, with room for, perhaps, ten people abreast. The ceiling arched overhead, broken by occasional wooden beams, hints of old paintings now faded beyond recognition, and small square shafts with sunlight bursting through too bright to look at.

The corridor was not straight but curved to the right. Repeated windows in the inner righthand wall opened into a central shaft of light with a view down to all levels of the ziggurat.

The left-hand wall was interrupted by doors and a few arches hinting at rooms—perhaps other pools or even, Jayde idly hoped, some place for refreshment.

The air was hot and smelled rather old.

People sat on benches along both sides of the corridor, talking or resting. Jayde wondered how long "The Walk" was going to take.

As they came by the arch to the pool once more, she commented, "That was quick!"

"Really?" asked Yarl.

"I didn't think we'd gone all the way round."

Yarl smiled. "Yes, complications exist throughout. Let's walk a little further and find a seat."

When they had found a bench with room for two, Yarl began to speak, his eyes shifting across the floor, hardly noticing the pilgrims walking quietly by. "You know Meoenan youth sometimes go on a retreat or a journey before they begin their adult duties."

Jayde nodded. "Yes, we say 'going walkabout.'"

Yarl smiled and continued, "A good expression. When I first came here to The Walk, I was young. Perhaps my family brought me here too soon. I didn't find what I sought. I then made other journeys. Much later, I returned here and sat for many hours on a bench such as this." He looked up. "Tell me what you see. Please, describe the scene before you."

Jayde was surprised but began, "I see pilgrims. People from all over Sonloi. It's nice to see everyone getting on so well. Especially after the...difficulties we've been facing."

Yarl held his palms upward but said nothing.

"The people walking have serious expressions on their faces, absorbed in what they're doing. I'm not sure I understand the point of it. But...I guess they do."

Again, Yarl held his palms upward and said nothing.

Jayde hesitated. "I like the different gear everyone wears. I see coats and cloaks, robes and suits, like from a period piece...I don't know. But—I hope you don't mind me saying—there's something a little odd about the variety of people going by. It's not like the streets outside."

Yarl turned and smiled. "Tuanomena is close to you."

Alarmed, she said, "What does that mean?"

His large eyes held hers. "We will see."

He sat back on the bench and pointed across the corridor. "As I sat here, I saw myself go by. I saw a young, troubled youth who saw almost nothing as he walked. I sat, realizing how much I had grown. How much more...myself I had become."

She smiled and said, "You'd left your problems behind?"

Yarl replied, "No, not at all. I realized how much I had grown to love my troubles and my limitations."

"That's interesting."

Yarl sighed. "But I think you don't yet understand me. I said I saw myself go by. As clearly as I see these students, those monks, those old folks leaning on each other as they walk. I saw myself go by."

Jayde said, "You mean, figuratively."

"No."

"In some spiritual sense?"

"No."

"Shit..."

Yarl pointed at a group of pilgrims across The Walk. "That style of robe hasn't been worn in two hundred years. That headdress? I've never seen such a thing before. Such are some of the 'complications' I warned you of. Sometimes, on The Walk, the pilgrims may thin out. At other times, one is pressed forward in a crowd. It can be different each time. When Tuanomena is close, and wishes to speak, it can seem as though The Walk extends for miles. We walk in hope. We walk in wonder. If you find yourself alone, it is said Tuanomena will speak."

The pair sat in silence.

"Perhaps you find it hard to believe?" said Yarl quietly.

"I do," admitted Jayde.

"Shall we walk around again?" Yarl suggested.

They walked. Jayde was reluctant to make eye contact with the other pilgrims. *I have to be careful. I'm an alien here.*

After several silent circuits, Jayde, mesmerized by the quiet repetition, stumbled on the sandy floor and grabbed for support. She found the sleeve of a tall Meoenan woman.

Jayde laughed and said, "Excuse me!"

Yarl approached the tall Meoenan and spoke a few words. It seemed to Jayde that the pilgrim did not understand Yarl at all.

He tried again, speaking slowly. A couple, walking arm in arm, stopped to listen.

"Yarl." He brought both hands to his chest.

She replied, "Nanji" with the same gesture.

"Lass oh garangu?" Yarl asked.

She did not understand.

The Meoenan male half of the couple nearby, said, "Mizzo! Lazz oh gurunge?" He opened his hands to Yarl, drew them to his chest, and said, "Faarl."

Nanji smiled, bowed, and said, "Firt o lazz." She looked over Yarl's shoulder, and her eyes fell on Jayde as if seeing her for the first time. "Quirz a ste, mernuge?"

With Faarl's help, Yarl and Nanji began to communicate and Yarl, half turning to Jayde, translated.

"My pronunciation is wrong, though the words are familiar. Her name is Nanji.

"Nanji, may I ask...what year is it for you?" he asked.

"Oh, that is difficult to say in here, isn't it? Outside it is 15,232 Gart 17."

"Thank you," Yarl replied. To Jayde he said, "So that's three hundred years ago. I guess Faarl is somewhere in between us."

"But," Nanji interrupted, "who is this stranger? Where is she from? I've never seen any creature like her!"

Yarl asked Jayde, "How much do I say about you?"

Jayde held up a hand and said, "I'd say as little as possible. Just say one day we'll be friends."

To Nanji, Yarl replied, "For us the date is 15,540 Frip 12. Her people are friends that your Sonloi has yet to meet."

"How strange! Tuanomena works in mysterious and astounding ways! Peace to you all." Nanji turned and walked on.

Jayde muttered, "This is freaking me out."

"Are you alright?" Yarl whispered.

Jayde flashed brightened eyes at him. "Oh, this is fascinating. And scary. And I'm sorry Alfie's missing it. Lead on!"

16 ALFIE

"This potghor isn't fresh," complained The Artist.

"I had some earlier. It was quite adequate."

"Adequate won't do. I told you I was hungry. And you serve me this!"

"Would you prefer something else?"

"I would prefer, when you are talking to me, that I see you. Why don't you come forward? Why serve the food through a slot when you could serve it face-to-face?"

Her jailer paused before answering. "It was decided that anonymity was to be maintained."

"But that was before you realized how uncomfortable that would be, how rude it makes you, what an insult it is to me."

"No insult is intended."

"As if kidnapping and imprisonment weren't insults enough! Well, if no additional insult is intended, you know what to do. Come forward and talk to me."

"That is not in accordance with my instructions."

"Baby! Aren't you of an age to decide that sort of thing for yourself? Shame on you!"

Alfie wondered if that had been too strong as she listened to the silence that followed.

"Anyway," she said, "Fresh potghor! And more of it. Do you have apples? I know the station had a recent delivery from Earth. I like to eat one a day. How many will you order?"

No answer came from the darkness beyond the light from her cage.

She sat down again in the wing chair. After so many years of humans learning to avoid accidentally insulting their alien partners, she now had to carefully and deliberately create ways to get under this one individual's pale blue skin.

She sighed.

So delicate physically. So introspective in their philosophy. So bloody annoying!

17 JAYDE

The city of Tuanomena boasted famous cafés. Before dawn, Yarl took Jayde to one of the most expensive, The Tuano, where news crews lay in wait to record the great and the good of Meoenan society rubbing shoulders.

Once they were seated, she asked Yarl, "Why all this? Why so public?"

Yarl handed her the menu and said, "For the potghor! The chef here is the best. And they probably won't arrest us in front of cameras."

She smiled and shook her head, "I have section leaders who say things like that. I'll say to you what I say to them. That 'probably' sounds like it's a major risk."

The waiter came, they ordered, and then neither spoke.

A few photographers peered in through the café window, but since the human was doing nothing of interest, they soon left.

Jayde asked at last, "What am I to make of our...walk?"

Yarl smiled and waited.

Jayde said quietly, "Time travel. Really? And you don't tell anyone about it?"

Yarl's shoulders rose, and he stretched his fingers. "We don't like to use that phrase. I'm not sure it would be completely accurate in this case. There is something, or someone—Tuanomena—at the temple that allows, creates, or maintains a blurring of the normal constrictions of time."

Jayde tried to process what he had said. "I would...Don't you try and make use of it? Haven't you thought to ask people from the future what's going to happen?"

Yarl nodded but said, "No. The role of our religious practices and the years spent in study and contemplation provide us with a perspective that overcomes such temptations. 'It' is not ours to 'make use of' in any way. We thank Tuanomena for what happens in the temple. We accept any gift that may be given. We are not owners. We are not in command."

Their food arrived and they ate in silence.

Jayde muttered, "You're right, the potghor is wonderful!"

"The best," Yarl agreed.

They finished their dishes, again in silence.

The waiter cleared the table, and Jayde asked, "Who else knows about this—about The Walk and its 'complications'?"

Yarl replied, "I am often surprised at how few. The daunting prospect of the many levels and long rituals, the study, the dedication. Few Meoena have the luxury or ambition to achieve The Walk and so know only rumors and folktales. Yet, I know at least one other human to have visited. The Caretaker spent much time at the temple, but what he experienced there I do not know. It is said he took The Walk more than once."

"Did The Artist ever come with him?"

"I don't think so."

"That's a shame." She asked, "What did you mean, Yarl, when you said Tuanomena was close to me?"

Yarl thought before speaking. "You spoke accurately and in wonder. The Walk is, as you said, not like the streets outside. Tuanomena gave you an insight into The Walk, and you responded to it. For which I thank you. The Walk is a place for absolute honesty, for clear seeing, clear thinking. Nanji spoke from her heart. She wondered what you were and asked, without fear of causing offense or of letting out a secret. The Walk is life in its raw state. It is unfiltered experience. We say it is the present moment stretched into a circle."

Jayde frowned and stared at her empty plate. She nodded. "Actually, yes, that makes sense. I get what you are saying."

"And now," Yarl said with a sigh, "we must make a leap of faith. Faith in Tuanomena and the rightness of our cause."

She said "Okay" with as much caution as she felt polite.

"To return to Chief Solma's office but bring what we have learned on The Walk with us. To stretch the present moment into a circle while we talk with them. To see them clearly and without filter. I trust in Tuanomena that it will be informative."

Jayde nodded and looked at her tablet. "Wait a minute!"

"Is there a problem?"

"I have a huge list of missed messages. They're still coming in."

"Ah."

"What the..? It's—"

"Complicated?"

"We were in there two days!"

Yarl smiled and sat back in his chair. "And this surprises you?"

A few moments later, Phil and a team of Sonloi-AC security officers made their way through the tables.

18 JIM

Jim woke to the ship saying, "A member of EBMS staff is requesting access at the rear airlock."

He heard voices down below. Looking around his module, he thought once again, *I have to clean this place up*. He frowned at the large plush version of Chin-Chin hanging on the back of the door.

At the airlock, Marhan looked Davey up and down and said, "Small monkey, are you related to Jim? You have a similar untidiness about you."

Davey nodded. "Is Uncle Jim here?"

Marhan frowned. "I think so."

"Who are you?"

"Marhan! Ernot Dirl Marhan from the great world of Tanna Gul!"

"Cool! You're a canid, aren't you? But..." Davey frowned and looked the Gul up and down.

Marhan's ears flattened. He turned his head slightly to allow his left eye a view of his own body. "Forgive me. I will dress."

Davey smiled as the large naked canid disappeared up the left-hand ramp to the sleeping modules.

Jim staggered down the right-hand ramp to the flight room, with a sideways glance at Marhan going the other way. "Davey? What are you doing here?"

"Are you okay, Uncle Jim?"

"Why wouldn't I be?"

"Um...you've got at least one undressed canid on board. Did you bring more of them?"

With a nervous glance to the upper level, Jim shook his head and said, "Don't think so." Taking a step toward his nephew, he added quietly, "I'll check."

Jim was halfway up the ramp when he turned and asked again, "How did you get here?"

"Um, I live here?"

Jim blinked. "We're back at EBMS?"

Davey nodded.

"Shit! Marhan! Get yourself down here!"

A string of Gul cursing was the only answer he got.

Jim turned back to the controls and sat heavily on the seat. "Raeda! Display the navigation log since we last docked at EBMS."

Both Jim and Davey were silent as he read and read. Jim put his head down on his arms and said, "Shit!" again.

"Can I...get you anything?" Davey asked.

Without looking up, Jim replied, "Food. Hot food. Better include whatever meat you can get for Marhan."

"Are you alright for water?"

"Raeda! Status of water supply."

"Water tanks are at one-third. Water reclamation is functioning at optimal capacity."

Jim looked sideways at Davey, "Sports drinks. Whatever you can get."

Davey nodded. "Is it okay if Clo comes?"

Jim said into his sleeve, "Assuming Marhan is dressed and alone."

Davey skipped along the corridor and left.

． ． ．

Marhan's voice came from the upper level. "Has the small monkey gone?"

"He's gone. He's getting you something to eat."

"He is part of your troupe?"

"One of my brother's boys. Call him Davey."

Marhan descended the ramp, dressed in a flight suit. "Where are we?" he asked.

"Europa Biological Monitoring Station. It's near Earth."

"And...?"

"How did we get here?" Jim offered.

Marhan sat in a chair and nodded.

"Just trying to figure that out."

Marhan was silent as he cast his eyes around the ship. Then he asked, "What do you remember?"

Jim frowned. "Not much."

Marhan nodded. "The same."

They caught each other's eye, and both began laughing. Marhan let out howls as Jim shook in his chair.

Jim snorted, "It must have been good!"

Marhan gasped, "Celebrations should always be such! If I had a tail, it would ache all the way up to my snout."

Jim's face became serious. " Are you alone in your module? Did we...bring anyone else on board?"

Marhan's ears spread wide, and he sniffed the air. "I don't think so. There was no one there just now."

"Raeda! Is there anyone else on board besides myself and Marhan?"

"No one else is on board."

Jim muttered, "That's a relief."

"Nonsense!" Marhan shouted, "Ha! We let them get away!"

Jim held up his hands. "Let's think who they might have been before we decide if it's a good thing or not."

Again, they burst into fits of laughter.

． ． ．

Clo and Davey returned with two boxes of food and drinks.

Davey nudged her as Jim unpacked and handed items to Marhan. "I told you."

She replied in a whisper, "He's so big. And those teeth!"

Marhan turned his snout to them and said, "He has good ears too, little monkeys."

A look of alarm crossed Clo's face.

Jim said, "Don't be put off by his bluster, Clo. He won't eat you."

"You sure?" she asked.

"Ha!" said Marhan with a snap of his jaws. "Better safe than sorry!"

"Thanks for all this!" Jim said, "How much do we owe you?"

Davey looked at Clo. "Um, I charged it to your account."

"My account?"

"Yeah..."

Clo said, "Davey set it up while you were away."

Jim rolled his eyes. "You'd better have done it legally. I don't want you—or me—getting into unnecessary trouble."

Davey smiled and said, "Clean job. Honest!"

Jim pointed his finger at his nephew. "You, sir, are a bad influence!"

Davey beamed with pleasure at the compliment.

Clo asked, "Do you know there's an EIA agent on station looking for you?"

Jim shook his head. "No. Is it Tella?"

Clo shook her head.

"No," Davey said, "she's pretty."

Clo punched his arm.

Jim turned to his displays and said, "Raeda! Show me waiting messages here."

While he read, Marhan stood and rummaged in the box. "Is there more of that white meat?"

"The chicken? I don't think so," Clo replied.

"What sort of creature is it?"

"A bird."

"Really? It's a long time since there were birds on Tanna Gul. I ate some as a pup. Never since."

Davey asked, "What happened to them?"

Marhan shrugged, "We screwed our ecosystems. Have you not heard? Our stupidity is such that we die from it."

Both Davey and Clo looked horrified, and neither said anything.

Marhan stretched his arms and yawned. He let out a growl that chilled Clo. "I will sleep again," he said. Without a glance at anyone, he leapt up the ramp and into his module.

Jim turned away from his messages and asked her, "What do you think of him?"

Her eyes widened. "Real scary! Are you sure he's safe?"

Jim smiled sadly. "No, he's not. Listen, he was almost in a position to take control of his whole planet. I don't know how successful he would've been, but he was ready to give it a try. Physically, he could catch and eat any one of us. He'd also do whatever the political equivalent is—if he thought it necessary. So, no, he's not safe. I rescued him from...a sort of prison, and he owes me. Don't worry. He has no reason to harm any of us. And I probably shouldn't say this to you guys..."

Davey encouraged him. "It's okay."

Jim continued, "I wake up at the end of a week like I've apparently had...and I feel almost comfortable having him around. That doesn't happen with many of my acquaintances. Not often at all."

Jim pointed his finger at Davey and said, "Listen. Your dad isn't wrong about me, Davey. I wish he was. I don't always keep things straight like he does. You should concentrate on being more like him than me."

Davey looked away from Jim, looked at Clo, and muttered, "Sure."

19 MATT AND JIM AND ALICE

Matt sat next to Jim at a conference room table.

"So, after all that yelling at me about the precariousness of your job, you went off on a bender? Is that it?"

"I...went...No! Yeah. Totally."

"Jim—"

"Don't even start!" Jim shook his head. "Just don't bother. Who is this woman we're meeting?"

Matt sighed. "An EIA trojan horse. She has an artificial eye streaming a huge selection of data out to her ship. She's made up to look cute. No, I take that back. She's made up."

"Spy bot rather than sex bot?"

"Front-desk-receptionist bot."

Jim laughed. "Got you."

The EIA agent opened the door and marched up to the table.

"Agent Able?"

"Please sit down," Matt ordered.

Jim stared at her as she sat.

"You are Agent James Able?" she asked directly.

Jim nodded. Then he said, "But with that nice prosthetic eye, you've already checked that."

She dropped her smile. "Yes, I have. Now, what can you tell me about the Neraffan?"

"Which one?"

"Tella."

Jim nodded. "Tall. Not much of a tan."

"I don't need a description, Agent Able. Where is it?"

"Who wants to know?"

"My name is Alice Brown. I assure you I have all the necessary authorization to ask you these questions."

"Then I'm sure you have the ID and the warrants to back up that assertion."

"I transmitted all the documentation to your flier four days ago."

"Which one?"

"I—I'm sorry?"

"Which flier?"

"Your agency-allocated flier. The one you are authorized to travel in."

"Hmm," Jim said.

She froze. "What?"

"I don't have a flier allocated to me at present."

She frowned and stabbed her fingers at her tablet for many seconds. "Impossible!"

Matt smiled.

Jim shrugged. "I don't, do I?"

"So what is going on? Where did those messages get sent?"

"Can't help you there. I'd get someone on that right away if I were you."

She sat, silently caught between several rude replies.

Matt said quietly, "Why don't you just explain to Jim why you want to see the Neraffan, and how you came to lose track of one of your alien employees?"

She stabbed Matt with a glance and then turned both eyes on Jim once more.

"Tella is absent without leave. It has registered a mission but has not attended or traveled as it has reported."

Jim nodded and said, "That would explain it not returning my calls."

There was silence around the table.

Jim asked, "How is this my problem?"

"As the agent most recently working with Tella, you are in a position to help us with our inquiries."

"I'd be in a position to help if I knew anything, yes. But I don't."

"Why did you rent warehouse space at Pier 78 and Makland Avenue, Unity City?"

"What?"

"It's on your expenses. What's it for?"

Jim sat up. "Show me."

She handed her tablet across the table. He read and reread the entry. Jim handed the tablet to Matt, shook his head, and replied, "Not one of mine."

"Did you rent it for a party?" Matt asked.

Jim glowered at him. "Not helpful."

"It has your authorization." She asked, "Are you telling me your account has been compromised?"

Jim smiled across the table. "I see. I accept that it is possible Tella could have used my account to make this transaction."

"How and why?"

"'How' is easy. We shared expenses on our previous mission. I could probably hack Tella's account if I needed to."

"That is not according to protocol, Agent Able."

Jim ignored her. "'Why,' I see now, is where you try and make it my problem."

"I would like you to accompany me back to Unity City. We'll examine the warehouse together. Any objections?"

"Many. But listing them won't do any good, will it?"

"Not at all."

"I want to find Tella too. And I want to know why you have that eye and what you do with it."

"You do not need to know that, Agent Able."

Matt asked, "Are we done?"

Jim nodded.

She said, "We leave from berth A2 in half an hour."

Jim nodded but stayed sitting until she left.

"What?" asked Matt.

"Got a friend on board my ship. He won't come onto the station."

"'He'?"

Jim nodded. "Like I said, a friend. I got him out of a jam a while back." Jim shrugged. "He likes beer too."

"Oh, I see."

"I'll get rid of him once I get back."

"If I need the berth, I'll cast him and the ship loose."

"I don't doubt you would." Nodding to the door, he added, "Piece of work, isn't she?"

"Be careful."

⬛

Jim threw his backpack into the luggage net of Alice Brown's flier.

"Anyone joining us?" he asked.

"Not at present."

Jim sighed and buckled himself into a seat.

Alice turned her head from the controls. "I have flown before; you don't need to buckle up."

"I'm sure you have. Which section do you work in?"

"You don't need to know."

"The EIA is a pain in the butt sometimes, isn't it?"

"Yes."

They didn't speak again for over an hour.

Somewhere near the orbit of Mars, Alice said, "That's odd—" She snapped her seat belt around herself as several thuds sounded on the flier's hull.

"Did we hit something?" Jim asked.

"No. Something's appeared out there. It's huge. I think we're now inside it."

The flier shook, an alarm sounded, and the lights went out.

"All systems are down," Alice called out above the continuing alarm.

"Any emergency lighting?" Jim asked, unbuckling himself to move forward toward her.

"Doing my best..."

An explosion near the rear compartments knocked Jim sideways. He had a glimpse of Alice's artificial eye glowing in the dark. His ears were ringing louder than the alarm.

A single blaster beam caught Alice in the neck, briefly illuminating her chin and one hand.

Jim shrank back against his seat.

Another beam caught his shoulder, and he felt a cold numbness spreading through his chest.

He pushed himself up and, despite the deepening darkness, tried to move toward their attacker.

Another shot hit him full on. As he froze, he wondered, *How do I explain this one to Tella?*

20 JAYDE

Yarl left Jayde and Phil eating dessert at the café. He soon returned with a large, flat parcel.

"I will talk to them about this."

Jayde nodded. "One of Alfie's paintings?"

"It is her portrait of me."

"Understood. Phil, call Solma and tell him we're on our way back."

"What shall I say about the fuss we've been making about your disappearance? It's been a major incident."

Jayde smiled. "Don't mention it. Ever. Gaslight them like they've tried to gaslight us."

The police chief had assembled about ten more aides to sit with him behind the long table. Several more Meonea stood behind, ready with notepads, tablets, and phones to prompt or rescue whichever seated Meoena needed it.

Again, Jayde was made to stand. Yarl was given the courtesy of a chair when he announced he had a statement to make and a painting to discuss.

Jayde thought back to the pool and the sound of many feet. She remembered the warmth of the temple and shivered at the cold air of the office.

Yarl did not address the assembled officials in Standard. The Meoenan tongue, as he spoke in his usual careful manner, became, for Jayde, a pool of pastel sound.

She became aware of herself standing apart from the room, watching the attendees across the table. She could see the body language, the nods, the glances, the repetitions.

She watched and pretended the Meoena were passing her by as she sat on a bench on The Walk. She became aware of the pattern in the Meoenan interactions as if they were the rhythm of quiet feet.

She saw one person controlled the room. Only one Meoenan did not check with any other. Only one person answered glances but never glanced.

Yarl stood and rewrapped his painting, but Jayde felt she wasn't finished yet. She was still watching, fascinated.

To Solma's surprise, Jayde left without saying anything to him or the others. This itself was the subject of hours of conversation in the room once they had left.

Yarl handed her a menu again, this time in a secluded side room at The Tuano.

"Do you wish to eat first or talk first?" Yarl began.

"I need to talk first," Jayde said nodding repeatedly.

"Who was the Meoenan male behind Solma's right shoulder?"

Yarl smiled. "I do not know his name."

She looked horrified. "But that's who's controlling all this! He's the one!"

Yarl continued to smile. "I do not know his name, but I know who he is."

Jayde opened the menu but looked sideways at Yarl. "Explain."

"He is not a government minister, yet he is at the ministers' sides. He is not a lobbyist; the elected approach him with deference. He does not come to this café and, so, is never photographed or filmed."

She asked, "Do you have a real Secret Service? Like we have the EIA?"

"If I knew of it, it wouldn't be secret, would it?"

"You know what I mean."

"I do. And I do not joke. There is such a thing, and it is such a secret."

Jayde sighed. "That explains a few things." She shook her head. "Why would they kidnap Alfie?"

"Perhaps they wouldn't or didn't, but they certainly would be the ones to try and cover it up. This is what we think," Yarl said.

They ordered and chatted about the other attendees. When the food arrived, Jayde asked, "Who's 'we,' Yarl?"

Yarl was still for a long time.

Jayde smiled and waited.

Yarl turned to her slowly and said, "I cannot answer. But know that I am not the only one alarmed by The Artist's disappearance. We want no harm to come to her. We want no retreat from our relationship with Earth."

Jayde nodded. "Okay. Of course, I'll accept that. I've suspected we've been getting help we haven't seen. For that, and all your own efforts, we are so grateful."

"If they can take The Artist—or cover the tracks of those who did—what hope does anyone less well-known have? If a beloved alien celebrity can be removed, how much easier will it be to remove an ordinary person?"

"I feel sick that one creep is so much in control and so invisible. What can we do about him?"

"We must be cautious. If you declare yourself too explicitly as an enemy, you will merely be a target to remove. You must act more like one of us. You must see who else can help."

"Agreed. We can't pursue this as we have been. It goes up too high. Solma, I could handle. This unknown person? No, we need to regroup back up on the station."

21 ALFIE AND JIM

Jim woke up on a bed under a blanket, still dressed in his flight suit. A small light shone over his head.

He sat up. Three of the sides of the enclosure were comprised of thin vertical bars. Outside was darkness.

The only other light came from a similar cage next to his. He could smell potghor.

He got up slowly and approached the bars.

The woman with magnificent, long, multi-colored hair was sitting—perhaps sleeping—in a wing chair.

He gripped the bars that made up their joint wall and said quietly, "Oh shit!"

She opened her eyes, smiled, and said, "Hello, dear."

"Hi, Mom."

JIM ABLE OFFWORLD

SHED

11

ED CHARLTON

AUTHOR OF "THE ALERONDE TRILOGY"

01 EARLY YEARS

Lem Able swallowed hard to control the wave of queasiness that hit him every time he approached Sonloi-AC. There it was—huge, skeletal, fragile. Maintaining an orbit means to fall constantly yet never to crash. For him, the station remained permanently caught between being whole and being wrecked, between becoming everything the team dreamed of and becoming a desperate waste of time.

And I bet my life and my family on this.

A year and half's work by the best construction engineers the Earth could muster had brought the station only to this primitive stage. The outline of the hemispherical main body was complete. The main struts for the arms sweeping back to the propulsion array were in place, but the array was not. A few floors of habitable rooms existed only as a temporary haven for those who did not live on Sonloi or on one of the attendant Earth ships tethered to the upper docks.

Home! God, what am I doing?

Fasta Kerit, Lem's Meoenan shadow, handed him a tablet. "Your wife."

"Alfie? What's up? We're on our way over."

"As soon as you get in, go to Taff Jones on T5."

"What does he need?"

"For you to get your son out of the way. He's been helping himself again."

Lem snorted and said, "Again?" He shook his head. "I don't have time for this, love."

"You do if you want dinner."

Lem laughed. "Will do. See you soon."

Taff Jones served as the controller of all construction supplies for the building of Sonloi-AC. Generally referred to as The Quartermaster, he was a Welshman who began calling himself Jones when he found the Meoena couldn't pronounce Llewellyn.

Taff greeted Lem at the main door of the stores. "Lem, if you don't get him under control now, what's he going to be like later? When we're done, this station will have more places to run and hide than you'll ever be able to search in!

"I know, Taff, I know. What's my little artful dodger been up to this time?"

"Walking off with six meters of cabling."

Lem shook his head. "Where is he?"

"My office. I've locked him in."

Jones led the way and stood back for Lem to enter.

"Jim? What is this? What were you up to?"

Jim Able sitting in a chair, his black hair pointing in different directions, swung his legs and stared at the floor.

Lem continued, "Jim, you're six years old. What do you need cabling for?"

Jim shifted in his seat. "Rolo and I found an intersection where the floor isn't finished. We couldn't get over. So we wanted to swing from one side to the other. We would've been safe."

"Did you steal hooks or snap rings to go with it?"

Jim shook his head.

"So you didn't really think it through, did you? Come on, you can draw me what you were going to do over dinner."

As they left, Jones said, "That it? You encourage him too much."

"Apologize to the quartermaster, Jim."

"Sorry, Mr. Jones."

"Well, you're banned from in here, Master Able. Don't you come back without an adult, you hear?"

"Yes, Mr. Jones."

Lem put his arm around the boy's shoulder and steered him out with a quiet, "Well done."

Later that night, Lem called Fasta Kerit. "Fasta, what did your Rolo tell you about today?"

"Not much. He was with Jim, wasn't he?"

"Oh, yeah, that's for sure. They were in Section 3 of Level 98."

"What? That's barely habitable! And why? There's nothing in there yet."

"Oh, I know. But they're curious. You can't blame them. If they aren't exploring, they're stuck in the same rooms they study in. I can understand it. For me, it's more important that they're honest about it. I don't want them thinking they have to keep it secret."

"That's not the Meoenan way, Lem. We expect obedience from children. We also hope for more common sense!"

"Well, good luck with Rolo on both those scores. We know that neither are Jim's best assets."

Fasta laughed. "See you next shift, Lem."

"See you, Fasta."

Mazette Able pulled on her father's leg. "Daddy!"

"Hi, love!"

"Daddy!"

"What is it, little one? Did you eat all your dinner?"

"Uh-huh. My bear's gone."

"Gone? Did he go for a walk?"

"No."

"Is he in the wash again?"

"No. He's gone!"

"Well, that's a problem, isn't it? How are you going to solve that? I tell you what. You ask your mother's help to find him. Daddy has some reading he has to do before the next shift."

"You're always reading!"

"I know, sweetheart. It'll get better as the station gets built. I won't always be reading." He smiled. "Go on now."

02 THE CAGES

"How are you, dear?" asked Alfie.

"Where are we?" Jim asked in return.

"In cages, dear, being observed by a middle-aged Meoenan who lurks in the shadows, not showing himself. So far, he brought me inadequately cooked potghor and not enough of it."

Jim smiled. "I'm fine, Mom. I see you are doing okay in difficult circumstances."

Alfie smiled back and said quietly, "It's a ship of some kind, but I don't think we're traveling. There's none of that irritating vibration you get when the D-switch is constantly working."

Jim shook his head. "No one can feel that, Mom; it's too fast. You imagine it."

"Were you hurt when they got you?"

Jim shrugged. "No, but I don't know what happened to the EIA agent I was with."

"Oh dear."

"You okay?"

Alfie nodded and said deliberately, "They have gone to a great deal of trouble to arrange this, haven't they?"

"Unless you've suddenly found a way of printing money, I can't see why either of us would be worth it."

A Meoenan voice spoke calmly through the darkness. "The reason we have brought you here will soon become clear. Do you require food?"

Jim peered through the bars, hoping for a glimpse of their captor. "No. I require my freedom and that of my mother."

"Excellent! That is what we want too. I take from that you will assist us in our inquiries."

"I very much doubt it," Jim replied.

The voice did not answer.

Jim sighed, looked at his mother, and then examined the edges and joints of his cage for weaknesses.

Jim called out, "So why do want us? What 'inquiries' do you want us to help with?"

"We will discuss this when my employer arrives."

"Oh now," Jim chided, "give us a clue."

An alarm sounded, echoing in the darkness in a way voices did not. Jim heard, in the difference, the echoes of a large cargo bay, the alarm sounding at the far end. Their cages were in a corner, he thought, with cladding or carpeting.

"That might be him now," the voice declared with some enthusiasm.

"Run along," Jim said. "Don't worry about us. We'll wait here."

The sound of Meoenan feet echoed across the darkened cargo bay, coming to a halt near Jim's cage.

The voice said, "We will begin."

Jim winked at his mother and sat down in the armchair.

The voice intoned, "The Meoena of Pec Sonloi are always grateful that humans were the first aliens with whom we made substantial contact. The station Sonloi-AC is the symbol of our harmonious partnership and the trust between our two species. It has been the springboard for many other fruitful projects over many years."

Jim was going to make a smart comment but decided to hold his tongue.

Alfie snorted.

"First among the people of Earth are the Family Able: The Artist who finds—in our faces—our hearts; the sons—the elder and the younger—who grew before our eyes in grace and wisdom."

Jim snorted.

"Most of all, The Caretaker. He who understood the plans of the station. He who stayed, with the Family Able, after the construction was done to maintain, to advise, to guard, to...take care."

Jim listened carefully to the emotion. He knew none of what had been said was in any way necessary. Formal Meoenan speech often took the shape of a spiral, walking around the topic before being concerned with any content.

The voice sighed and continued, "And yet, we hear in these latter days, long after Lemuel's passing, that he appears not to have had our people's interests in his heart, that he used his position with us to further the ends of others. That he betrayed the trust we placed in him."

Jim frowned and slowly turned his face toward his mother, who was turning her puzzled frown toward him.

"You two," their captor said steadily, "can put this right. You can correct the error Lemuel made. You can redress the affront to the Meoena."

Jim held his hand up toward his mother and asked, "Do you want to express your outrage, or shall I do it?"

Her face betrayed no emotion. "I think it's up to our 'host' to explain himself. Kidnapping is one thing; disrespecting my husband is quite another."

Jim turned back to stare into the darkness. He smiled and waited.

The voice came again. "Your husband, Madam, acquired a piece of technology that may be valuable to the Meoena. It is both written and accepted that all such alien technology that comes aboard our stations is under the option of Meoenan authorities. All must be declared. None may be stored, investigated, duplicated, sold, bartered, or advertised for sale without the express permission of the relevant authorities."

"What piece of technology?" Jim asked.

"A piece of technology not so declared."

"Yeah, but what is it?"

No answer came.

"Come on," Jim encouraged, "don't be shy."

No answer came.

"What's the matter?"

Alfie interrupted. "Jim—"

"Not yet, Mom."

"Jim—"

"Mom! What?"

"They don't know, dear. This is all gossip and rumor. It's a fairy tale of hidden gold."

Jim looked to her and back to the dark. He laughed. "Really? That's all you've got? Lem had some tech that you never saw, don't know about, but whatever it is you're sure it's worth doing all this to get your hands on?" He shook his head.

The voice replied, "You will find it for us. You have the knowledge of both the station and your father's ways. You know where he might hide such items. You will find it."

"You're out of your minds!"

"Your mother will remain our guest until it is found."

Jim swore.

Alfie said, "He's right."

Jim glanced at her, frowned, and pointed out of the cage.

"No, dear, you're right. They're completely out of their minds. We've been kidnapped by lunatics."

Jim nodded. "Glad we're agreed on that."

A new voice spoke in the dark. "How long will it take you to search the entire station and inventory all devices left by your late father?"

"What? That's insane! It would take months!"

"How many months?"

Jim spluttered a little. "I'm not doing it. What does it matter?"

"You will search. Your mother's safety is assured only once the search is conducted."

"No way."

"How will the search be done?" Alfie asked with a smile. "Will Jim be free to look where he wants, as he wants? Will you have armed guards parading around the station, terrifying the residents? Have you thought about how that will look?"

Jim caught her eye and stopped protesting. He knew she was on to something.

They waited for a reply.

"We will extend liberty in the planning and execution of the search. If the residents and their concerns become a problem, we will evacuate the station until the search is concluded."

Jim nodded. "I see. So you have the power to do that, have you? That places you within a highly select group."

"Such speculation will assist neither you nor your mother. Do you agree to conduct the search, inventory all that your father left behind, and deliver all technology, parts, plans, and notes to us?"

"How? Where will you be? How will I travel?"

"All is arranged."

"And what am I looking for again?"

"We will monitor your search, but we will not interfere with it. You will be observed. You will be given facilities to arrange and catalog your finds. You will be provided accommodation."

Alfie immediately asked, "Where? There are no spare suites."

"Your rooms are currently vacant."

She snorted again but did not reply.

Jim turned to her and whispered, "What do you think? Am I doing this?"

She smiled. "That's up to you, dear."

"Anything you need me to send?"

"A change of clothes would be nice. Especially if it might take a while."

Jim nodded. "Dad was everywhere. He knew every nook and cranny, inside and out. It won't be quick."

She nodded.

Jim stood at the bars. "Can I bring in help? There's someone from Earth who is really good at this sort of thing."

"There will be no contact with the outside. You will tell no one of your mission or its circumstances."

"Hmm."

"We will return."

No more words were spoken. Jim and Alfie heard only the sound of footsteps fading away.

"I assume our jailer is still here," Jim whispered.

His mother nodded and, in English, said, "Probably. We'll just have to talk in English and hope he doesn't understand."

"So, where did Dad hide things?"

She laughed. "In the shed, I suppose."

"Right!" Jim laughed also. "Whenever he was mad at you, that's where he said he was going."

"As the years went on, he spent more and more time 'mad at me,' and I with him. Though I know now he was also at that temple a lot in Tuanomena City."

"You never knew where else he went?"

She shook her head. "No. He could have hidden himself away in a hundred different places on the station."

"I always loved the thought that there was a little wooden garden shed stuck somewhere on the outer shell of AC where he'd go to be alone and tinker with his machines." Jim sighed. "I miss him."

Alfie nodded. "I suppose I do, too, in a way."

03 TELLA

The noise of chains and heavy machinery echoed throughout the warehouse.

Tella shouted to be heard. "Are you sure you have enough height for the engravers? I told you both the depth of the cuts and the angles have to be exact."

The foreman rubbed his chin gently and looked at the Neraffan over his glasses. "Yeah, you said. I heard. It's enough. I've installed enough of these to know. You'll get the accuracy. It'll be as good as your scans. No better, mind you. No better. Garbage in, garbage out."

"Accuracy is essential. Payment is hinged upon it."

"Yeah. You said."

Not knowing what else to say, Tella moved to one side to observe in silence.

The crew was installing sixty-four laser engravers in a ring, suspended from the rafters of the warehouse.

Below, they had built an enormous piece of simulated rock two feet thick across the floor. It was circular, perfectly flat; it almost filled the entire warehouse.

Tella stepped into the tiny office, newly constructed for the laser controls.

A young woman sat plugging a series of cables into the back of a large panel.

"Was the data uploaded successfully?" Tella asked.

"Yes, sir, no problems. We'll get it done!"

"Thank you. I appreciate your efforts."

She nodded and said, "I've got to get back to work."

Tella left, sighing.

It looked at its list of messages, many of them from Jim Able.

Soon the EIA will move to track him and see if he has news of me.

Tella left the team at the warehouse and traveled to the nearest rental agency. It hired a small, one-person flier and flew out over the ocean south of Unity City and back toward the warehouse. The Neraffan landed as close to the warehouse's rear doors as it could safely manage.

Nodding in silence, it thought, *escape route secured.*

Tella stripped off its long white tunic and entered the warehouse again to stand invisible, watching and listening, to ensure the work went according to its instructions.

04 JAYDE'S DESK

Jayde returned to her office to find a short middle-aged Meoenan male sitting behind her desk.

"Who are you? What are you doing in my office?"

He looked up at her with a degree of control meant to intimidate. She recognized that face. She had seen him on the news. She had seen him wither a young reporter with a look—a look just like this one.

Jayde didn't hesitate. She walked up to the side of her desk and put her face too close. "Get out of my chair."

The Meoenan smiled, nodded deliberately, and stood, his shoulder jerking toward her face. She turned away from him, spinning round to catch the back of her chair with one hand and pull it back and away from the desk.

He turned to stare at her, but she had the chair and was also behind the desk.

"Please take a seat over there," she said quietly.

He stood, silent, as if he were about to deliver a blow. He nodded, moved around, sat, and put his feet up on the front of the desk.

"Do you know who I am?" he asked.

She sat and quickly surveyed the items laid out on the desk. *Nothing confidential. Good.*

"You are Lert Carn, and you have no business being here."

"Nor do you have any business disrupting the work of our police chief or upsetting the good religious people at the Temple of Tuanomena."

"Have they complained to you? Are you now part of either of the station administration committees?"

He laughed. "Don't play games. I heard you were back. I decided it was time for a chat."

"Make an appointment."

"I hoped we could have dinner. In an hour?"

"You don't want anything on the record then?"

"I think we can chat a while before it comes to that."

"The café has an excellent view."

"The Mafali restaurant is more discreet."

"The café. Or go home."

He bowed his head, withdrew his feet, and stood up. "One hour."

She did not reply.

As soon as he left, she called Yarl. "Yarl, get in here!"

"Madam Administrator," Yarl said dutifully, as he came through the door.

"Lert Carn is here. I'm eating with him in an hour. Suggestions?"

Yarl almost gestured, "No." Instead, he smiled and said, "Walk with him."

Jayde nodded. "Nice thought. And here's a better one. How many ships are currently docked at the station?"

Yarl punched a few commands into his tablet. "Twelve."

"Did Carn come in his own?"

"Yes."

"Arrange an immediate full inspection of all ships. Whatever regulation, ruse, feast day—whatever you can think of to justify it."

"I'm sure a proper reason exists somewhere."
"I want his navigation log. All of it."
"Ah."
"And I don't want him to know we got it."
"Ah."
"Call in whatever help you need. Now! The clock is ticking."
Yarl hesitated. "There is danger in this strategy."
"Who for? Us or Alfie?"
He nodded and left the office.

Jayde put her hand to her mouth and drummed her fingers on her desk. *Why am I suddenly not hungry?*

05 TELLA'S PROJECT

Silence reigned through the warehouse at Pier 78 and Makland Avenue, Unity City. The builders, the laser technicians, the painters, all had gone.

Only Tella stood, silent at the edge of the huge circular slab. What lay recreated in a smaller form across the warehouse floor, Tella had once seen on TMV-I. The Turcanian religious sect, the Regdenir, had performed their ceremony, the B'Goron Trahsa, on the original. They worshiped there but with no regard for the writings on the stone.

Tella had seen the lines, knew who had carved them, and had determined nothing would prevent it from studying them.

The government of TMV-I was preparing the population for the shocks that would come from opening up their world to interplanetary society. While they still forbade any offworld contact, Tella had no access to the original platform. The Neraffan had taken extremely high-definition scans from their flier, but Jim Able had kept the images.

But now, before it, lay the best recreation it could manage. All was ready.

It raised its transparent arms and took two long breaths, as an athlete might prepare for a jump. Then, slowly and with care, it stepped onto the flat surface.

Immediately thin lines traced over its feet. It walked close to the edge, watching the lines come and go as the etchings in the stone echoed and distorted across toes and feet.

Less than one-third of the way around, the lines changed. A circle appeared on the top of Tella's left foot. Throwing itself down onto the stone, it drew its hand over the etched circle. More detail showed on the back of its hand—not just a circle but also five curls within.

"And we begin, where you began, my friend, so long ago. Lead me," Tella muttered, its voice a mere whisper in the silent building.

Tella stroked and touched the stone and read its story for more than four hours. Each mark on the stone rose up through the Neraffan's skin, sometimes distorting, sometimes expanding. Details showed through its fingers, broader strokes through its arms. The whole platform was etched with the ancient secret writing of the Neraffan-jong, which could only be interpreted by the living hands and arms of one such as Tella.

Then Tella's tablet sounded an alert. Reluctantly, it stood, walked to the tablet, and read, "James Able abducted on flight from EBMS to Earth."

06 NEARLY DONE

Lem ran his gloved hand over the white enameled panels under the wide glass expanse of what would one day be the café's window. Through his visor, he could see the leaking joint. A faint jet of moisture froze a few inches from the hole. "Fasta, it's here. Panel 47a by 02g and 48a by 02g."

"Got it!" Fasta's voice came through the helmet comms link. "I'll have the lads take it apart again. We'll get it this time."

"I hope so. I don't want to see any more of this. What do they think they're building here, a colander?"

"What's a colander?"

"Never mind. Coming back in."

"Okay."

Alfie fidgeted with a paint brush as she sat with her husband at the dinner table. "I'm not sure. She's so young!"

"She won't be on her own. Johan and Maggie will be there to meet her. The flight attendant will look after her during the journey."

"But she's only nine! Jim's twelve and we're not letting him travel anywhere on his own."

"Alfie, love, we trust Mazette. She'll sit quietly, read her books, and be no trouble. She's a good girl. God! Let Jim loose on a ship and he'll have it half dismantled before they get underway."

"I know. I suppose it's not a fair comparison. I still worry."

"That's your job. It'll still be your job when you're ninety. She'll love it on Earth. She's only seen a little bit of Sonloi. She's never seen the sea—I mean, *our* sea! Can you imagine?"

"I'd prefer to be the one showing it to her."

Lem shook his head. "Been through that, haven't we? We can't go now. She'll be back in a month."

Alfie sighed, unconvinced. "Maybe Matt could go with her?"

"He's studying. I don't want him missing those extra credits."

She sighed again. "Oh, well. I guess we have no choice."

Lem watched her as she took her brush over to the easel. He remembered his grandfather's adage: "A woman convinced against her will is of the same opinion still."

07 YARL AND JAYDE

The alarms on Sonloi-AC were quite specific in their function. One sounded to announce an external threat, such as a possible damaging collision. Another sounded to warn of an internal threat, such as a fire.

The biological threat alarm, ringing now, hardly ever sounded. All ships had contagion protocols; all visitors underwent decontamination. Anyone causing such a threat accidentally would be severely embarrassed. Anyone thinking to deliberately bring contagion to a station would probably decide to use armaments as a much faster, more effective, and cheaper method.

In the event of the activation of the bio-alarm, all personnel knew to stay where they were. Someone somewhere would deal with the threat, and no one wanted to be the one to get in their way.

After the alarm, the air in the café became a little warmer and somewhat less fresh, but dinner continued, accompanied by an elevated buzz of conversation.

Teams of Meoenan technicians, all dressed from head to foot in protective gear, boarded each of the docked ships. The crews shuffled reluctantly through additional decontamination. Cleaning teams worked room by room through several of the vessels.

Within an hour, the station had returned to normal.

Jayde had a few strongly worded protests waiting for her.

"Yarl! What did you get?" she hissed, leaning over his desk.

He drew his hands together and said quietly, "Everything you asked for."

"Great! Let me see it."

"No."

"Wh-what do you mean?"

"I had the resources to begin the plan as you instructed. However, the disposition of the requested material is beyond my power to fulfill."

"I"—she stopped and frowned—"What did you say?"

"We extracted the navigation log. No one saw us. But I couldn't keep the copy. It has gone elsewhere."

"Where?" Jayde's eyes widened.

Yarl did not look at her. "You said to 'call in whatever help' was needed. I called. They acted. But I was—am—not in charge."

"I see."

"Once I made my request, and the importance of the log became obvious, others made their own decisions and calculations."

"Look, I don't care what—how—you guys organize yourselves. This is about getting Alfie back!"

"Yes."

"Yes, what?"

"The information gained will be used in returning The Artist to Sonloi-AC."

"'Will be used' by your contacts. You're telling me it won't be used by me."

"I believe not. We must wait and trust."

Jayde snorted, turned her back, and then faced him again. "You say you're not in charge. Look at me!" She waited until Yarl's eyes were focused on her face. "I'm in charge, remember? This isn't what I wanted, and you know it. You people are just so frustrating— the...contorted...way you do things!"

"I'm sorry I have disappointed you. Perhaps I should take some time off?"

Jayde frowned. "Sure. Though I doubt I'll be any less mad at you after."

"I'm sorry. I shall go at once."

Jayde nodded and said, "Clear your desk."

08 ANNE

Tella approached its rented flier, parked at the back of the warehouse. A slight reflection on the metallic paintwork caught its eye. It swung around ready to defend itself.

A woman stood facing it squarely, blaster ready to fire. She said, "You're damned hard to find! You are Tella, right?"

Tella replied, "Firstly, not as difficult as I would like, it seems. Secondly, if you know my name, you must be confident that I am indeed Tella. How many Neraffans are there in Unity City?"

"So far, just you. I'm Anne Brewer. I'm with the OEA Tactical Response Unit. I've worked with Jim Able, and I'm looking for him."

"What is that to me?"

Anne bit her lip and half smiled. "Can we talk somewhere private?"

"You don't trust me," Tella replied, looking at the blaster.

"Not yet. I've heard good things about you. However,"—she gestured to the warehouse, the flier, and the sea—"all this is quite a setup. You're up to something. You're EIA. You aren't expecting me. I think I'm right to be careful."

Tella nodded. "We can talk inside the warehouse or the flier."

"The flier."

Tella turned to open the steps up to the flier. Anne holstered her blaster but did not fasten its strap.

Inside the small craft, Tella sat in the pilot's seat, and Anne squeezed herself onto a luggage shelf to one side.

"How much did Jim tell you about his experiences at Ch'Garratt?" she began.

"He has told me of it on several occasions."

"I was there, just after, to extract him."

Tella smiled. "This he has not mentioned."

"You know about Jack Katrigg?"

Tella nodded.

"Well," Anne hesitated, "I recently gave Jim some intelligence about a sighting of Katrigg. And I'm afraid Jim might be off doing something stupid."

"Always a possibility."

"So, I came to find you. Damn, it took a while!"

"It should not have been possible at all."

Anne laughed. "Typical EIA arrogance. The OEA does good work, mister."

Tella smiled and showed Anne the report of Jim's disappearance.

"He was on his way to Earth?"

"From the Europa Biological Monitoring Station."

"Last I checked with them, they hadn't seen him."

"He was in an agency flier, rather than his own ship, when the incident occurred."

Anne nodded, "I know about his ship. He described it as 'mobile lodgings.'"

"It must still be docked at EBMS."

Anne held Tella's gaze. "We should check it out."

"We?"

"Damn right! Who else?"

Tella turned to the controls. "I can in no way guarantee your safety. Nor can I officially work with you in your capacity as a member of the Tactical Response Unit. Our agencies would require several months of agonized discussion before agreeing to such an arrangement."

"I'm on vacation," she replied.

"So am I," Tella said quietly. "Please try and secure yourself for the flight to orbit."

She glanced around the small cabin. "Okay. Looks like I'll go sit on the toilet."

Tella said, "I must send a message before we depart."

"Sure."

To: Pritas
From: Tella

In Quavvour's name, greetings.

Come to Unity City, Pier 78 and Makland Avenue, Warehouse 42B.

Examine the carving therein.

A living colony of Jong may survive on Turcanis Major Five.

I have done what I can. Now you must act. Be aware there is no clear path. We must involve the Cott. Let them preserve the carving and deal with Earth authorities.

A friend's life is in danger. To this matter I must dedicate myself.

I entrust this matter to you and your best judgment. Do not let me down.

---

09 THE TEMPLE OF TUANOMENA

"What does the sign say?" Lem asked his guide.

"First was built the temple; then came the city."

"Really? So, why did they build it here?"

"Tuanomena was here first."

Lem laughed. "Okay! I know enough not to ask more. Whatever I ask now, the answer is 'It's really quite complicated.'"

The guide smiled and continued, "Like you, the young ask many questions. 'Is the temple far?' 'Will we stay there long?' And their elders will answer, 'It is not far, though it may not be visited quickly.' Not all questions may be answered simply."

"Lead on!" Lem said, smiling.

Lem Able had visited the temple several times but had thought it no more than an archaeological artifact, the unchanged bequest of a distant culture from Meoenan history.

Fasta had told him of the large community of male and female monks who lived within the ziggurat, maintained the structure, and perpetuated the ancient rituals of the place while largely staying out of public view. Some served visitors, some taught students, but many lived entirely hidden lives.

The resonance between their purpose and Lem's own brought him back again.

He had helped bring Sonloi-AC to life. He was staying on to maintain it. How long would the station last? Did the temple builders understand how many years these stone walls would stand? What did they put in place, in those early days, to ensure generational care would be bestowed on the structure and its activities?

The thought of time stretching beyond the reach of his own efforts humbled him. The vision of the things he must leave behind falling through the hands of others appalled him. It fascinated him.

When I'm dead, who will care about the internal structures of AC? Who will read the documentation we're writing? Even if they do, how much of it will they understand?

He looked up at the sign, "First was built the temple; then came the city." *Maybe that's the answer. The station will acquire what it needs. It will develop its own friends, its own monks.* Lem chuckled at the thought of being an acolyte to a ball of steel, glass, and plastic.

The guide moved on to a large open square lit by brilliant sunlight streaming from the high roof. The party of visitors, including several humans, clustered around him.

"'Is the temple dedicated to a deity?' the stranger may ask. But what answer can we give? Tuanomena reveals some knowledge to some students, different knowledge to others, gifts to some recipients, while others come empty away. You must find your own answer to that question. Come back as you will. Come and study if you wish. Be open to all that Tuanomena may give to you."

"We could come and study here?" Lem asked, surprised.

The guide made an ambiguous Meoenan gesture and said, "I see no problem with that. We have had no interplanetary students as yet. But such opportunities are new to us all. If you wish a more detailed answer, I will ask the office of the Chatse to speak with you."

Lem frowned as he answered, "Sure. I'd like that." *Would I? Why? Maybe the early monks can give me a clue on setting up a proper legacy.*

10 JIM'S SEARCH: PART ONE

Jim knew better than to hurry, only firing the jets on his pack when he had to. He remembered what his father taught him when he was still too small for a full-sized suit: it's easy to build up too much momentum with jet thrusters and perspective is tricky when you are a small human next to a huge ship or—in this case—station.

Sonloi-AC was spherical but not a complete sphere. The planet-facing half was full, its surface smooth and white.

Rising seamlessly from the front end, four elegant arms curved to meet at the equator behind the station. At their farthest point, the arms held the main engine block that day by day and night by night kept the station dancing smoothly.

Corralled by these long graceful arms were the service accesses, the fuel and material stores, and all the workings—the "back end," as Lem Able used to call it—that would otherwise mar the circular beauty of the front end.

Shuttles came and went from the planet to the north pole of the station. Larger ships, visiting flagships, supply vessels, and passing military ships docked at the south pole.

Jim came down from the north, under one arm, into the shadows. He flew over large areas of antennae, relays, and aerials. He saw blocks the size of large buildings clustered in groups according to the function of the machinery hidden inside. He saw small, dimly lit windows, begrudging the light they lost from maintenance passages, workshops, and crew break rooms.

He saw areas deliberately blackened to avoid unnecessary reflected light interfering with the telescopes and research instruments that grew like mushrooms on any surface that would hold them.

This had been his father's domain. Lem had known every block, every shadow, every curve. He knew what machinery was behind each wall, what services and why, where the redundancy lay, and where empty areas stood ready for future expansion. Jim knew some of these from helping his father in his day-to-day work. He had learned much of the station's inner workings but not all. Lem had spent most of his working life building the station and then caring for it.

If Lem Able had hidden anything, it would be back here somewhere. But Jim had no specific idea where to begin.

He maneuvered himself below the arm, out toward the propulsion array. The bulk of the station hid him from the light of Pec; little light shone up from the back end.

An idea began to form as Jim repeatedly asked himself, *Okay, Dad, where would you hide something?*

The idea was twofold. Lem wouldn't just paint something black to hide it from casual view. That sort of disguise, easily overcome by close-range observation, was not subtle enough for Lem. Jim's father was better than that; he would have done it with style.

You would have positioned it just right, wouldn't you? The positioning would be part of the fun, part of the disguise. Something as simple as putting it where no one could look out a window at it. That would be step one.

Step two?

Actually... Jim held his thumbs on the jet controls. He laughed. *That's a really difficult thing to do back here. Passing ships can, if they want, come around this side and see almost everything. It's all plainly on display.*

Jim's heart sank for a moment. He wondered if he should just go back inside and work from a model.

No, if it's here, it'll only be seen and accessed from out here. And only once you know it's there.

Where would no one ever need to go?

Jim slowly worked his way down the arm, passing a few passive nodes built to record the humdrum data on the local radiation levels and the stresses in the arm.

The arm began to narrow as it curved to meet the other arms out farther at the propulsion array.

The point where the four sweeping arms met was a huge cylindrical core, one end facing the station, the other blossoming into a rosette of thrusters, exhausts, and five massive engine housings. The face of the core was a solid wall showing no maintainable parts. Inside the core were, of course, technical wonders, but outside held nothing of interest.

The station could only move forward, its habitable parts leading the way, though with a propulsion array of such power and delicate complexity, it could spin on a pinhead. In fact, it constantly moved —tiny adjustments, up, down, to one side or another, so subtle and quiet the residents could hardly tell.

Jim approached the inner face of the central cylindrical core; it was black to avoid unnecessary reflection. The core was hidden from the outside of the arms and unseen from all the maintenance windows directly overhead.

This is the place, Jim thought.

The shed hid in plain sight.

Jim hovered above it for a long while, slowly casting his small flashlight beam along what features he could see.

Against the black metal of the core wall was a black rectangle.

As he came a little closer, he moved down one side, and the shape revealed itself. The whole construction was a simple outer frame and an inner rectangular body. The far end held to the core wall with a minimum of girders and beams, less neat and clean than the rest of the station.

Jim positioned himself to look down the gap between the frame and the inner object. They were only about six inches apart. He was looking at a rectangular column some fifty or sixty feet tall and fifteen feet wide. The top consisted of a typical airlock.

He laughed. When Jim was eight years old, his father had helped him make a gun. It fired a steel bolt, and the firing mechanism was an array of electromagnets. This building used the same technique. Given the right trigger, Jim thought, the interior structure could fire straight out, into the back of Sonloi-AC. It also meant that, given the right setup, the interior structure would never touch the outer frame at all.

What were you thinking?

Jim drifted off to consider the door.

It was a regular outer airlock door, with the regulation ease-of-use handle and warning signs. But this had a coating of nonreflective black and had no window.

Jim thought of his father: always ready for fun and always ready with a laugh—much to his wife's annoyance. Also, to the alarm of his children, he was often a practical joker.

But he was, also, always a teacher. His pranks usually had a point, a lesson to be learned. Jim remembered several lessons learned at the cost of a blow to the nose, a black eye, or an embarrassing time in helpless weightlessness.

Still not risking a better light, he opened the airlock door. His left hand went up, inside, and to the left. He felt the spring-trap in his hand.

Classic, Dad.

In the dark, Jim was faintly aware of the jointed arm that connected the trap to something to his right, something darker than the surrounding shadows. He briefly turned on the flashlight again.

A large round punch bag stretched between two arms. If he hadn't caught the spring-trap, the arms would have swung across the doorway and the punch bag would have smacked him back out of the door at speed.

Smiling and still holding the trap mechanism, Jim stepped inside. The trap reset with a faint click, and he let go. The airlock door shut smoothly behind him.

He pressed the control to equalize the air, but an alarm warning lit up. *How many years since anyone came through here?*

He overrode the warning and opened the inner door.

Low-level lighting came on.

Down the length of the single room, Jim could see workbenches, storage shelves filled with plastic boxes of different sizes, and a small cloud of papers, floating weightless.

No air, no gravity. But it's full of your stuff, isn't it, Dad? You actually built a damned shed, didn't you?

11 GROR GUTE

A monk, yes. A leader, that too. A monk, though, with ambition. Gror Gute studied harder than his peers.

The life of the temple held both hardships and comforts. No one became thin while living as a monk. But much else had to be left outside. No one became rich while living as a monk.

The pinnacle of the ziggurat, the uppermost layer, also served as the spiritual apogee to which all thoughts rose. Every monk longed, one day, to be educated sufficiently and worthy enough, yet optimally humbled and disciplined in attitude, to be able to ascend to The Walk. There Tuanomena would select, at will, certain individuals for special blessings.

Those not chosen would also be changed in many ways, perhaps by The Walk itself or by mere proximity to the mystery that is Tuanomena.

The tales of those who had walked The Walk were precious reading in the temple library.

"Why did Tuanomena choose these souls?" a novice might ask, only to be rebuked for spiritual jealousy.

"It is not our place to ask, or even wonder, but to accept in gratitude. Tuanomena owes us no explanation. We have no call upon the mystery. Leave outside the temple such considerations. We are here within the walls to learn, not to possess, not to attain, not to grasp. No, our place is to let go. If we later are to receive, it is to the exultation of Tuanomena, not of ourselves."

Gror Gute studied harder than his peers.

Mit Apogan. Gror rolled the name around in his mind. Never once, in forty years, had he heard such a name pronounced until—on reading the name in a note—he negotiated passage offworld and heard the name formed and pronounced in alien mouths.

A star called Mit—cold, white, and dimmer than Pec—shone through the high clouds and onto the flat stone of the cave's entrance.

The light carries little warmth.

Such an observation encapsulated the constant constraint of a monk. He or she may observe but not follow the fracturing, distracting thoughts that might spread from such an observation.

Such a fact of bodily experience should never be a source of complaint. It should not become a wish that things were other than they are.

The weaker light must not be considered subordinate to its warmer peers. Warmth must not be something one aspires to. Nor comfort. Nor safety.

One welcomes what it is.

Hunger, likewise, often leads to a fracturing of purpose. Seldom a challenge in the comfortable and stable temple. Here, on an alien planet with a flight bag of dwindling supplies, it presents itself as a problem.

But one welcomes what it is.

How long will I meditate here?

A long time must not be spoken of as subordinate to its shorter peers. A conclusion, or an event, or an ending must not be something one aspires to. Nor comfort. Nor safety.

On Mit Apogan, on whatever continent that spread across the dark horizon, in whatever country that surrounded this mountain, and here inside this nameless cave, the night was full of noise.

Echoes in the hills below: *The cracks of branches, perhaps.* The sudden tumble of pebbles above the cave's entrance: *A creature, certainly. A danger, perhaps.* Gror listened with the dispassion of a monk.

The quiet brush of fur on stone: *At last, I am not alone.*

Every monk must be admonished, occasionally, for wishing his or her meditation was other than it is. It is not rare to find the desire for company giving rise to a distraction.

One welcomes what it is.

I am not alone

12 JIM'S SEARCH: PART TWO

Jim walked a short way in and noticed the trap at the airlock had more to it than a punching bag. Wires ran from the inner doorway and attached to a long rectangular device on the nearest table inside.

He looked and looked again.

"Dad?" he said out loud. His heart was thumping.

The device was a D-switch. Where a regular D-switch had three sets of coordinates that could be input for each jump, this one already had some coordinates set.

The device had a clean, but old, metallic surface. It had seven sets of numbers in addition to the familiar three, making it almost three times as long as a regular D-switch. Two of the seven displays, Jim could see, were changing slowly. Two more were changing much faster.

Jim knew all D-switches were the same. They all came from the same source, all fitted by spacecraft manufacturers the same way. They only had destination settings.

"What are those other parameters, Dad? And why—how?—do you have this thing?"

The D-switch was clamped to the table with two metal bars. At its base, two pieces of tape held a simple timer with what looked to Jim like a toggle switch.

In his father's hand, in black indelible pen, the tape to the left was marked "Outgoing" and to the right, "Back."

What does that mean?

Jim sighed and straightened up, rolling the tension from his shoulders.

You've set the switch. The door opens and you jump to a destination of some sort. That's your 'Outgoing.' The punch bag deploys, and then this egg timer flips the switch 'Back.' Why?

Jim's mind raced through several impossible scenarios.

Why doesn't Sonloi-AC go with you? What is this for? Am I the first person to see this? What the hell is going on?

Two answers came immediately.

No, the electromagnets! The shed doesn't touch the station, so only the shed moves. Nice.

And if whoever gets hit with the punch bag isn't hanging on, you come back without him. Not nice. Not nice at all.

Jim felt sick. This was no ordinary engineering toy of his father's. This was a D-switch that did something else. What something else could be better than timeless, effortless, universally available space travel? And why had his father set a deathtrap to guard it?

This is too much! Sorry, Mom, there's no way I can give this to anybody! I guess Dad felt the same. This setup is rigged so no stranger would be able to get at it. Depending on what it really does and who created it, it's probably worth a fortune.

Jim looked down the length of the room.

Which is why Dad couldn't let anyone else see it. And why someone would be motivated enough to kidnap us to get to it.

Jim floated down to the next workbench, reached up and reset the gravity control. The papers floated softly to the floor. He untethered a stool and sat down.

Okay, Jim, priorities! How he got this can wait. What it does is something he would've spent a lot of time on. I need to find your notes, Dad, which won't be just lying around. You secured them somewhere, didn't you? But now, I have to keep it out of the wrong hands! That's the problem. That's number one. Sorry, Mom, you just got relegated to second place.

Jim looked back to the airlock and the punch bag mechanism.

So far, so good. You've rigged it to prevent access. But, that was only ever a temporary fix. Why didn't you—

Jim's thoughts were interrupted by a click in his helmet radio.

He pressed the button on the wrist of his spacesuit. "Hello? This is Jim Able."

Instead of a reply or another click, a knock came from the airlock door. Someone was outside.

Jim looked quickly at the D-switch. His father had fixed a cloth cover in place above the switch. Jim rolled out the cover and clipped it into place to conceal the device.

Nice.

Jim repeated his reply. "Hello? This is Jim Able."

"I know damn well who you are. I know where you are too. So open the damn door!"

"Who is this?"

There was silence.

Jim said, "Hello?"

"It's your dad, Jim. Open the door."

Jim turned slowly from the switch toward the door.

His heart pumping, he walked back into the airlock, reached up to the spring trap to prevent it activating, and opened the door.

Jim could see a familiar face through the clear visor of another spacesuit.

"Hoo, now," said Lem. "Take a breath."

Jim growled, "What is this?"

Lem floated in through the door. His hand went up to the trap and Jim's glove. "I've got it. Thanks."

Jim let go and backed into the shed.

Lem waited until the door had shut itself and then followed Jim.

"First question," he said cheerfully. "Is this the first time you've gotten in here? Tell me. It's absolutely the most important thing."

Jim nodded. "Yes. But—"

"Okay. Right-o. So you've only just seen the tin monster."

"The what?"

"That D-switch that isn't a D-switch."

Jim nodded and said nothing.

Lem looked at his son. "I hope you came with plenty of oxygen; this is going to take a while. I've moved through time to speak to you."

Lem unzipped a large pocket on the front of his suit, revealing another—or, rather, the same—D-switch.

13 LEM AND GROR

"What are you?"

Lem thought the question both odd and rude. Meoena, noted for their politeness, are rarely so direct.

He turned to the monk who had spoken. *And who are you? Did you just mean 'Who are you?'* "I'm Lem Able, senior engineer for Sonloi-AC. At your service."

"And I am Gror Gute. I did not ask 'who' you are, but 'what.'"

Lem nodded. *Right-o, deliberately rude. This is a first. Maybe being short and a little overweight gives you a bad attitude.* "I'm a human. How can you not have seen one of us before?"

Gror replied slowly, "I have seen humans. Indeed, I have recently returned from traveling to other worlds and have made the acquaintance of several interesting species. I refer, however, to you —I will admit, a human—sitting here in the Temple of Tuanomena. You have our holiest books laid out before you. You are unaccompanied by any temple staff. How is this possible? You work in space, in orbit of our world, as you say. And so, I question what you do here. What are you that such behavior is tolerated?"

"I have permission to study here. Your librarian has been kind enough to lend me these books. Perhaps this was arranged while you were traveling, but I have permission."

Lem felt the weight of the silence that followed. Gror stood across the table from him and stared, unmoving.

The Meoenan said something Lem didn't catch.

"I'm sorry? What did you say?"

Gror sighed and through gritted teeth asked, "Do you have permission from Tuanomena?"

Lem smiled and said, "I'm sure there's no easy answer to that one!"

"Come to The Walk."

Lem sat back in surprise. "I-I'm sure I do not have permission for that! I know how hard you guys work to get ready for The Walk. Years of study! I'm just a beginner. Though I have been reading a lot about it."

"There are paths through the temple that some may take with greater ease than the masses. If you desire to encounter Tuanomena, you must come to The Walk."

Lem was instantly suspicious. He had heard the monk's name, but it meant nothing to him, other than it being similar to one of the authors he'd come across in his studies. "I'm not sure I should. I wouldn't want to get you into trouble for taking me where I shouldn't go."

"At each step up the temple, we leave behind the dust of what we have carried. Do not carry the dust of concern for me. Shake it off. Come with me! Now!"

Gror accompanied Lem on several circuits around The Walk. The crowd thinned, gathered, and thinned again. Lem saw it all, wide-eyed. As the repetition continued, his spirit calmed. He began to understand more of what he had been reading.

He whispered to Gror, "I should be getting back. I have to go to work."

Gror laughed.

A while later, Lem tried again, "I really have to be going. This is wonderful, and I don't want it to end, but I have to get back."

Gror hissed back, "Be at peace! Tuanomena may yet grace us with his presence."

Lem stopped walking. "I would like that. Very much. But I'm not a monk. You asked me what I was. Well, here is something I'm not. I cannot spend any more time with you. Thank you for bringing me. Now, please, take me back."

Gror glowered. "You will come again?"

Lem nodded enthusiastically. "Of course! This is a wonderful privilege. It's an honor I would never refuse."

Gror looked at him with something Lem thought might have been the beginnings of respect. "Very well. I have hope yet that Tuanomena will clarify your position here."

Lem nodded but said nothing.

Gror led him back to retrieve his shoes. They walked down some steps, and suddenly they were in the library again and everything was as it was before.

14 MAZETTE

Johan and Maggie met Mazette off the flight. She greeted them formally and asked about her luggage.

Johan's first thought was *There's a kid who has her act together.*

Under a beach umbrella, Maggie sat with the girl and sipped a cold drink. "What do you think of life on Earth, Maz? Is it very different from what you've seen on Sonloi?"

Maz didn't answer right away. Maggie watched and waited.

"I think it's confusing. There are so many people doing so many things. Across on Sonloi, it's only been trips with Mom and Dad, and they take us places where nothing is happening. At home, it's a lot less noisy than here."

"I know what you mean. A lot of people seem to think they must rush around and talk loudly all the time. That's what I love about coming to the beach. Everyone relaxes."

"The sea is awesome, though I wish it tasted better."

Maggie laughed. "Next planet you build, dear, make sure you order a sweet ocean."

Mazette nodded sagely, "I will. And I'll make it—for the whole planet—that no one is in a rush."

"That sounds like somewhere I would love to visit!"

The front door of Johan and Maggie's house was guarded by two ornamental cedars. Maggie had warned Mazette not to disturb the pair of sparrows nesting in one.

"Can I hold one? Just once?"

"No, dear. They're wild birds. We don't pick them up. We can watch them and make sure they have food when the weather's bad, but that's all. We have to give them their space."

"I wish there were birds at home."

Maggie smiled sadly. *Life in space is so limiting for a child!* "Do you have no pets at all?"

"Matt had a fish tank, but it started to smell, so Dad got rid of it. And someone has a cat we see once in a while."

"Oh, that's nice."

Late in the evening, Mazette sat on the front step listening to the chirping. One bird flew out suddenly.

The girl jumped up and ran down the path after it. "Where are you going? It's late!" she called.

Maggie's voice came from within the house. "Don't go out in the street, Maz!"

She waited at the end of the path, at the open gate, watching the trees across the road. The bird started to fly back toward her, but the sound of an engine frightened it. Swinging low over the road, the bird turned, and went back to the other trees.

She stepped out of the gate.

The engine coughed and whined. The hovercar lurched down, crashing onto the garden fence. Maz disappeared underneath.

. . .

Lem came to Earth alone for the inquest. The whole family came for the funeral.

Sonloi-AC was not the same when they returned.

The Meoena of Pec Sonloi all grieved with the Family Able. Books of remembrance cluttered the side table in their small apartment on the crew level.

Jim lay in bed, listening to the low voices of his parents talking in the main room.

"We never will, love. We never will," Lem said.

"That's no comfort."

"I hear grief is something that stays with you. It's something everything else has to adjust to. We have to give it time."

Alfie snorted.

Lem pressed on. "It won't be easy. For us, or the boys."

"No."

"I'll talk to them. Try and find out what they're feeling."

"I think we probably know that, don't we?"

Lem shrugged. "It's better to ask. Jim has hardly said a word since we got back."

After a long while, Alfie said, "I want to paint her. I wish I had—"

"You did. We have that beautiful portrait of the three of them!"

"That was too long ago! I want to paint her as she was when she left for Earth. Full of hope and excitement..."

They both sat with silent tears.

Jim was still listening as his parents went to bed, but he didn't hear one final quiet comment from Alfie. Even if he had, he wouldn't have understood what it meant for the Family Able.

"You insisted she go."

Alfie sat awake in her chair. "Where's my food?" she called.

"Being prepared," replied the voice.

"What's taking so long?"

"Please be patient."

"What does your wife think of you being away for so long?"

No answer came.

Alfie persisted. "I've been thinking of her. She must be a very patient wife to put up with it all. I grew disgusted with my husband when he spent too much time helping you Meoena, and less and less time with me. You should watch out she doesn't leave you."

She heard a faint reaction, less than a word, quieter than a grunt. She smiled to herself. "I suppose, this being a secret operation, you haven't been able to tell her where you are. That must be so uncomfortable. I mean, not just for you—for her! Imagine! You disappear for days on end, and then it turns to weeks. Has she reported you missing? What lies did you have to tell her?"

"These matters are of no concern to you."

"Oh yes they are. You're here worrying about home. What's she doing? Who is she with? How worried is she? With all this going on in that quiet orderly mind of yours, what chance do *I* have? How much of your attention do *I* get? It's a recipe for mistakes, and you know it! They've left you here, on the spot, making decisions minute by minute, knowing you're distracted and worried about her. Worried about home—Oh, my goodness, I hope you don't have children! Oh, I hope not, poor dears."

"These matters are not your concern!"

"You'll make a mistake. I'll come to harm. And then what? What will happen then? Do you think your employer is the understanding sort...or...?"

"Be silent! I will check on the progress of your food."

She went on, talking to his retreating footsteps. "Really, how much do you know about him? How trustworthy is a person who would arrange all this? How much will he care about your family in the end?"

Alfie enjoyed the silence that followed. *Oh, such dull sport. But what else do I have to do?*

A noise interrupted Alfie's nap. A noise she had never heard or imagined before; metal raked against metal; seals burst, and the air popped. The noise came not once but again and again in rapid succession—an enormous ratcheting sound that shook the bars of the cage and hurt her ears. It persisted for three or four painful seconds.

Then all was quiet and still. The small lights in the cages went out.

She felt no movement. No air flowed, but the temperature had dropped.

"I don't think that came from the kitchen," she said to herself.

Fast footsteps came across the cargo bay floor. Flashlights swept the cages.

"There she is!" called a young Meoenan voice.

Several other voices whooped and cheered.

"Who's there?" Alfie called.

"Don't be afraid. We are here to help."

She waited.

Six Meoena appeared next to the bars. They wore space suits, visors open.

"Hello, dears. The door is round the back, I think."

Five moved behind the cages. One remained.

"I am relieved to find you unharmed."

"Yarl Breen? Is that you?"

"Yes, dear Artist. We must hurry. As soon as you are free from here, we must run. My colleagues have a suit for you. We must get you into it immediately."

"Oh, I see. I can tell the air pressure isn't right. You've done something drastic, haven't you. Is Jim with you?"

"The Younger Son? No, was he here?"

Alfie nodded. Before they could say more, the back part of the cage, where the food slot had been, blew inward with a burst of white sparks. Alfie put her hands up to sweep her hair behind her and walked out to the helping arms of her rescuers.

Alfie followed Yarl and the others to the flight room of their ship. She recognized the large commercial vessel—the kind that came to resupply the station occasionally, large enough to carry structural pieces for the station, large machinery, or enormous quantities of necessities.

She looked out of the observation windows down the ship's length to another—the vessel she had come from. The other ship was a small transporter, a vessel only designed for shuttling smaller items from planet to station or vice versa or for keeping artists imprisoned in secret.

Alfie stared at the two vessels, incredulous. They had not docked together but intersected. The larger ship had somehow engulfed the smaller's bridge area. A cloud of material expanded from the join: air and debris, jets of liquid freezing in the vacuum.

Alfie clicked the communicator on her suit. "What did you do?" she asked.

Yarl answered. "No two D-switches will occupy the same space at the same time. However, one vessel may be stored in or docked with another. The D-switch of the larger takes precedence. The switch of the smaller will not operate while it is stored. Had your vessel been traveling on regular propulsion, we would have appeared in front of it with our cargo bay open and enveloped you that way. Instead, we used small adjustments of our course until the D-switch of your vessel was encompassed by our ship."

"You've breached the hulls of both. Both are leaking atmosphere!"

"We will soon be near Sonloi-AC and the emergency call for evacuation has already gone out."

She laughed. "I've never heard of such a thing!"

"When we learned that Lert Carn's ship spent an hour docked with another vessel, we had to act quickly, before it could retreat. This was the best we could come up with at short notice."

"Lert Carn? Oh, dear."

"Our station administrator will be happy to see you."

"And I her. But you didn't know Jim is on the station?"

"I had not heard it, but, yes, I'm told he is there now."

"Good. What happened to the crew of the ship I was on?"

Yarl hesitated. "They put up little resistance."

Alfie sighed. "Oh dear, oh dear. How did such an organized rescue happen? You're a capable person, Yarl, but not that good! Who is behind all this?"

"I cannot say. But you can thank your husband that Sonloi-AC and those most closely associated with it are watched and protected."

Alfie frowned but asked nothing further.

16 LEM AND TUANOMENA

Gror found Lem reading in a quiet alcove.

"Will you ascend to The Walk with me again?"

There're no social niceties with you, are there? Lem nodded. "Always! It's an honor."

"What have you been reading?

"Someone called Miqlu. I'm not sure I understand it all. Or even some of it. It's very mystical."

Gror laughed. "We accept what is. If it is incomprehensible, we accept that. If it is mystical and pregnant with meaning, this too, we accept."

"As I think I have told you before, I am not a monk. I'm an engineer. I seek facts and explanations."

Gror growled in his chest, a sound Lem had never heard from a Meoenan. "That is why it is you who build space stations and we who live in them."

Are you patronizing me? "Perhaps we have complementary skills and interests. I look forward to seeing how your people use Sonloi-AC. I think it will be a great place for the sharing of your culture and your encounters with your neighbors."

Gror rolled his large eyes. "Do you take part in The Walk to analyze it, to find out how it works?"

"Of course! I want to know everything about it!"

"Even if you find out how it works, you will merely know how it works, not what it is."

"You're an irritating and challenging guide, Gror. I won't hide that you rub me up the wrong way—and I believe that's mutual. But I appreciate what you are doing for me. I need to know more about The Walk. I see the surface; I see what it seems to be. But it's a whole lot more, isn't it? You know way more than you're telling me."

Gror was silent as they took the stairs to a higher floor. Then he said, "The Walk is where we encounter Tuanomena. There is no need to know more. There is nothing more to tell you."

"Who is Tuanomena? Or, perhaps, I should use your first question to me? *What* is Tuanomena?"

Gror howled with laughter. He was slightly out of breath at the top of the stairs. "At last! As a student, you begin to ask the right question."

As Lem stood on the top step, Gror grabbed his shoulder. "Tuanomena is a blade that slices people. He carves one member from a family, one student from a class. Tuanomena chooses one from another. He breaks through our every bond. We are the carved, not the carver. We are the broken, not the breaker. Study The Walk all you wish, human. You hold no sway here. This place is Tuanomena's. Humility is your only protection."

Humility? Me? You arrogant son of a bitch! Lem swallowed, partly at the unexpected confrontation, partly for fear of being pushed back down the stairs. "I hear you. I know I am a stranger here, a first-year student. I'm not claiming any special treatment. But I am who I am. I see things through a human lens, through an engineer's lens. I won't apologize for that. Any more than you should for being a monk."

"Tuanomena will decide."

Decide what?

Gror led Lem on to The Walk.

.   .   .

Lem lost count of how many times they circled The Walk. Their feet and those of their fellow pilgrims marked out a meditative yet subtle rhythm.

Suddenly, the sunlight dimmed in the shafts and windows. Lem felt cold and alone.

Ahead, the path no longer had the comforting curve. It ran straight into a shadow.

A thought that was not his own pounded in Lem's mind. His knees failed and the ground rose up.

As he fainted, Lem was aware of the presence. The presence was neither hostile nor friendly but almost amused. Tuanomena felt like someone of sure and overwhelming confidence who found Lem's presence somehow a pleasure.

It was Gror's eyes that Lem awoke to. He knew many Meoena, but none who had ever looked at him that way. He didn't know what it meant. *Alfie should paint you.*

Gror was talking to another pilgrim. "He wakes. Tuanomena has blessed him."

"Praised be Tuanomena!" was the reply. Lem was aware of the walkers moving steadily by.

"Here!" Gror encouraged him. "A bench."

They sat for many minutes. Neither spoke.

"I guess...I met Tuanomena."

"It would seem so," Gror chuckled. "You, who sees the surface, sees what seems to be. What do you see now, engineer?"

Lem thought. "I don't know. I met someone. That's for sure—someone, not something."

Gror swung his arms. "Did Tuanomena speak?"

"Yes...though it's not what I'm used to as far as speech goes," said Lem. "He called me a name...What did he mean by calling me 'Lem-Jim-See'?"

"That is not your name?"

"No. I'm Lem. My younger son is Jim. What does he see? Does he want me to bring Jim here?"

Gror shifted uncomfortably on the bench. "Unlikely."

"I guess it'll be okay, as a student, if I take a while to process all this?"

"I, too, must 'process all this.' I had not expected Tuanomena to appear to you, yet not to one who stood next to you."

Lem nodded. *Yeah, for someone like you, that's got to hurt!*

Gror rose and turned, offering both hands to help Lem to his feet. "Your presence here alters so much. I don't understand all the consequences. Of course, I do not know the mind of Tuanomena. Expect me to visit you again."

Lem nodded and took the Meoenan's hands, which were hot to his touch and, he thought, trembling slightly.

17 DAD: VISIT TWO

Jim returned to The Artist's suite. Two Meoenan guards were waiting.

"I brought these. You can check them out. I don't know what they are. Do you?"

He dropped the tub of gear on a table and went straight to the kitchen.

The guards slowly took each item out and spread them across the table.

One made a call. "Eight items for review. Yes, sir."

Jim watched his mother's kettle boil, smiled, and thought. *A nav system from a Nuin transporter, two data storage units from Fos Gatelle, a hairdryer, a Duran army coin-sorter, a walkie-talkie radio of Dad's own design, an old Earth blaster with a leaking power unit that will give everyone who handles it a nasty rash in a few days, and an incomplete surveillance probe of some sort. A good selection to begin with.*

After his drink, Jim announced, "I've been up for twenty-four hours. I'm going to sleep."

The Meoena nodded.

Jim awoke to the sound of an argument. Even without hearing

all the words, he knew enough colloquial Melu to understand a superior had arrived and was not pleased.

The Meoenan officer burst into the bedroom. "Up! This junk does not fool anyone! I will accompany you to the structure at the navigation core. No more delays! Now!"

Jim got up slowly, yawned, and said, "Suit up, then. I'm not hiding anything."

The Meoenan's eyes studied Jim's face, but he said nothing.

Out at the far reaches of the back end, Jim clicked his comms unit and said, "I need to go in first. Wait behind me when I open the door."

"Why?"

"Trust me. You'll see when we get in there."

Jim placed his gloved hand on the shed door and opened it. The Meoenan was immediately at his shoulder and pushed himself into the opening. Jim swung himself back and held the door ajar.

Pec Sonloi and all its satellites disappeared as the door trap triggered the switch.

The punch bag slammed across the doorway, catching the Meoenan's arms and chest, propelling him back out.

Jim held on tight to the handle.

Watching the space-suited figure spin away, Jim felt a pang of guilt. Beyond this victim of his father's trap, Jim could see a series of faint bright dots stretching out into the emptiness.

The timer on the switch triggered, and Sonloi-AC reappeared overhead.

Dad, that was an ugly thing to do. I wish you'd found a better way.

He swung himself in through the door, and it closed behind him. He watched the trap reset and wondered how many of their operatives they had lost.

How long have they known about the shed?

A space-suited figure waited on one of the benches.

"Hi, Dad."

"Oh! You're not surprised to see me?"

"Second time for me. First for you?"

Lem gulped. "Ah...yes, it is. I hadn't thought of that—that I might cross over myself."

"It makes it quicker this time. You just have to remember to tell me everything next time."

"Right-o," Lem said looking at Jim. "it's so good to see you!" He turned quickly and added, "So, you already know what this is about."

"Roughly. You came by this thing." He indicated the D-switch still bolted to the table. "And I'm stuck with dealing with it."

Lem said, "'Bout it. Did I say how sorry I was?"

"No. But I'm wondering if it has something to do with your death. Do the rules of time travel cover us talking about that?"

"I'm dead? Oh, if I die because of this...Well, I won't know about it yet, will I? Come on, Jim! Think clearly. I'm not dead yet, but I do have limited options. Now, you tell me I may have limited time. This is the best one I can come up with. Bear with me, please."

"Sure, Dad. I'm sorry I mentioned it. I won't tell you when or how. I know I wouldn't want to know."

Lem nodded.

Jim continued, "But I don't think my options are any better than yours. I don't have anywhere to hide the switch. If I move this thing away from the station, they'll track me and kill me. No one's going to mess around acquiring this. It doesn't just move in space, does it? It's a time machine! There will be governments, generals, dictators, and the ultrarich bankrupting themselves and killing each other and anyone else so they can own it—or use it at least once."

Lem nodded. "That's what I thought. That's why I'm here. How much did I tell you—last time—about Tuanomena?"

"What? The city? You didn't mention it."

"Really? Okay. Must remember that. I'm not talking about the city. It's a bit difficult to explain. And it's really hard to explain it in the right order."

"I don't follow."

"It's okay. I'll work it out."

While Lem collected his thoughts, Jim waited patiently.

Lem began, "The Temple of Tuanomena is where I got the T-switch."

"Is that what we're calling it?"

"Yeah, that's a good working name for it, don't you think?"

"Okay."

"I don't mean it was lying around and I picked it up. Tuanomena gave it to me."

"What? Or do I mean, who?"

"The temple isn't named for nothing. It took me a while to understand and pick through the mythology. There's something there, in the top level. Well, not there...it comes and goes."

"There's an entity called Tuanomena?"

"Oh yes. I've met it—a couple of times."

"What is it? Meoena of some sort?"

"No nothing at all like that. Not like us." Lem was silent again.

Jim prompted, "Why did it give you the 'T-switch'?"

Lem stood and went over to a workbench. "I can't really answer that. I hope, perhaps, I'll find out—or you will. I had a guide who took me to The Walk. A couple of times, Tuanomena...chose...to communicate. One time—and I can't really remember how it came about—I was walking down a temple corridor and found myself next to The Walk. Almost right away, Tuanomena was there and so was this thing. Just lying there on a table! Maybe he just thought I'd like it? It is"—Lem fished for words—"the ultimate gadget, isn't it? I mean, it's truly amazing."

"More so than a regular D-switch." Jim nodded. "And they are bad enough."

"Bad enough? Where's your curiosity? You're the son of an engineer! This stuff is in your blood; you must be at least a little interested in how they all work, how they do what they do?"

"I'm also the son of an artist who can spend a week painting something two inches square and then declare it complete crap."

Lem's face colored up, but Jim couldn't see it through the visor. "Well, I don't want you to paint it; I want you to take it back."

"Do what? Take it back? Last time, you said I was supposed to keep it safe, to keep the mechanism set, and not tell anyone!"

"Okay. So that was the first time you were hearing about it. That was probably enough, so you could think about what it all means. I don't underestimate the difficulties you'll face. I can rig up—I did rig up—a mechanism to keep it safe. And you, I was sure, would know how to get in here. That's my limit, I think. For the reasons you said, I'll be trampled in the rush if anyone else hears about it. I can't think what to safely do with it beyond these bounds." He gestured to the walls of the workshop. "This is what I've worked on"—he paused, unwilling to voice the admission—"to distract me from actually using it."

"How can I do any better? The secret's out—or, at least, a good enough rumor."

"What do you mean?"

"I told you! No, sorry, I *will* tell you the next time we meet—and you knew all about it, because I'm telling you *now*—Mom was kidnapped. Then they came for me. I'm here searching for something they think you left hidden. I'm not certain the people who have Mom know what it is yet. But I can't keep searching unsuccessfully through your stuff much longer. You must have heard the trap deploy before I came in. That was the guy supervising my search. Another casualty."

"Okay, okay, that's not what I expected to hear. That's bad. Did they hurt her—or you?"

"Not yet."

"Meoena or someone else?"

"Meoena grunts. Well trained not to give any clues as to who their bosses might be."

Lem sighed and sat down again. "I'll be honest, son, I'm not sure I can control the T-switch accurately enough. This is the first time I've found you here. I've been doing a kind of binary search from— never mind when—trying to find you here. Do me a favor; write up a log of when you're in here. It'll help. I'm struggling...and not just with you having already heard part of the story from me."

"Yeah, I can understand that."

"Well, I found you. That was my next step, after securing it in here. How about we work with what we have, like we always used to?"

Jim said, "I've missed you. Apart from your...next...visit, it's been a long while since I saw you."

Lem smiled. "You're on Earth, just started working for the OEA I'm hoping it works out for you."

Jim nodded and wondered how much to say. "It'll work out. For a while. I get sacked eventually."

Lem held up his gloved hands. "Don't tell me too much. The temptation to go and try to fix things is enormous. As I try to use it, I'm so conscious of being able to go anywhere, anytime. It's not just thinking 'Oh, I'd like to go back and see an Apollo mission take off.' I lost that joyride feeling almost immediately. It's...an impossible temptation. How could anyone resist; just one trip, just one time, just put one mistake right?"

"I already know that's why I don't want it, Dad. My life is a whole series of mistakes that are down to no one else but me. I could stop myself making any one and change everything, couldn't I?"

Lem nodded. "You could. But I really fear that in fixing one thing, I'd cause something else to break. And then? You know, what do you do? Switch somewhere else, sometime else, and fix what you just broke. Whoever starts down that road will never come back, never finish tweaking...correcting...things."

"Maybe that's why Tuanomena gave it to you. You're the guy who repairs stuff, 'The Caretaker,' the one the Meoena look up to."

Lem shook his head. "Not me. No way. I'll fix a machine or the plumbing, not people's lives. I couldn't fix my own marriage—or you guys! How dare I meddle—interfere—with anyone else's life? There's just no way of knowing what would happen..."

Jim sat quietly, trying to imagine what his father would be tempted to go back and change. He knew. His stomach sank.

Mazette.

She could have a full life. She could grow to be a woman, a mother. There may be generations, absent from history, who would get to live.

Jim looked anew at the silent, hunched figure in the spacesuit.

Oh, Dad! How can you resist? To have her back!

Almost instantly, the thoughts of other children he'd known of or heard of dying rushed upon him.

How do you stop with just one? Who could decide which lives to save, which deaths to leave unchanged? Save your sister and let all those others die?

You're right, Dad, taking a week's vacation in ancient Rome isn't where the problem lies.

He sat and looked at the T-switch, his heart thumping with the temptation. His limbs trembled as if he were fighting to hold against a riptide. He announced, "Okay, Dad, we're agreed. How do I take it back?"

18 JAYDE AND ALFIE

In the medical suite of Sonloi-AC, Jayde and Alfie stood hugging a long time.

"Are you okay?" Jayde asked eventually.

"Sawbones says I am. It'll take a while to get my head around it all."

"But they didn't harm you."

"Oh, no. It was all very polite and Meoenan. You know—irritating as hell!"

Jayde laughed. "Now, Alfie, two things. Someone was in your rooms. We don't know who exactly, but they disappeared as soon as you all appeared off station."

"It's okay. I had heard that they might use my place as a base."

"Okay. Second thing is—"

"My son?"

"Yeah. Rumors but no definite sightings."

Alfie nodded. "He's here. The deal was that Jim would find some 'thing' Lem had and hand it over to them, and I'd be let go."

"Really? So, I need to know what that might be. And where is he looking?"

Alfie narrowed her eyes at her friend and said, "I can tell you neither, I'm afraid. I was just the bait. And, of course, if he found it, Jim wasn't going to just hand it over to them."

Jayde began to laugh but stopped. "Of course."

"Do you know who was behind it?"

"Oh, Alfie, you know I'm not supposed to say. It's all about to blow up, and I need to control what gets said when."

Alfie smiled. "Jayde, this is what they employ you for. You're damned good at it! I...am just a painter."

Jayde leaned closer and said, "That's a front that your family has used for years. You are way more than that."

Alfie looked away still smiling.

Jayde continued, "Oh, and you're damned good at it too."

Alfie said, "You're making me blush. But, since you're in a good mood, let me ask you a favor."

"Anything."

"Give Yarl his job back."

Jayde's smile disappeared. "I didn't fire him."

"He's a good person. And he has talents you could use."

"I know. I know. He's also...not one of us."

"Jayde? Shame on you!"

Jayde blushed and nodded. "Okay."

19 DAD: VISIT THREE

A click sounded in Jim's helmet radio.

"Dad?"

"Yes, it's me. I'm coming in. Which meeting is this?"

"The third."

"Right-o, we're in sync for this one!"

Lem made his way in from the airlock.

Jim said, "Mom's back. I haven't heard all the details yet. Some of the Meoena she's painted over the years got together and pulled some stunt to get her back. I came out here in the confusion hoping no one saw me."

"Good! Good news!"

"Have you found out more about controlling the T-switch?"

"I think so. I've...done a fair bit of experimenting."

"Is it enough to get me into the temple at the right time?"

Lem waved a glove. "Yeah, slight change of spec on that one. I'm thinking we should go together."

Jim nodded. "Okay. You can make the introductions with Tuanomena."

"Hmm...Yeah, it's not really like that."

Jim bit back irritation. "Okay, I guess I'll soon find out. How do we get over the fact that you are using the T-switch from your time and I have it here from mine?"

Lem was silent. He looked at his switch. He looked over to the bench where the switch was bolted down. "I have no idea. Which one do we use?"

"I guess Tuanomena didn't include a manual with 'what if?' scenarios?"

Lem laughed. "No, no documentation."

Jim smiled. "Since when did that stop us?"

They both sat, thinking, looking from one device to the other.

Jim spoke. "Both. I'll use mine; you use yours. Can we arrive at the same place at the same time?"

"Sure...I think."

"Okay. Will Tuanomena be there?"

"What do you know about The Walk?"

Jim nodded. "I remember hearing about it. Like a meditation area at the top of the temple."

"That's it. You walk around in one direction with all the others. Sometimes there's a bunch of people walking. Sometimes you find yourself on your own. That's..."

"What?"

"That's when you might meet Tuanomena."

Jim snorted. "Okay. Doesn't sound as definite as I'd hoped. Especially with dangerous cargo."

"It'll be okay. I'm sure. We may just need to walk a while."

"Okay." Jim pointed to the bench. "Shall I dismantle this, or do you want to?"

"I'd better."

Jim turned to his dad. "What else is there? What did you do?"

"Fail-safe."

"Shit."

"I'll disarm it. No trouble."

"Would I have found it if I'd tried to unbolt the thing?"

"Probably."

"That's not a great comfort, Dad."

"You must always check, Jim. If I've taught you anything, that should've stuck with you."

"Yeah, I guess so."

As Lem worked on dismantling the fail-safe and removing the T-switch, Jim sat thinking. "You know what?" he said.

"What, son?"

"You have to take the switch you're carrying back to your time and travel from there. No, wait, that's wrong too..."

"I'm listening."

"You can't do anything that will stop the thing being here for me to find. You can't do anything except set up what you're now taking apart. Back then, I mean."

"Okay," Lem replied cautiously.

"I have to go from here—I mean, now. But how are you going to get here if you don't have it with you?"

"Yeah, yeah, I see what you mean."

Jim continued, "The goal is to get both of us there—at the same time—with the T-switch from now. That one. My one."

Lem nodded and said, "Well, okay. It's like they say about Tuanomena, it's—"

"Say 'it's not really like that,' and I'll either throw you or myself out of that door."

Lem laughed. "I was going to say 'complicated.'" He leaned back against the workbench and held up a wrench. "I've spent a long time studying at the temple. Did I mention that bit? Anyway, there are a whole bunch of written accounts of pilgrims encountering Tuanomena. They are all remarkably similar. It's confusing. It's awesome. It's hard to express clearly."

"The Meoena say something like that about Mom's paintings."

Lem looked away. "They do...you're right. Isn't that something?" He put down the wrench and sighed. "Anyway, Tuanomena meets them when they're on their own. While we need to meet there and hope he'll meet us together. We may not need to arrive together."

"Is Tuanomena really male?"

"Oh, no! An 'it' if ever there was one, but that's so difficult in both English and Standard. 'It' is just awkward."

"I work with a Neraffan who insists on being called 'it.' Gets offended if you slip up."

Lem laughed. "I don't think Tuanomena gets offended. It's not really"—he held up a hand and stopped himself. "Anyway, on The Walk, you're not supposed to bother the other pilgrims. They allow talking, but there's a real unspoken rule to leave people you don't know alone."

"Sounds like a church."

Lem nodded. "Very much so. The strange thing is, in the written accounts—well, they often mention seeing people from other years, other ages, doing The Walk."

"What?"

"I guess Tuanomena will bring us together if he wants to. The Meoena have a long history of theorizing about time, time travel, and all that stuff. I've read a lot of it. It all comes down to Tuanom-ena. It's like he encourages them to speculate but doesn't provide any answers"—Lem sighed—"I tell you, I have seen some strange stuff on The Walk. His giving me this thing isn't completely out of the blue. I'm thinking I'll go back with my switch, set everything up, and leave it here. And then get the shuttle over to the temple as usual. Right now, we'll input the coordinates for you to get to the temple about the same time I get there. And then we hope for the best."

"What if it doesn't work out the way you think? What's our backup? Mom is back, but the fallout has yet to happen. They aren't going to give up, so she might still be in danger. And I'm going to go back to your time without knowing how I get back here to now. Do I just wait in the temple and hope never to meet my earlier self?"

Lem stood without replying, then said, "We'll ask Tuanomena to send you back here, to this time. If people are coming and going from different times, he must be doing it somehow. There's another reason I think it'll work, but it's a strange thing."

"Try me."

"Tuanomena calls me by a name: 'Lem-Jim-see.' Never been sure what to make of it. But I guess he thinks of you when he thinks of me." He held the T-switch, newly unbolted from the bench. "This may be the reason. That's why I think we should go together —besides watching each other's backs."

20 THE CARETAKERS

"Fasta, how long have we worked together?"

"Too long! You've made me half-human."

Lem mulled over the reproach. "You've done as much damage to me. Look how I spend my spare time, disappearing into the temple and reading Meoenan mystics!"

Fasta nodded. "Something that still surprises me."

They sat at a window in a tower at the back end. Barely visible in the starlight were shadowy forms of buildings, armatures holding telescopes and scanners, aerials and dishes. The sweeping arms of Sonloi-AC carved the blackest of silhouettes.

"We did good, didn't we? Building this station?" Lem wondered.

"Of course! This is the first, the best! This got our world thinking as a world. This is where we can see ourselves and the beauty of Sonloi. We built a kind of lens that brought the galaxy into focus."

"This is going to sound crazy..."

"I doubt it."

"Really. This station is going to outlast us. It's not built of stone like the temple, but it will still last for a long time. It should—"

"If we've done our jobs right." Fasta finished the sentence.

"What do you think of the teams they're hiring for maintenance?"

Fasta hesitated. "You're a tough act to follow. Not just you. You humans, in general. We're not like you."

"It worries me."

"What can we do? We can't, despite our best efforts, live forever. We'll retire. So, we leave it all to someone else."

"What if we could have a say in who that might be?"

"We do! You interview new technicians every couple of months."

"That's not what I mean though. I can see the technicians training up okay. I can even hope that some of them will read the damned documentation!"

"Ha! Some hope that is!"

"But I mean more...something more..." He waved his hands vaguely.

"Mystical?"

"If you like. Who will *care*?"

Fasta remained silent. He reached forward, took Lem's flask, and poured some of the drink into his glass. Then he said, quietly, "You can't teach that sort of thing. They have to discover it for themselves."

Lem smiled. "Isn't that why your young folk do walkabouts?"

Fasta nodded solemnly. "That's right. That's exactly right. No young person worthy of his or her independence will obediently follow what the family says they must do. Of course, they must rebel —kick against the barriers. They must find out why the family believes the way it does. For themselves."

"What can we do to help them discover why we care about AC?"

Fasta shook his head.

A while later, Lem said, "I met a monk. Odd fellow. I think he isn't sure having dealings with other worlds is a good idea."

Fasta nodded but said nothing.

Lem continued, "If I'm right, there'll be a backlash against it all. A retreat, if you like."

Fasta frowned. "Our politics move slowly. There's a general common sense about it all. I don't see that sort of thing becoming a problem."

"Think, Fasta! What if it does? We're in the best position to do something about it. You and me. Right now!"

Fasta focused his eyes on Lem's. "Us? We're engineers. We're not politicians. I'm certainly no one to start a movement, if that's what you mean!"

Lem shook his head. "Not a movement. Something less...obvious. Something more like the monks at the temple."

Fasta laughed. "In what way? Overfed? Secretive? Ignored by everyday folk?"

Lem leaned forward. "Yes! Apart from the overfed bit."

"You're crazy!"

"I told you! Where are the people who care? We don't even have to lead it; it isn't about us. It's about them...them caring enough about Sonloi-AC to make sure no one turns the lights off up here prematurely. Do you see?"

Fasta looked out of the window at the shadows. "No, you're crazy. You want them to do something you won't be here to help with. To start something you can't control. You want to create an organization that will work in an environment you can't predict."

Lem followed his gaze. "Yeah...'Bout right. What do you think?"

"What do I think about what?"

"Give me the name of five families who think like we do. Find me someone who can arrange walkabouts for the children of those families when the time comes."

Fasta's eyes returned to Lem's face. "Seriously?"

"Never more so."

Fasta poured another drink. "What do you mean 'think like we do'?"

"Believing in the same approach to interplanetary cooperation that we have. People who have made friends with humans. People whose kids are growing up with humans—or, at least, think that's a good idea. Like us!"

They sat in silence for a long time.

"The Breens," Fasta said.

"Who?"

"A family. Lots of connections in the government and in the temple. I'd be surprised if you haven't seen at least one of them. Boring a clan as I ever met. I mean, old Klate has about nine or ten children. They all look and dress alike. All terribly formal and self-controlled. Some would say the parents are doing something right, creating upright, polite citizens. Others—and, honestly, I've been one of them—say it's all a bit creepy."

"Go on."

"Sometimes you hear rumors of one kid or another breaking out of the mold. But I think they end up making names for themselves and still being part of the family where they started. Go and meet them. See what they think of humans and the wider galaxy."

"Okay. But that's a strange sort of recommendation."

"You're looking for a strange sort of Meoenan. They've got what it would take to do what you want. But—and I say this as a warning, not a cop-out—I don't know them well enough to tell you to trust them."

Lem felt a surge of confidence he had rarely experienced. "Right-o!"

21 EBMS

"EBMS Control, this is Officer Brewer, OEA Tactical Response Unit, requesting docking permission."

Several minutes passed before the reply came.

"We have no warning of your visit, Officer Brewer. Please explain your presence at this station."

"I need to see Jim Able."

"Stand by."

"There is no one of that name on station."

"I know. Let me at his ship. That's all I need."

No answer came for many minutes.

"OEA vessel, this is Dr. Matthew Able. State your business."

Tella spoke. "Along with Anne Brewer of the O.E.A., I, Tella of Neraff have returned to your station, Dr. Able. We are in search of Jim. I have had a report that he is missing. I wish to start my search on his ship."

"Tella? You're EIA, aren't you? You should know what happened to him!"

"I know some of what happened. I need to piece together the rest. I'm sure you want to do the same. Please allow us to dock."

"Use the dock next to Jim's. You'll be escorted to his ship. Do not attempt to enter any other part of the station."

"Agreed. Thank you," Tella replied.

Once the call ended, Anne muttered, "A bit paranoid, isn't he?"

"He is in charge and wants all to remember it. Jim doesn't like him."

"Huh. Well, siblings don't always get along, I suppose."

"I find that surprising, but then, I am not human."

"That's for sure."

22 THE SHED

"Come on, Jim! Something you can help me with. Maybe cheer you up a bit."

Jim shrugged his shoulders with the inelegant lack of enthusiasm only a teenager can conjure.

Jim followed his father through seldom-used corridors of the back end.

"Where are we going?" he eventually asked.

"New project. A sort of workshop area."

"What's wrong with the other...forty-nine workshops?"

Lem laughed. "You'll need one of those soon—your own space—won't you? I'm sure you'd like to spread out your gear when you're working on something."

"Sure. Somewhere to work on my own would be great. Everyone treats me like a nuisance."

"Well..." Lem didn't say "The way you act, you are, more often than not!" Instead, he continued, "Space is always tight on a station. There's never enough room."

.   .   .

"Here we are!" Lem unlocked a door and led Jim into a large empty room lit only by a single emergency light.

Jim noticed the room was cool. *Hmm...on or close to the skin.*

Opposite the door, in the center of the wall was an emergency access hatch.

"Know what that is?" his father asked.

"E.A.H. Why is it on the inside?"

"Good question. What's your guess?"

Jim sighed. "I don't know! It's cold here...so the hatch is breeching the skin...There's something out there."

Lem waited.

"You've put the hatch in this side of the wall to go out, not come in. What's out there isn't always going to be there."

"Let's go and see."

Lem approached the hatch and typed in a code. Then he stood back, checked his tablet, and input something there.

Jim frowned but didn't ask "Why the extra security?" He shook his head. *The old man's going crazy.*

Lem opened the hatch and led Jim inside. Stepping slightly to the right, Lem reached up and turned on the lights.

Immediately, Jim was alert. His foot hovered over the black floor plate directly inside the hatch. He leaned back, keeping the weight on his trailing foot. He glanced at his father and caught a glint in Lem's eye as he watched his son.

Smiling, Jim tapped the floor plate gently.

A hiss of smoke or steam erupted from above, and the plate lurched up and forward into the room.

Jim laughed. "Nice one!"

"Well done, son! You'd have been flat on your face, wouldn't you!"

Jim swatted his father's arm as he stepped around the trap. "Psycho!"

"Hey, less of the cheek, you! Always check! Always check!"

Lem turned on more lights, and Jim saw the whole of the workshop.

Its dimensions were like many other rooms on Sonloi-AC: long and thin, with a central aisle and workbenches on either side. In this case, only one side had benches. On the other side stood stacks of utilitarian transport cases.

"This is it?"

"Yep! I'm thinking of positioning several of these at different places around the back end. Use them to store stuff we'd otherwise need to carry out there. Make repairs more efficient. Do them nearer the site. What do you think?"

Jim shrugged. "Suppose so." He went over to the transport cases and read some of the labels. "Won't that make inventory more difficult? I mean, scattering this stuff around in so many different places?"

Lem shrugged. "Maybe. Central control of stores and equipment was Taff Llewellyn's obsession. I think decentralization makes sense some of the time."

Jim sighed. "Suppose so."

"There's no hurry in creating these. I work on them when I can, and I'll deploy them as they're ready. Maybe put a hatch on the station end and an airlock on the other." He looked around the unprepossessing unit with pride. "Over here! I need to put the next workbench together. Give me a hand."

Father and son settled into a well-practiced routine. Jim fetched the components, and Lem arranged and fitted them. Where necessary, they used both pairs of hands or arms, like a human octopus, to hold sections in place while being secured.

As they worked together, they talked.

Lem asked, "Heard from Rolo yet?"

Jim shook his head.

"Well, don't worry. Part of the point of their walkabouts, I think, is maybe being somewhere it's difficult to communicate from."

"Yeah..."

"Did he say anything about where he was going?"

"No..."

Lem paused in his work. "You okay?"

Jim nodded.

They worked in silence until Lem added, "He'll come back. It's only a walkabout."

Jim shook his head and looked away. "I dunno..."

"What?"

"He..."

"Go on. What did he say?"

Jim shrugged. "I dunno. I'm not sure he's coming back."

Lem continued to work. "What makes you say that?"

Jim didn't reply. They worked on.

Then Jim said, "He never felt comfortable...living here, on the station. His family—aunts and stuff, when they visited—were kind of funny about me being his friend."

"Huh!" Lem said, "Fasta never said anything. He was okay with you two hanging around together." He paused. "Except when you were blowing things up."

Jim shrugged.

Later, Lem asked, "Did something happen with Rolo? When he was leaving?"

"No."

"Jim?"

Jim sighed in annoyance. "He just said, 'Teo Ma!' That's all."

Lem looked surprised. "Well, that's not goodbye, is it? That's *au revoir*. That's what I'd expect him to say."

"Yeah..."

"But you think otherwise? Really?"

"I don't think he meant it. I think the walkabout is an excuse to get away."

"From what? You? Us?"

"Yeah...The whole thing, the being with humans, the being with me."

Lem shook his head. "You wait. He'll be back. Back and full of stories."

"Maybe..."

"Look, Jim...It's not all that unusual to have feelings of not fitting in. That's just part of being the age you are. And don't forget, both you and Rolo have had an unusual life. Not every kid gets to grow up in a station like this—to see it grow alongside you!"

Jim shrugged.

"It'll work out is what I mean. Your mother and I both know neither of you will end up in ordinary office jobs. You'll both find your niches. I'm looking forward to seeing where you guys end up. Damn what anyone else thinks! He'll find his path. So will you, son!"

Jim shrugged again, "Yeah...guess so."

23 TUANOMENA

Jim looked back into the shed as he and Lem moved out through the airlock. He remembered helping his father furnish it. He had thought at the time it was one of many, but he now realized the others were never quite like this one. He wanted to ask his father if he'd known then what he would use it for. It seemed so long ago.

Lem waved, pressed a button on the T-switch attached to his suit, and vanished. Jim briefly looked up at the rest of Sonloi-AC and pressed the button to activate his own T-switch.

A stone wall appeared a few inches from his visor, and he dropped a small distance to the floor. Recovering his balance, he breathed a sigh of relief.

Checking the outside air, he opened his visor. The air smelled stuffy and warm. Voices, hushed in private conversations, came from behind him, beyond an arch.

Good shot, Dad!

He removed his spacesuit and folded it over the helmet in the corner of the otherwise empty room. He hugged the T-switch to his chest and zipped up his jacket, then turned and went through the arch.

Several Meoena waited their turns at the edge of a pool. *Okay, we're washing feet and hands. Good to know.*

He stored his boots and socks with the many others, noting the large number of pilgrims represented.

Crowds filled The Walk. He and a Meoenan couple waited patiently for a gap before stepping out to join the quiet shuffling.

Sooner than he realized, Jim came to an arch, beyond which he could see a pool. *Is that where I came in?*

He left The Walk to check. *Hmm. My boots. Fewer shoes in all. That's odd.*

He returned and circumvented The Walk again.

Okay, Dad, where are you?

He walked around again and then sat on a bench.

As he waited, he noticed a human pass by—a young woman with dark hair, cut short and a little unruly. She wore the same robes he saw on several Meoenan pilgrims.

Why the frown? he thought. *What's troubling you?*

She walked on, not noticing Jim.

I'll catch you next time around.

He waited. He sat and watched the pilgrims go by. A large Meoenan strutted past, her jewelry sparkling. Among the pale colors of the other pilgrims, she stood out as if she walked with a trumpet chorus. She held hands with two older, small, and drab attendants.

Jim continued sitting on the bench until his backside began complaining.

The bejeweled Meoenan came by again, followed later by the young woman, the same concerned look on her face, neither looking left nor right.

There you are!

Jim stood up and began to follow her.

The Meoenan and her two attendants stopped in the middle of the Walk in a huddle; two other pilgrims stopped to converse quietly with her. The young woman stepped around the gaggle and moved on. As Jim tried to do the same, he heard a stage whisper from his left.

"Jim! Jim! There you are!"

"Hi, Dad! Where have you been?"

Lem waved from a bench. He patted the empty place next to him and said, "What do you mean? I've been waiting ages for you!"

Jim sat down. "I've been here a while, and you weren't sitting here last time I came around."

"Oh, right-o. Like I told you, things can get a bit odd up here."

"I'm beginning to notice. There's another human here, a young woman."

"Concentrate, Jim! We're here for a purpose."

Jim looked sideways at his father. "Yeah, I know. She looks...I don't know. If we see her, I want to speak to her."

Lem laughed. "Sure, Jim, sure. Let's start walking. Remember, we're looking for the crowd to thin out."

Jim shook his head. "When's lunchtime? This looks like a ton of people and few gaps in between."

"You'll see."

Jim lost count of how many times they circled The Walk; the walking became meditative. Lem talked a little of the monk who had first brought him to The Walk. Then father and son spoke less and less. Jim found the rhythm of their footfalls, the low murmur of other conversations, and the slight stuffiness of the air calming.

Later, after many more rounds, a voice broke the silence.

"Gentlemen!"

She spoke in English with a strength, enjoyment, and certainty that woke Jim from his walking reverie.

He and Lem turned. The young woman stood alone in The Walk.

"Hi!" said Jim.

Lem touched his arm. "Look, we're alone!"

The young woman stepped closer and said, "I'm Sea. It's so good to meet you!"

Jim was lost for words.

Lem replied, "And you, Sea. That's an unusual name."

She smiled and didn't reply. Instead, she motioned onwards.

As they walked side by side, she said, "We are honored to have The Walk to ourselves. Do you think Tuanomena will speak with us?"

Lem nodded. "That's been my experience. Are you ready?"

She smiled. "Oh, yes. You have no idea."

Jim asked, "Have we met? You seem...familiar."

She wore a mischievous smile. "Not that I recall."

The sunlight streaming through in bright shafts dimmed suddenly.

Ahead of them The Walk straightened, and in the middle of their path stood a large stone table.

Jim thought he had seen a table like it but couldn't remember where.

"Tuanomena is here!" Lem whispered.

"Tuanomena will speak!" said Sea.

Jim swallowed and put his hand under the T-Switch in his jacket to make sure it was secure.

With Lem standing at the table to the left and Sea to the right, Jim found himself trapped in the middle.

Silence encompassed them, though Jim could hear his father's faint breathing.

Into their minds came a thought that was not their own. With it came a vibrant feeling of calm enjoyment.

Lem-Jim-Sea, to be with you is Tuanomena's pleasure.

JIM ABLE OFFWORLD

SEA

12

ED CHARLTON

AUTHOR OF "THE ALERONDE TRILOGY"

01 EBMS

As two EBMS guards escorted them from their flier to Jim's ship, Anne asked Tella, "How are we going to get in?"

"The ship may allow me access. I'm not sure."

"Great."

At the airlock of Jim's ship, Tella pressed the comms button. "Raeda, this is Tella. Open the door."

The ship replied, "Tella is not authorized for access."

"Shit," Anne muttered.

"Raeda," Tella tried again. "In Jim's absence, you require a pilot. I am qualified to pilot you until Jim is located and returns."

The ship replied, "Tella is not authorized for access."

Anne sighed and leaned her back against the airlock. To her surprise, the door began moving.

Marhan's snout emerged, sniffing. "More monkeys? What do you want?"

Tella stepped back quickly. Anne drew her blaster.

The enormous canid stepped out of the airlock and put his face level with Tella's. "You!"

"Ernot Dirl Marhan, an unexpected meeting."

"Why are you here?"

"You guys know each other?" Anne asked.

Tella ignored her. "Why are *you* here? What are you doing in Jim's ship?"

Marhan snapped his jaws and growled at Tella, then turned his gaze to Anne. "Who are you, monkey?"

She pointed her blaster at him. "A friend of Jim's. Got a problem with that, dog breath?"

Marhan laughed.

A young voice spoke from behind Marhan. "Is that Tella?"

"Davey, I told you to stay hidden," Marhan hissed.

"Yeah, but it's Tella. Uncle Jim was trying to contact it!"

Marhan glanced back at Davey, looked again at Anne and her blaster then at Tella again. He growled, gestured to Anne to put her blaster away, turned around, and followed Davey back into the ship.

Marhan sat in the pilot's chair. Davey sat next to Clo, who was staring at a display full of streaming data open before her.

"Explain your presence here," began Tella.

Marhan growled again but answered, "I found Able on Hon Hen Flereat. I was celebrating. He joined me, and we went to...various other sites. Until I return to Flereat to retrieve my own vessel, I live here." Marhan snapped his jaws at Tella again but turned to Anne. "And you? What is your name and business here?"

"I worked with Jim. I'm Anne. Did he tell you about the affair at Ch'Garratt?" Marhan nodded, and Davey looked up. "I was there to extract him. We also worked on a related matter. I gave him some information recently that may be why he was at Flereat."

"Yeah," said Davey to Marhan, "We saw those messages, remember?"

"Shush, small monkey! Say no more than you need."

Anne and Tella exchanged a glance.

Marhan continued, "Jim went off with an EIA agent and has not returned. They search for him. Do you think he is dead?"

"We don't know," Tella replied.

Clo offered, "He might be at Pec Sonloi."

"Where's that?" both Anne and Tella asked at once.

Clo replied, "Umm, it's where he grew up. There's a post here on a gossip site that someone had seen him. They're asking why it wasn't announced that he was there. I'm Clo, by the way. Pleased to meet you both."

Anne smiled at her and said, "Good to meet you too. Listen, we're all here for the same reason. We want to find Jim." Looking at Tella, she continued, "So let's work on it together, shall we?"

Marhan stood and put his face close to Tella. "Ground rules first. The snot person is to remain visible at all times." With a swift turn toward Anne, he added, "And your weapon remains strapped in its holster and set in safe mode. Understand?"

Anne narrowed her eyes and said, "When I assess that you are not a threat to us—or these children."

Marhan towered over her. "I *am* a threat to you, monkey! But ask yourself why your blood is not already soaking the carpet of this pretty ship. It is to protect the small ones that I insist you act in a responsible manner! Keep your weapon away, and your chameleon dressed!"

Davey grunted. "I'm not a child."

"Tella is not *mine*," Anne replied coolly. "He's Jim's boss."

"Nonsense! It works for Jim."

"Ah, I can explain that—" Tella began.

Marhan interrupted. "I don't care about your explanations. I know how you acted when we first met; you followed Jim's orders. And I know it was Jim alone who came back for me. Him, I owe a debt. You, I owe nothing but contempt!"

Anne sighed. "This is going to take some work, isn't it? Listen, both of you. I didn't come all this way to waste my time. First let's find out what's happened to Jim. Then you boys can sort out your pasts, okay?"

She stood close to Tella and looked from its face to Marhan. "Okay?"

Tella turned its face to hers and said, "I am not a 'boy.' Please do not offend me by using your gender-specific language."

Anne's face colored, and she grabbed Tella's robe under its chin and put her face very close to the Neraffan. She said, "Not helpful!

I'll offend you until the cows come home if it helps us find Jim. Got it?"

Tella's face, white from the proximity to the robe, also showed a faint glow from Anne's hands. The Neraffan nodded once.

Letting go of Tella, Anne asked Marhan, "And you?"

He laughed and said, "A monkey with spirit! Good." He turned to Clo and Davey and said, "Now, young ones, what is this you have on Pec Sonloi?"

Tella mumbled, "What in Quavvour's name are cows?"

02 TUANOMENA

Lem, Jim, and Sea stood by the ancient stone table and felt Tuanomena's presence in their minds.

Lem-Jim-Sea, to be with you is Tuanomena's pleasure.

Lem said, "It's a pleasure to be with you again."

Again.

The thought hung in the air as if Tuanomena was tasting it.

Jim began, "We've come with this." He brought the rectangular T-switch from under his jacket.

Sea gasped. "Is that it? I imagined it would be bigger."

Jim frowned and was about to say "What?" but Tuanomena's thought interrupted.

To travel. Without restraint.

No one spoke.

Lem finally said, "That's what he says every time. That's his name for the T-switch, I think."

Jim coughed. "Well, Tuanomena, we've come to bring it back. It's too dangerous." He placed it on the stone table.

To travel. Without restraint.

"Too dangerous?" asked Sea.

"Damn right," Jim answered.

In the blink of an eye, Sea picked up the T-switch and said loudly, "I'll take it! The guys think it's too dangerous. I don't."

"Sea!" Lem shouted.

"Wait a minute!" Jim said.

To travel. Without restraint, again the thought repeated.

Jim asked her, "How do you even know about this?"

She smiled. "Oh, I've heard all about this. How you guys were given a time machine and gave it back! How you stopped anyone else from seeing it, investigating it, using it." She turned the device to examine it.

"No one gets to use it," Jim said. "It's way too risky—the damage we could do!"

Sea smiled again. "The good we could do!"

"No," said Lem. "We've thought this over, young lady."

"Who are you to make that decision? Who did you check with? You didn't ask me! I've spent a long time getting here—just for this moment. You don't deserve more explanation. I'm taking it, and there's nothing you can do!"

Jim's stomach sank. He saw himself reach out to try and take it back from her, knowing he would fail. He saw her maneuver the T-switch just beyond his reach. He was too late. He felt stupid, more than he had ever felt before. *Why didn't I see the danger in her?*

To travel. Without restraint, once more the thought echoed.

Sea moved with the skill of a dancer. She turned, T-switch in hand, away from Lem and Jim, skipping back down the straight path.

"Dad, we have to stop her!"

Lem's laugh hit Jim like a slap on the face. "Not worked out who she is yet?"

Jim stammered, "No-no idea."

"I have. Leave it to me." Lem ran after the young woman.

Jim steadied himself against the stone table.

Lem-Jim-Sea, to be with you is Tuanomena's pleasure.

"What have you done here?" Jim shouted in embarrassment, alarm, and anger.

Darkness flashed over him, and the sand of The Walk rose to catch him as he fell.

Several concerned pilgrims guided him to a bench and encouraged him.

"Tuanomena has blessed you!"

"Those who are chosen always have this look!"

"It is wonderful that Tuanomena even appears to aliens such as this one!"

"It is hard for any pilgrim to return from such an encounter. How disappointing it must be to return to this dull world."

Jim wiped sand from his face and muttered in English, "Fuck off. Leave me alone."

03 SONLOI-AC

The station administrator called down the corridor, "Alfie!"

The Artist turned and smiled. "Jayde! I was just going for a coffee. Coming?"

Jayde shook her head. "I don't have time. We need to talk."

Alfie grabbed her arm and said, "Yes, dear. You need a break, a coffee, and a friendly face. Come on."

Jayde allowed herself to be led to the café.

With drinks in front of them, Alfie said, "Now, dear, in your own time."

"How is Jim?"

Alfie sighed. "Still hiding in my rooms. He won't say what happened. I haven't seen him like this in a long while. If he weren't here, I'm sure he'd be drinking."

"Shit." Jayde hesitated but then continued, "I have a Neraffan and a Gul who just washed up in the strangest damned ship I've ever seen. They're demanding to see Jim. What do I do with them?"

"How odd! Do you think they are after money?"

Their conversation was interrupted by a cheery cry from the door of the café.

"Grandma! Grandma!"

Alfie turned, and her eyes widened. "Davey? Little Davey! Is that you?"

The teen ran over to her, and she rose to envelope him in a broad hug.

"Hi, Grandma! Is Uncle Jim with you?"

"My, how you've grown! Well, well. Where's your father?"

"Umm"—Davey turned—"Clo? Grandma, this is my girlfriend, Clo. It's short for Clodagh."

Clo had followed Davey and said, "Hi! Is Jim here? We came looking for him. It's a lovely station, isn't it? You must love living here!"

Alfie held one of Davey's hands and looked from his face to Clo's. "Girlfriend, you say? Well, that's news in itself." She took Clo's hand and said, "Welcome, dear. It's lovely to meet you. Now, you two, have you had breakfast? Come and sit with us."

She corralled them into the two seats opposite Jayde and herself. "This is the station administrator. Her name is Jayde."

They both shrank a little and mumbled, "Hi."

"Jayde, this is my grandson, Davey, and his girlfriend, Clo. They are just about to explain how they got here and why they suddenly need to see their Uncle Jim."

Jayde smiled and said, "So lovely to meet you both. Which ship did you come in on?"

Clo glanced at Davey who answered, "Umm, it's a bit complicated."

Alfie said without smiling, "There's a lot of that going around at the moment."

Jayde asked, "Was it that ugly ship with the spherical modules all over it?"

Davey nodded. "It belongs to Uncle Jim."

Surprised, Jayde said, "Oh!"

Alfie smiled and asked, "Since you are big enough and old enough to have a girlfriend, are you old enough now to pilot a spaceship?"

Davey's face fell, but Clo answered, "We're with Uncle Jim's boss. He's from Neraff and is kind of creepy. He can make himself disappear, sort of, not like a ghost, you know, more like a chameleon. Marhan—he's a Gul—doesn't like him, I think."

Davey interrupted and said, "But Anne is with us. She worked with Uncle Jim and got him out of Ch'Garratt when all that happened."

It was Alfie's turn to be surprised. "How do you know about that?"

Jayde held up both hands. "So, the Neraffan, the Gul, and Anne. She's human, right?" Clo and Davey nodded together. "Anyone else?"

Davey shook his head. "Just us."

Alfie and Jayde exchanged a glance.

Alfie looked around and called a waiter.

The Meoenan was immediately at the table, smiling and bowing slightly. "Madam. What do you wish?"

"Please arrange for afternoon tea in my rooms. Seven"—she glanced at Jayde again, who nodded—"eight people. The full works. Three o'clock."

"Three o'clock, afternoon tea for eight. With servers?"

"Oh, why not?"

Jayde spoke over her, "No, no servers, thank you."

Alfie nodded and looked to Davey, "I suppose the Gul eats meat."

Davey nodded.

To the waiter she said, "So a leg of something large, roasted, no sauces or gravy."

"Of course, madam."

As the waiter retreated, Alfie said, "Now you two, your uncle is here, but he's not feeling well. He may or may not join us for tea. You go back to the ship and invite the others, please."

Clo blurted out, "Is Uncle Jim drinking again?"

Alfie had picked up her cup but put it down again. She smiled. "Well, you are completely without boundaries, aren't you dear?

That's lovely. But no." To Davey she said, "It's best not to discuss such things in public, dears. That's why we're all having tea together, so we can talk freely then."

Davey's eyes widened, "Oh...gotcha, Grandma! Okay."

04 LEM'S DEATH

In the shed, Lem Able tidied his tools. He pinned several wrenches and screwdrivers into their places on the wall. He closed the lids of storage bins and slid the bins under their workbenches. Wadding up some paper, he fed it into the reclaimer.

He checked again through the contents of his tool bag.

An alarm sounded at his wrist.

"Here we go!"

He sealed his spacesuit and his tool bag. He approached the T-switch where it lay, clamped to the workbench, and examined the settings.

He checked the spring trap inside the airlock door and stepped outside.

Glancing up at the infrastructure of Sonloi-AC, he smiled with satisfaction. He turned his attention to the jet thrusters, set their firing power to maximum, checked his position, checked his position again, checked his direction, checked his direction again, and pressed the "Fire" button.

Alarms rang in his helmet, but he did not react. The seconds seemed to stretch. Time enough to wonder again if he was about to die in the cold of space.

A net enveloped him, its mesh digging into the bulk of his suit. A seal broke. Another alarm sounded.

He felt himself swing around, and Pec's intense light blinded him.

Two gloved hands clutched his helmet, and he was in shadow once more.

He could see into another visor. "Hi, Sea," he said, "Glad you're here."

"The future is this way, Lem!" she replied. Her hand left his helmet, and she engaged the T-switch.

05 AFTERNOON TEA

Jim lay on the spare bed staring at the ceiling.

Who is she? What did I miss about her?

He realized his teeth were clenched hard. *Again with this?* He remembered his counselor teaching him as a teenager: Deep breath, relax the jaw, deep breath, be aware of your body.

Again. Relax. Relax the jaw. Deep breath.

Again. He remembered how Tuanomena had repeated the word "Again." How it had hung in the air. In his mind. The strange noncommunication of the presence in The Walk.

What is Tuanomena? No wonder we don't have contact with beings like that...so unlike us.

He heard Alfie come back into the suite. He sighed. *Don't come nagging me, Mother.*

Jim's thoughts plowed down familiar paths.

No one knows I'm here. Tella is missing. I could just check out. No one would be any the wiser.

List the positives, Jim, list the positives!

I have a ship. Not sure I can trust the Praestans Rapax's motives for giving it to me...Ha! I know I can't. Damn Marhan for being right!

I have a job. But Tella's missing.

I have a family. Sort of. But who is Sea? What did I miss about her? Where did Dad end up after The Walk?

Alfie glanced at the closed door to the spare room and smiled sadly.

Counting around the sitting room, she was pleased. *Enough seats. Need a couple of small tables.* She fetched them from a closet. "Very good!"

She sat in her favorite chair, picked up her tablet, and made a call. "Hello, Frank, it's Alfie. I'd like to place a call to my son on EBMS. Can you make the connection for me?"

"Certainly, Alfie. Encrypted or public?"

"Not public, I think. The fewer people hearing him swear, the better."

Frank laughed. "Understood. There you go!"

"Thanks!"

A faint beeping tone repeated until a voice answered at EBMS. "This is EBMS. How may I direct your call?"

"This is Dr. Able's mother. I trust I may speak with him."

"I'll see if he's free, Alfie. Please hold."

Almost immediately, Matt's face appeared on her tablet.

"Mother?"

"Hello, dear."

"Is everything okay?"

"Oh yes. I think so. I'm calling with news." She laughed lightly. "Do you want the good news or the good news?"

"What do you mean, Mother?"

She smiled at him. "Jim is here."

Matt's jaw dropped.

She continued, "And to my great delight, so is my grandson Davey. And his lovely girlfriend. They've come looking for his uncle, it seems."

She waited until Matt's storm of temper and swearing subsided.

"Now, dear," she continued, "they are all coming for tea this afternoon. If you like, I can have young Davey talk to you after that."

Matt chewed his tongue for a moment, then replied, "No, just tell him he's grounded for the rest of his life."

"Yes, dear. I'll call you again later."

Matt nodded.

As she ended the call, she heard him faintly mutter, "Thanks."

Alfie came through the door to Jim's room and sat down next to him on the bed.

Jim sighed.

She said quietly, "Make yourself presentable, dear. You have visitors coming for tea."

"Meoena?"

Alfie frowned. "No. They don't seem to know you're here. It seems you've done a good job of avoiding them. You are second only to your father as far as the station and its secret ways are concerned."

"I could stay here for months without having to speak to anyone."

She reached out and began to straighten his more-than-usually untidy hair.

"As much as that might suit your mood, you're coming to tea, or rather, tea—and the guests—are coming to you."

"I really don't need to see anyone right now. I wouldn't be good company."

"Yes, dear." Alfie stood. "It's not optional. I'll drag you out of here by your ears if I must. I've done it before!"

Jim snorted. "I'm a bit heavier than I was then."

"So it'll hurt more. Be ready in two hours."

Marhan sniffed loudly on entering the suite. "What is that smell?"

Alfie suggested, "Meat? We arranged a roast for you."

"No, the other smells—paint, solvents. It's like a fabrication shop in here!"

Alfie reached up to take his furry arm in hers, "Yes, dear, I paint. It's the oil paints and the brush cleaners you smell."

"What do you mean?"

Alfie looked sideways and upwards to his face. "Come through to the studio and see."

Tella, in its white robe, went to take up station behind one of the armchairs.

Davey and Clo threw themselves onto the sofa. Davey pointed out several of the paintings on the walls. "Those are hers too!"

"Who's that little girl in that one?" Clo whispered.

"That is Auntie Maz. She died."

Anne sat next to Jayde and said, "How long have you been administrator here?"

Jayde said, "A couple of lifetimes. And that's just this week."

Anne laughed. "That's why I could never do a desk job. Too much like work."

"What, blowing the crap out of things isn't work?"

Anne shook her head. "Not at all. If they didn't pay me, I'd pay them!"

In the artist's studio, Marhan looked closely at the latest portrait of a young Meoenan. "This is your work? You create these?"

"I do."

"I am an engineer. I draw, but only dull reality. This is different. In this face you have put more than can be seen."

"Thank you."

"Your perspective is wrong. The face, even this ugly Sonloi face, is stretched. But I see why. You have the eyes both clearly shown. In fact"—the canid stepped back from the canvas and nodded vigorously—"the eyes are all, the rest is"—he waved a paw—"fiction!"

"The eyes are the window to the soul."

Marhan snorted, turned his snout to Alfie, and said quietly, "Only when the creature has one."

Alfie held his gaze and said, "You are a most interesting person. Come, we must join the other guests."

· · ·

Marhan squatted next to the empty chair in front of Tella, holding some meat in one paw but uncertain how to handle the plate in his other.

The chatter stopped as Jim emerged from the spare room.

He looked around, puzzled. "Anne?"

"Hi, Jim! Good to see you."

Jim nodded to Tella, who bowed in reply.

Jim looked around the room again. "What the hell are you all doing here?"

Alfie answered, "They've all come because they care, Jim. I don't think you realize quite the effect you have on people."

Jim shook his head, "I'm not drinking, so an intervention or whatever would be misplaced."

"Mr. Able," Jayde said, "We've got a lot to talk about."

"You're mother's friend, the administrator?"

"I am. I'm Jayde Duke."

With a glance at his mother, Jim said, "Good enough." Then he said, "Wait a moment."

Jim returned from the bedroom with a small silver sphere the size of a golf ball. He placed it on the table in the center of the room and tapped it once. Its silver sheen changed to a shimmering rainbow.

Marhan stared at the device and sniffed.

Jim sat down in the armchair and said to Tella, "Remember that?"

"I do. This is a more appropriate occasion to activate it."

"What is it, Uncle Jim?" Davey asked, reaching out to pick it up.

"Don't touch it! It's jamming all electronics in the room. No one will be able to eavesdrop."

Jayde looked alarmed.

"Anyone want to start?" Jim asked.

06 PLAN

"You came in my ship?" Jim asked Marhan.

"Of course," Marhan replied. "And soon, perhaps, I can reclaim my own ship before the docking charges at Flereat bankrupt me!"

Jim smiled. "Be a shame to waste your newfound wealth that way."

"So be quick, monkey!"

Jim looked at their faces. "Okay. Your help will be appreciated in solving a problem. How many of you know about Tuanomena and The Walk?"

Jayde said, "I've been on it. If you need, we can have Yarl join us. His family has something to do with the temple; he got me in. He knows a whole lot about it."

Jim nodded, and Jayde tried to send a message.

She said, "That device is very effective."

"Ah, right..." Jim tapped the sphere again. "Try now."

She sent her message and nodded.

Jim indicated to Davey to turn the device on again. Davey grinned, leaned forward, and carefully tapped the sphere.

"Okay. I was there. I met Tuanomena."

"Oh my..." Jayde gasped.

"But I also recently met a couple of other people. Mom, I met Dad."

Alfie's eyes widened. "How?"

"Tuanomena gave Dad a time machine. Dad called it a T-switch."

No one spoke.

Jim continued, not looking at anyone in particular. "He and I decided it was too dangerous to keep. So we were trying to give it back."

Everybody spoke at once.

Jim raised his voice. "But someone stole it—from right in front of us."

Anne was the first to ask, "Who?"

Jim shook his head. "That's what I need help with. Dad said he'd worked out who she was, but I can't see it. She's human, about thirty or so. Your kind of build, Anne. Dark hair, but a bit messy. She was dressed in the anonymous stuff the pilgrims wear in the temple. She moved like lightning. She was well prepared."

Silence fell again.

Jayde said quietly, "A time machine in the wrong hands could be real trouble."

Davey muttered, "Yeah...but..." and smiled.

Tella spoke. "We must approach this logically. We must not let our fear or apprehension overtake us."

Marhan snorted.

Jim asked, "Anything strike you so far?"

Tella nodded. "Yes. You have never met her before."

"So?"

"She has not traveled in time to appear in your past."

Marhan half turned his head to look at Tella.

Tella asked, "Did she know who you and your father were?"

"I guess so. She was expecting us. And she said she thought the T-switch would be bigger. So she had heard of it but not seen it."

Frowning, Anne asked, "How does that help?"

Tella answered, "If her plans are not to engage with you in your past, perhaps her plans involve your future."

Alfie laughed skeptically, "Her plans might not involve you at all."

Jim nodded. "True enough. But my plans involve getting it back. I may not know who she is, but I don't trust her with it. Just like I don't trust anyone with it."

"You may yet meet her," Tella said. "To know the things she does, I think it likely you will. Or she will become known to one of us here."

Davey asked, "So what does it look like?"

"Like a D-switch but longer, more complicated."

"Cool! Does it work in the gravity well? Can you carry it around with you?"

Jim nodded. "I used it to get from here to the temple. Dad set it up so I could leave here and travel back in time to before he died and travel in space across to Sonloi."

Davey gave Clo a wide-eyed glance.

Anne said, "I was going to ask if you'd tried it."

Picking a piece of meat from his teeth, Marhan said, "You will never find her. If both time and space are your search area, where could you start? Already your part is over, Jim."

Jim shook his head. "I can't accept that. It's my fault. She shouldn't have been able to get hold of it. I should have been more careful."

Tella said, "Both of those things can be true. However much fault may be laid at your feet, it may not be your place to rectify the situation."

"Do you know her name?" Jayde asked.

"Sea."

"As in 'the ocean'?"

"I guess so. Though, that's the funny thing. Dad said Tuanomena always called him Lem-Jim-Sea. And, now that I think about it, Tuanomena called me that too."

"A chain of ownership, perhaps?" offered Tella.

"I guess so."

A knock came at the door. Everyone froze.

Jayde said, "Probably Yarl." She rose and let the Meoenan in.

Alfie watched Yarl carefully as he was introduced to the company and Jim briefly retold the story. As she expected, Yarl was unfazed by anything he heard.

Yarl's immediate and only response was to say, "No dealings with Tuanomena are...uncomplicated."

Jayde smiled.

Yarl asked Jim, "How do you know it's a time machine?"

"My father used it to come here. I met him in a...workshop at the back of the station."

"Pardon me," Yarl continued, his eyes on the carpet, "but your father's ultimate fate was not properly ascertained; his body not recovered. Is it possible he has been alive all this time?"

Jim sighed. "He appeared several times and not in the right order. His first meeting with me was the second time I saw him. I'm convinced the device works...like a D-switch, but with time parameters. And it works near stars. That's the other weird thing."

Anne offered, "And you used it yourself?"

Jim nodded. "But I only went to the temple...and The Walk. So, saying a particular year or date is..."

"Complicated," Yarl finished for him.

"But I came out of meeting Tuanomena at the right time. Yesterday morning, a couple of hours after I left. I have no idea how."

Yarl nodded. "It is highly significant that this woman was unaccompanied on the Walk. To be allowed to access The Walk on her own, your opponent must have studied diligently, as your father did, and earned her place there. But I know of no other human student than Lem."

"I was there alone at first," Jim countered.

"True," Yarl replied, "but you had your father's help, and you used a device as wrapped in complications as The Walk itself."

Alfie watched Yarl's face. Something in his eyes reminded her of when he had returned to the station as an adult. She saw an enthusiasm for life, a fascination for what was being said, an engagement so deep she was almost envious. She said, to no one in particular, "I wish I'd known earlier that's where Lem had been going. Stupid ass, why didn't he tell me?"

Tella said, "Again, this is evidence of Sea's place in the future; she is not known at the temple yet."

"Are you worried news about the time machine will get out?" Clo asked.

Jim nodded. "It already did. Before I knew about it."

Jayde added, "Lert Carn and his associates kidnapped The Artist and Jim in order to track down some mysterious device that The Caretaker had left behind. I don't know if anyone outside this room knows it's a time machine, but Carn went to a lot of trouble to retrieve it. He knows there is something. He knows it's valuable."

"Between Yarl's friends and Dad's ingenuity," Jim answered, "Carn doesn't have the device. The switch is no longer here—in the present. I guess it will still be in Sea's possession when it appears next. I would like to be ready for her."

Marhan growled and Clo looked alarmed. "Jim," he said, "Your pride is hurt. She might not appear for years—tens of years! She might not ever come close to you again. Prepare all you wish, but do not wait. It is gone. This is a tale to tell your children. Nothing more."

"I agree," said Tella.

Jim looked over his shoulder at the Neraffan, to the Gul, and back again. "That, I suppose, I should take seriously—the two of you agreeing on something!" He groaned. "But it's not the answer I was looking for."

Marhan snorted.

Alfie sat up straight. "Is this time for me to offer more tea? I agree with our canid friend. There isn't much we can do. It's safe from Lert Carn. It's safe from us and all our thoughts of what each of us would do with it if we had the chance. I think that's something to celebrate!"

Anne stared at Alfie. "I begin to see where he gets it from."

Davey and Clo began a whispered, but animated, conversation about what they would do with a time machine.

Anne asked Alfie, "The Lert person kidnapped you?"

"Oh yes, to ensure Jim's cooperation."

"Are you going after him?"

Alfie looked down her nose at Anne. "He's a popular politician, dear. My best would be to paint him unflatteringly. I don't think he'd notice."

"No, I suppose not. But someone has to get him."

Alfie shook her head. "I don't see how."

Anne persisted. "Look, one of Earth's best friends, a Meoenan, kidnapping a human? The Office of External Affairs has to know about it! They can do something. I'm happy to kick up a stink until they do."

"Young lady, talk to Jayde. Talk to Yarl. They're best placed to advise you. I am just a painter."

Tella addressed Jim, "If this matter is at a dead end, as Marhan suggests, perhaps I must return to Earth. I have a project I must complete in Unity City."

"And I must return to Flereat and soon," Marhan added.

Jim sighed and nodded. "Okay. Flereat, then EBMS, then Earth. Oh God, it'll be a long rant from my brother when I drop those two off."

He indicated Davey and Clo giggling together on the couch.

Jim sighed and sat back in the armchair, muttering. "Sea, this isn't over."

07 ON BOARD: FIRST NIGHT

Once they were all on board his ship, Jim said, "Let's all get some sleep. We all need to be sharp over the next few days."

Davey shuffled his feet.

Jim smiled. "You two were in module three on the way here?"

Davey nodded.

"Okay then. Marhan, were you in two?"

"I was."

"Tella, you know four is for you."

Tella nodded. "As the arch-manipulators, the Praestans Rapax, decided."

Davey's face was alive with curiosity, but he didn't ask.

Anne slid her arm into Jim's. "I've already tidied up in our module. You're such a slob!"

Jim smiled and blushed slightly. "Thanks! Show me what you did."

They all retired for the night.

In the early hours, in module one, Jim lay thinking.

When everything seemed so bad, so much just clicked into place.

I've got two friends on board. Though, technically, one is the boss, and they don't get on, but...

I've got a wonderful woman in my arms. Though, technically, I'm in hers, but...

I've got family on board. The ship isn't empty.

I don't have to force myself to see the positives. It really doesn't get any better than this!

08 SONLOI

The next day, Jayde and Yarl sat in The Artist's living room. The smell of roast meat still hung in the air.

"Lert Carn has been released," Yarl said. "It has been declared that, although his ship was docked with the kidnapper's ship, he himself was not identified at the scene. And so, his subordinates will take the blame—but not he."

Alfie snorted. "Impossible!"

"Inevitable," Jayde replied. "He has high level—meaning secret service—support."

Yarl sighed, nodded, and arched his fingers in front of his face. "However, we may have something."

Jayde shook her head.

Alfie glanced from her face to his. "Go on."

"A friend of a friend of a friend...Well, the child of a friend of a friend of a friend asked a question."

"Get to the point, Yarl," Jayde pressed.

Yarl nodded again. "Dear Artist, may I send you an image and have you display it on your larger screen here?"

"Of course! Please do."

Yarl tapped a few commands into his tablet, looked up, and said, "Please proceed."

Alfie picked up her tablet, stood, and switched on the large screen embedded in the wall at the other end of the room. Colors washed from gray to a swirl of rainbows to settle into a still scene of Lert Carn in his office on Sonloi, in the second city of Galleno.

"I take it he's no more handsome here than in person?" Alfie asked.

Jayde answered, "Less odious; his mouth isn't moving."

Yarl ignored them and said, "The question concerns the toy on his desk. What is it?"

"Where?" asked Alfie, approaching the screen.

"Bottom left. Near his right hand," Jayde answered, "What does it look like to you?"

"A marble. A glass bead?" Alfie leaned into the screen a little more. "A human eyeball?" She turned from the screen with a look of horror.

Jayde was nodding. "I was afraid you'd say that."

Yarl was watching Alfie steadily.

Alfie returned to her chair, and the three sat in silence.

Alfie opened her mouth to speak but stopped. Then she said, "Who would have such a thing? Obviously, it's artificial. But look at the circuitry on the back of it. That's not just a glass eye...not just..." She picked up her tablet and made a call. "Hello, Frank. Alfie. I'd like to place a call to my son on EBMS. Can you make the connection for me?"

"Certainly, Alfie. Encrypted or public?"

"Encrypted. Best encryption you have, please."

Frank replied, "Understood. There you go!"

"Thank you."

A faint beeping tone repeated until the operator answered at EBMS. "This is EBMS, how may I direct your call?"

"This is Dr. Able's mother on an encrypted link. I must speak with Dr. Able urgently."

"I'll see if he's free. Please hold."

"No. Immediately!"

"I understand, Mrs. Able. Please hold."

Matt's face appeared on her tablet.

"What's the problem, Mother, I'm in the middle of—"

"The EIA agent who went missing when they kidnapped your brother...Was there anything odd about her? Perhaps about her eyes?"

"W-what? How do you know about that?"

"Answer the question, dear. Her eyes?"

"Sh-she had an artificial one. Scanning constantly. Why? What's going on?"

"That's it! That's all I needed to know. Thank you, dear. I won't keep you." She hung up.

Yarl and Jayde stared at her.

Alfie smiled back and said, "So, how do we retrieve it, and how do we use it to glue Carn's ass to the floor of a cell?"

"It won't be easy," Yarl replied.

Jayde shook her head. "I don't want to waste my time on Carn at all. I want the one who pulls his strings."

Yarl nodded and said, "No. You cannot get to him. But if we can force Lert Carn to choose between his self-interest and his loyalty, it may yet work in our favor."

Jayde nodded and thought.

Alfie smiled at her. "I told you Yarl was good, didn't I?"

09 ON BOARD: DAY

The kitchen area of Jim's ship sat below the airlock. A ramp to the left of the flight room led down to the lower level. The equivalent ramp to the right led to storage and the launch bay of the one-person flier.

Anne's head rested on Jim's shoulder. It made eating breakfast tricky.

"Can you—"

"What?" she asked, sleepily.

"I'm eating."

She shook her head and looked around the galley. "Hmm. I should probably be checking in with work. You're a bad influence."

"You're welcome. More coffee?"

"Sure."

He poured her another cup.

Across the table Marhan yawned and grunted.

Jim asked, "What was that?"

"I should have brought the rest of that meat from your mother's. Your kitchen is ill stocked."

"Well, pardon me." Jim smiled. "To paraphrase someone I once met, 'You expect tender gazelles leaping across the plain? Make do!'"

Marhan narrowed his eyes and ground his teeth in reply.

Anne stood and yawned. "See you in a bit. Calls to make."

"I thought you were on vacation?"

"Still need to check on things."

"See you later." Jim held her hand for a moment as she drew away.

Marhan watched her go.

Jim drained his mug.

"We need to talk," the Gul said seriously.

"Sounds bad."

"On Flereat—before our celebration—I told you what I thought the Rapaxan monk had done to you. Here we sit in the ship they made for you. You have said nothing about it. Done nothing about it. Why not?"

Jim shrugged. "Been busy."

"Do you not believe me?"

"No—I mean, sure I believe you. I j—I just don't know what to make of it."

"In the meantime, what are they making of you? It will be nothing good, Jim Able, nothing good."

"Marhan, I know. But the Praestans Rapax play very long games. They didn't build this ship in a day. They didn't plan whatever Tamric did to me in a hurry. Whatever I do, I have to plan equally carefully."

Marhan gave a quick nod of his snout.

"I *have* been thinking it over. First, I need to find an independent doctor. Preferably one with multi-species experience but who is good with human anatomy and who is also absolutely discreet. That's a tall order."

Marhan's eyes wandered around the galley. Then he asked, "Which species has the longest experience with humans?"

"The Meoena of Pec Sonloi. Where we've just been."

"Where you grew up?"

Jim nodded.

"Did a Meoenan doctor treat you when you were young?"

"Yeah...a trainee under supervision."

"Does he still live? Is he trustworthy?"

Jim's eyes widened. "Maybe."

"Then visit your mother again. She can arrange things without arousing the suspicion of Rapaxan spies." Marhan's claw screeched across the square pattern of the tabletop. "They have spies on the station. Be sure of that."

"You are paranoid. But that doesn't mean, of course, you're wrong. Good thinking."

"When you take your revenge on the Praestans Rapax, Jim Able, I hope I may be with you—to take my own."

Jim looked Marhan in the eye and said, "Of course. I haven't forgotten. You have as much, if not more, reason than I."

Tella came down to the galley. "Good morning, Jim! Marhan."

"Morning, boss," Jim replied.

Marhan said nothing.

"Are you eating breakfast?" Jim asked.

"Nothing yet, thank you. But I do need to talk to you, now that we have some time."

Marhan nodded to Jim and said, "We will continue this another time, monkey."

Jim smiled and said, "Sure."

Marhan left, and Tella took his seat.

Jim asked, "Mind if I get more coffee first?"

"You might need it."

Jim's fresh mug of coffee grew cold as Tella spoke.

"You will remember our trip to TMV-One. We went to a promontory where the Regdenir performed one of their rituals. When I had the opportunity to question them, they seemed to know little of the history of the promontory, of the carvings etched into the circle beneath their feet. They called it the Pongret M'dar."

"Sure, I remember. You took pictures of it."

"I did. I spent a long time in the flier getting as accurate a set of images of the carvings as I could. I told you several times how important I knew the carvings to be."

"Don't remember that. But I remember you taking the pix."

"I was injured on that mission."

Jim nodded. "I packed you off onto an EIA ship, and they wouldn't give me a receipt."

"No. I think you miss the point. The images were in the flier. A rented flier. You had charge of them."

"Sure. I downloaded them onto a data capsule for you."

"You kept them from me."

Jim frowned. "No, I kept them *for* you."

Tella's face showed no reaction. It continued, "From the moment of your return, you made no effort to contact me. Despite my medical condition, despite my stated interest in the images, you made no effort to deliver them. You kept them *from* me. And—as much as I am experienced with humans—I did not know how to interpret your actions."

Jim laughed. "Tella? What is this? I got back to a world of trouble! Liz was all over me about TMV-One. She used what we did there as an excuse to fire me! Your pictures of some ancient carving weren't foremost in my mind. Your health was certainly a higher priority. And I tried—repeatedly—to contact you! The EIA don't acknowledge your existence to anyone. Especially not to staff at the Office of External Affairs, which is where I still was then. No way were they letting me know anything about you."

"I heard nothing from you. I did not hear that you had even tried to contact me. What conclusion do you think I could draw, Jim?"

Jim frowned and did not answer.

Tella continued. "The logic of the situation was inescapable: that your apparent friendship with me was merely the exercise of good technique in working team relationships and did not persist past the mission's end; that you understood the images to be something of value and you intended to realize that value for yourself. You intended to sell or trade the images."

Jim swallowed. "You crazy bastard! No..."

Tella placed its hands on the table, and the check pattern swelled up through its skin.

Jim asked cautiously, "Wait...What did you do?"

"I understood that I needed to keep you close and monitor your movements. I needed to find out if you still had the images of the Pongret M'dar or had already sold them on."

"What did you do?"

"I asked my superiors at the EIA about hiring you."

"And?"

"When they said 'no,' I devised a way of entering you into the human resources database and other key systems—without my boss's knowledge. I created a job for you. I employed you myself."

Jim put his face in his hands. "Tella! Tella! Tella!"

"I have recently come into possession of the data capsule with the images."

"Where was it?"

"In your apartment. At the bottom of a PR backpack."

"Oh...that's right." Jim nodded, remembering. "That's where I put it!"

"I now have it and have recreated the Pongret M'dar."

"In a warehouse in Unity City."

"Yes."

"That's why Agent Brown came looking for me. She was taking me there when I was kidnapped and she went missing."

Tella nodded. "As I suspected."

Jim drank a mouthful of cool coffee. "So, let me just get this straight." He sighed loudly. "Do I actually have a job?"

"No."

"And you think I'm pretending to be your friend."

"That is something I am still uncertain about. Humans are, in many ways, confusing."

With his eyes firmly on Tella's, Jim said, "Really? Not as much as others I could mention."

Tella said, "When I heard you were missing, I was concerned."

Jim said, "I'm glad. But I need to extract myself from the EIA! Before I get put in jail or shot. So do you. How the hell do I—we— do that?"

"I have ways of protecting myself that you lack."

"For someone who has been around humans for as long as you have, you show some awful gaps in your understanding of us. How did you think you'd get away with manufacturing a position for me?"

"Technically, it was no great challenge. It involved being unseen in the offices of several high-level officials and using their computers briefly when they stepped outside."

"That's not what I meant. I don't mean pull it off; I'm sure I could have done something similar if I'd tried. It's the not-being-found-out-after! People notice eventually. Everyone makes mistakes, but no one is permanently stupid. Even in the EIA"

With its face still showing neither concern nor humor, Tella said, "Really?"

"Anyway, I kept the data capsule *for* you, you transparent idiot! I had no idea the images meant so much to you!"

"They are of incalculable worth. I have already sent word to Neraff and to our embassy in Unity City. Our ambassadors should, by now, have ensured my recreation is preserved until access can be gained to the original on TMV-One."

"What's so important about it?"

"We are a persecuted people. We are dying out. But over a thousand years ago—a thousand TMV years—the writing on the Pongret M'dar shows there were Neraffan-jong on TMV."

Jim did not, at first, react. He said thoughtfully, "On Mainworld —on Beauty—itself? And on TMV-One, Madhar Nect told me they have legends about people of glass..."

"Jim, I am not concerned with legends. My people may still be there! I must go! I must go back to TMV-One."

10 ON BOARD: SECOND NIGHT

In the early hours, in module one, Jim said quietly, "I thought you girls—sorry, women—in active service took hormone suppressants to prevent pregnancies."

Anne replied, less quietly, "What? Why should we? Who gave you that idea?"

"Well, I..."

"What was your mother thinking!"

Jim smiled in the dark and said flippantly, "That's something even my father never figured out."

Anne continued, ignoring him, "I mean, every teenage boy gets his tubes blocked! Now you tell me you didn't? Why the hell didn't you?"

"I don't know...I grew up on the station. Maybe because we didn't always have a human doctor? We didn't have the same...I don't know."

"And it's completely reversible! Why would you—why *have* you —been taking such a chance with the women in your life?"

Jim shrugged. "What can I tell you? It didn't happen then, and I never really thought about it."

"I just don't believe this! You thought it was up to me to put chemicals in my body? While you didn't even bother to have the simplest of operations? I just don't believe this..."

Later, at the table, Davey and Clo sat leaning on each other. Anne sat on a stool away from the table, near the coffeemaker. There was no sign of Marhan or Tella.

Jim poured himself a cup of coffee and stood at Anne's shoulder. "You okay?"

"Sure."

Jim sighed. "Really?"

"I'm thinking," she said quietly, glancing at the others. "I've always known I was unlikely to be a mother. Nowhere on the horizon, really."

"You have a career you're good at and enjoy."

"But I've also thought that if I ever did get pregnant and it was a girl, I might go through with it. I mean, with a boy, obviously, I wouldn't, but...Does that sound weird to you?"

Jim gagged. "Umm, a little on the strange side, yeah."

"I thought you'd think so." She glanced up and then looked back into her mug. "There are enough entitled males in the galaxy. I could bring up a girl. Wouldn't know where to start with a boy."

"That's...the whole thing is"—he sighed—"complicated."

"No. Not for me. It's the way it is."

"Right."

Davey asked, "Uncle Jim? What's so special about Tella's module?"

"Hmm? Well, it's all decked out for Neraffans. It's...you can ask Tella yourself."

"Okay."

The ship intoned, "Approaching Hon system!"

Anne stood up. "Later."

Jim replied quietly, "Sure."

11 SONLOI: THE EYE

For Immediate Release:

The Institute for Art announces a new series of commissioned portraits.

In a gesture of goodwill and healing from both sides of the recent unfortunate events, famous artists are coming together to produce portraits of the movers and shakers from both Human and Meoena communities.

Initial sketches will commence immediately, with completed works to be shown during the Tulbar Festival in Tuanomena.

Dr. Emily Jones of Galleno will paint First Minister Cran Mular

Erta Brien of Sonloi-AC will paint Station Administrator Jayde Duke

Miles Fontainebleau of Renbacoi will paint celebrity dancer Miran Flad

The Artist of Sonloi-AC will paint business leader and author Lert Carn

The collective 'Why?' based in Tuanbass, will render youth icon Gort, in a special 3D format

———

"You think they will fall for it?" Jayde asked.

Yarl answered, "Only Lert's vanity is important. Will *he* fall for it? Nothing else need happen but our access to his office."

"Well," countered Alfie, "a great deal more needs to happen. But it'll be a good start. *If* he falls for it."

"Am I speaking with the infamous Artist of Sonloi-AC?"

"You are."

"This is Lert Carn."

"Yes, dear. Will I be painting you?"

"We'll see. Please come to my office later today. There are things we need to discuss."

"Of course. Do you mind if I do some preliminary sketches while we talk?"

"You can do what you like."

"Thank you."

"He didn't fall for it, did he?" Alfie said.

Yarl nodded. "He will be difficult. Dear Artist...I wonder if the eye is still functional."

Alfie shrugged.

Yarl's eyes searched the floor. "Would it be possible for me to speak to The Elder Son?"

Lert Carn's office dominated the suite of offices that dominated the building that dominated the most politically significant street in Galleno.

Alfie was not impressed. She arrived with a swirl of her most stained smock and the smell of paint fumes. She carried an over-sized sketch pad and an inconveniently large bag of pencils and charcoals.

A Meoenan technician, in an overall and cap, followed her with a long, awkward light stand.

Lert heard them crashing and grunting through the doors. His secretary had not returned from lunch, and he already felt irritated.

He smiled, exhaled slowly, filled his lungs, then shouted, "Watch the furniture, you fools! Where do you think you are?"

Alfie stopped in her tracks and replied, "Well, aren't you lovely? I brought up my children to help a lady when they could. Didn't your mother do the same?"

Lert laughed and stood up behind his desk. "Sort yourself out! Quickly!"

The technician erected the stand at the edge of the desk and switched it on. The light flooded the desk—and Lert—with an intrusive white glare.

"Ah! Is that necessary?" he asked.

"Do you want to look good or not?" Alfie asked testily.

Lert waved his hand at her and sat down again. While he waited for her to choose a pencil and select a sheet of paper, he mindlessly picked up the eye from his desk and began tossing it gently and catching it again.

He asked, "Any ill effects from your recent...adventures?"

"We call it Post Traumatic Stress. There are many symptoms. Some can take a long time to surface. Some can be quite debilitating."

"I'm sorry to hear it." He smiled and tossed the eye.

"Now," said Alfie, "there was something you wanted to talk about."

"What are you really up to?"

"My dear, what can you mean?"

"This portrait nonsense. So suddenly organized. So transparent! What are you up to?"

He tossed the eye one more time.

Moving behind his desk, the technician reached out calmly from behind Lert and caught it. He was across the room to Alfie before the politician could react.

Yarl removed his cap and spoke into his sleeve. "We have it!"

Several explosions rocked the ceiling of the office. Smoke filled the outer room and erupted down the outside of the windows.

Lert was on his feet but stopped dead at the sight of human soldiers filling the room. Turning, he saw several suspended outside the wide windows.

"Do not move!" shouted a soldier next to Alfie.

"Who are you? What are you doing here?" Lert shouted back.

The soldiers steadied their weapons.

Alfie and Yarl faced Lert.

Yarl said, "These are agents from Earth's External Intelligence Agency. They have come for this." He held up the eye. "When you extracted it from their agent, you perhaps did not realize it would still be active. It has been continually sending out its signals."

"Nonsense!"

"The First Minister thought it was worth allowing our human friends to find out for themselves."

Lert laughed. "No one will believe it. Look at the damage these aliens have just done! No one will believe their lies."

Alfie countered, "The Caretaker, my husband, installed many of the devices your astronomers use on the station. It was a simple matter to find one that had picked up signals on the right frequencies. The electronic record is there, in the hands of Meoenan scientists."

Yarl added, "But, by order of the First Minister, you are to surrender yourself to these humans for custody on Sonloi-AC pending transport to Earth."

"That, boy, will never happen!"

"We will see."

12 HEN FLEREAT

Jim sat waiting for Flereat docking instructions. He looked up from the ship's controls and asked, "Is there something wrong, Davey?"

"No. Nothing."

"Just that you're lurking. Come on, spit it out!"

"Well...Don't be mad."

Jim smiled. "What did you hack this time?"

"Flereat Customer Service."

"Why?"

"I got us all Black Tickets—you know, unlimited passes."

Jim paused before saying, "Huh! Nice one."

"You're not mad?"

"Sure I am! That's stealing. But...you'd think they'd have good security on that sort of thing."

"Yeah, totally. I mean, I thought I'd never get that far into their systems!"

"How do we collect them? Don't they have headshots and signatures?"

"Well. Yeah. I did all that."

Jim frowned. "Yeah, well, that's disturbing. Under our real names?"

Davey shrugged. "Sure."

"Even Marhan?"

Davey nodded.

"How did you get his signature? I don't think I've ever seen it."

"It's not hard to find."

Jim shook his finger at the boy and said, "Don't do anything like this again. I don't want to see you in jail."

"Sure. But that hacking program of yours is genuine awesome."

"Wait, I didn't show you that!"

"Sorry. But its name was a bit of a giveaway."

"So you went snooping through my personal files as well?"

"We needed to find you! We thought there might be something that would help."

Jim shook his head. "And I was worried about how your dad would treat you when you get back." He smiled. "You deserve every bit of it."

The parking system at Flereat was a masterpiece of unfriendly automation—until Jim sent the number of his Black Ticket. Then it transformed into a masterpiece of obsequious fawning.

They were redirected to a good berth, a short walk from the entrance to the Hall of the People, the main dome and center of Flereat. There, the uniformed staff lined up to present each of them with an electronic tag—the Black Ticket. Each ticket displayed a photo and a couple of icons on the front and a signature on the back. Stuffed in between were more sophisticated electronics than the average spaceship.

Anne was the first to spot the Group Voice feature. "Hey every-one. Check this!" She tapped a sequence of icons and whispered, "Chin-Chin is listening!"

Her voice came clearly out of each of their tags.

"Whoa!" said Clo.

"Uh-oh!" said Davey.

As they walked on together, Marhan drew Davey close with his long arm. "You are a fool, small monkey."

"W-what? Why?"

"This ticket bears my wife's signature."

"Really? Sorry."

Marhan laughed. "I can draw a fair copy of it if I ever have to. I was about to ask how you came by it, but perhaps I do not wish to know."

Jim asked, "You have a wife? How did I not know that?"

Marhan shrugged. "Perhaps you never asked. Tanna-Gul mates do not always live together. The younger ones do so more than we." He waved at Davey and Clo. "We do not behave as you monkeys do."

"Do you have to share your money with her?" Jim asked.

Marhan snapped his jaws. "Careful! That is one question too many."

Jim held up his hands and said, "Fair enough. Let's decide how we're going to spend the day. Since I'm here, I should continue the investigation I started–before I got interrupted." He glanced at Marhan. "So, I'm working."

"The courier who tried to kill you?" Marhan asked.

"That's right."

"I will come with you. You are not safe on your own."

Jim was going to object but merely nodded.

Anne muttered, "I didn't come here to work. I'm officially on vacation." She asked Tella, "How about you?"

"I know nothing of this place" Tella said, impassively. "I have never been. I am curious to see it. If Jim has Marhan at his side, perhaps I may take the day off."

"Never been here?" Anne exclaimed, "My parents brought me here several times! Oh, I can show you around."

"Thank you."

Leaning in she lowered her voice to say, "And I'll explain to you why Meko is the real hero of this place!"

Davey and Clo were deep in conversation. Jim said to them, "It's ten hours station time. You two are back on the ship at twenty-two hundred hours. No leeway. No complaints."

Both, looking a little crestfallen, nodded back.

"Okay!" Jim said, "Everyone have fun! Use that Group Voice thing if you have to."

Jim returned to The Golden Lasso Hotel.

With Marhan towering behind him, he stood at the concierge's desk. Jim showed a picture of Jack Katrigg. "This man caused some trouble here a while back. What can you tell me of him?"

"I'm sorry, sir," the concierge replied formally. "Who might you be?"

"James Able, of Sol Earth's External Intelligence Agency. I am not here as a tourist."

"May I see some identification, James Able?"

Jim flashed his EIA parking pass.

The concierge briefly looked Jim in the eye. "Please wait while I bring someone who can speak with you."

"Thank you."

They waited several minutes, surrounded by the hum of weary tourists.

"James Able? I am Arnit Hough, manager of The Golden Lasso. Let us sit together."

"Thank you," said Jim, gesturing for Marhan to follow and hoping Arnit Hough would find the Gul even more intimidating for not having been introduced.

They sat in a partly screened area off the main lobby.

The manager's skin varied through shades of light green. His eyes hid in the folds of a large and round face. Teeth, white and rounded like those of an herbivore, flashed as he spoke. Constantly nodding, he began, "How may I be of assistance?"

"This man." Jim showed the image again.

"I remember him."

"Has he been back?"

"No."

"How can I contact him?"

Hough smiled and shook his head. "Without a warrant from an

appropriate judicial authority, I'm afraid it is not possible for me to answer."

"Who are the 'appropriate' authorities?"

Again, Hough smiled and said, "That is a matter of some dispute. And it has been since the station was first opened. We live in something of a legal and regulatory gray area here."

Jim sighed and sat back. "That I did not know."

"It makes such business as yours more difficult, for which I apologize."

Marhan growled, "And business such as yours more easy."

Hough's smile remained fixed.

Jim glanced at Marhan and then put his face closer to Hough's. "I'm willing to pay a considerable inducement for word of this man. Perhaps someone in your position would welcome some extra income?"

Nodding, Hough said, "Thank you, thank you, for being so kind as to think of me. But no. No, no, I cannot undertake any such arrangement. Many people visit Flereat. Most come for pleasure; some come for business. Most are good people, yet some are not. I would not dare put myself at risk of the latter. You, too, should be wary of putting yourself at such risk. Though this is a place of entertainment, do not underestimate the dangers that some bring with them into the domes."

Jim shook his head. "Don't you think that those of us who understand that distinction have a duty to protect the former from the latter? Don't you think the families that come here deserve your consideration over those who are criminals?"

Hough continued to nod and smile but said nothing. At length, he put his green hand on Jim's and said, "No. The tourists can go fuck themselves. I run a hotel. Enjoy your trip home."

The manager stood and left Jim and Marhan staring after him.

Marhan laughed softly. "Jim Able, there is an honest person!"

"Ha! Of a kind. Of a kind."

"Who else would you ask?" Marhan said.

Jim shook his head. "I felt sure I could bribe some information from someone. Who else would Katrigg have dealt with?"

"He will have eaten, drunk, and had sex. Where will you start?"

"You are a practical fellow, Marhan. But this is a big place, and there's a lot of all three going on."

"Have you accessed the cameras from when he was here? Is there anyone he can be seen with?"

"Not the bits I've seen so far. But I know someone who can find out for us. Young Davey is a natural hacker."

"He is sloppy. He cannot tell the difference between my wife and me!"

"Yeah, he needs to travel more. Being cooped up on EBMS isn't good for him in the long run."

"Perhaps you could ask someone in Flereat Security about Katrigg? They may remember him."

Jim nodded. "True."

Like all entertainment, Flereat's business was to maintain an illusion. A vast infrastructure lay unseen by visitors between the floors and the ceilings. Networks of cabling, vacuum tubing, tunnels, and—in some areas—roadways housed the security and catering apparatus, the staffing and the cleaning, the retail logistics. All used vastly more energy, resources, and money than anything the public saw.

To visit a security office, other than a lost-property stand, meant Jim and Marhan had to first gain access to the Flereat infrastructure.

It only needed two bribes.

They walked, in dim light, along a road. Sudden flashes of brightness came and went as automated vehicles shot by.

Ahead of them shone the lights of a grim office block squashed between the road and the roof.

Marhan's claws curled around Jim's shoulder. They both turned their heads to the left toward a large tunnel mouth, dark and void. Voices whispered in the shadows.

"Shit!" Jim whispered.

"Go carefully. We are almost there," Marhan whispered back.

The pair walked faster toward the security building, but footsteps echoed out of the tunnel.

"Hey, humaa-aan!" came a call.

Jim glanced back. Four figures were following. Jim saw no guns, but they carried sticks or bats.

"Four, with sticks."

Marhan replied, "Fools!"

Three automated vehicles zoomed past. Under cover of the noise, the four ran up behind Jim and Marhan.

Marhan stopped suddenly, turned, and rose to his full height.

Jim turned and rose on the balls of his feet, ready to dodge the first blow. "What do you want?" he shouted.

"We waa-aant nothing, humaa-aan dirt!" one said.

Another raised his weapon, cried something Jim didn't understand, and rushed forward.

As Jim put up his arm in defense, he realized it wasn't a stick but a blade. It made contact as he changed strategy, dropping low and turning in to give a body check with his shoulder. He heard his attacker grunt and felt him stagger sideways. Jim swung the other way to see Marhan pick up one of the others and toss him casually to one side. Another lay bleeding at the Gul's feet. The fourth attacker glanced from Jim to Marhan, unsure what to do next.

Jim turned back to find the blade already coming toward him again.

The next few seconds were a blur of punches, pulls, grabs, and twists. Jim, at last, was on top, punching a narrow, boney face, blue blood on his hands.

Then two things happened at once. From the tunnel came the cries of five or six more hooded thugs running to support their fellows. From the direction of the security building came a thump like a burst of air, a woman's voice gave a command, and blaster fire flashed around them.

All their attackers, even those flat on the ground, twisted under the blasts.

Jim and Marhan stood frozen in confusion.

"Hi, Jim! How are you doing?" the woman said.

"Who are you?" he replied, gripping his bleeding arm.

"Forgotten me so soon? I'm Sea, remember? And I just saved your ass. Aren't you going to say thanks?"

Jim felt a wave of nausea as the pain from his arm finally broke through his adrenaline. He clenched his teeth to shake it off and stared at Sea. He recognized the face, but she was otherwise covered in body armor.

"Y-you're using the T-switch?" he asked.

"Of course!"

Marhan muttered, "This is her?"

Jim nodded and asked Sea, "Who are your friends?"

She glanced at the six other armored figures lining up behind her.

"My boys? Oh, you don't want to know. But they're kind enough to help me on my little adventures."

"Okay. So, thank you. I know 'how,' now tell me 'why.'"

Sea laughed. "Maybe you should be sitting down for this one, if you still haven't worked it out."

"Worked what out?"

"I'm changing the past. My past. These jokers would have left you with a broken back and brain injuries. Injuries that would have limited you the rest of your life."

Jim looked around at the bodies. He shook his head. "So..."

"It's my past too, Dad."

Marhan looked at Jim. Jim said nothing.

"I grew up without a father. That's the past I'm changing. Looks like I'll be seeing you!"

Turning to her associates, she raised her arm. They formed a circle, each touching a hand to hers.

The air thumped, and they were gone.

Marhan caught Jim as he sagged to the ground.

13 THE SHIP

Davey and Clo arrived back, out of breath, at 22:10 station time. The ship was eerily quiet.

"Think anyone's here yet?" Clo whispered.

"Tella might be."

"Don't!" She punched his arm.

The pair walked arm in arm up to their module. On the corridor floor, up against the wall, they saw Jim's soft toy Chin-Chin. Davey picked it up, saying, "We forgot to buy one!"

"You're not buying one of those!"

"Why not? It's what this place is all about."

Clo reached over to the toy and started uncoiling Chin-Chin's penis. "That's why! It's disgusting! And—ew, it's got a wire in it."

"Oh, so you can pose it! Awesome!"

The ship intoned, "Unauthorized access attempted at main airlock."

Davey stared at Clo. "Who...?"

A small explosion sounded beneath them.

The ship intoned again. "Unauthorized access. Unauthorized access. Main systems entering shutdown protocol."

Clo whispered, "What does that mean?"

Davey was halfway down the ramp peering over to see what was happening.

A lone figure walked deliberately from the airlock through a cloud of smoke. The intruder was dressed entirely in an armored battle suit. One arm was raised, a weapon primed to fire.

"Oh shit!" said Davey, a little too loudly.

He ran back up to Clo. Whispering, "We're in real trouble!" he grabbed both her and the soft toy. He led her down the other ramp, keeping their heads down.

"Don't know if this will work..." he said.

He left her with Chin-Chin's body, unrolling the rest of the penis as he crouched low and scrambled across behind the pilot's seat.

Blaster fire erupted from the intruder and hit the ship's controls, narrowly missing Davey's back.

He hid behind the low wall at the base of the left-hand ramp. Clo matched him from the other side.

The intruder walked on unafraid. As he reached the point between them, Davey shouted "Now!" Both pulled up on the wire.

Their grip wasn't strong enough to trip a soldier in a fully functioning battle suit. But the wire was strong and thin enough to slide up under one armored ankle plate. The plate popped slightly from its anchor and caught the top of the foot on the next step. In his attempt to regain his balance, the soldier lost what remained and fell headfirst into the back of Jim's chair.

His vizor shattered, and his helmet flew off. Rolling onto his back, the creature swore.

Davey stood in panic. He had never seen a member of this species before. The creature's face was beak-like, white and triangular, flared at the jaw, narrow at the forehead, and sweeping back to a faint hint of eyes and ears behind. Davey thought the soldier seemed dazed but soon might recover.

Clo shouted, "What do we do?"

Davey looked at the suit. Each arm bore a built-in weapon. The belt carried several pouches of different sizes and one obvious, large blaster.

"Oh, fuck!" Davey shouted. He reached down, unhooked the gun, and pointed it shakily at the face of the soldier.

The white face rolled to point directly at him, the arm of the suit rose from the floor, the built-in weapon whined, and Davey fired.

Jim and Marhan spent several hours at a first-aid station tucked carefully out of sight near the main dome. The attendants were polite to the point of never addressing how the injury to Jim's arm had come about.

"Do you know those things that attacked us?" Jim asked Marhan.

"Those bony faces? I've seen them on news reports. Lim is their star; I forget the planet. They're called Limarc. Refugees from some sort of global catastrophe. The planet is in a sorry state, much as Tanna Gul."

"What happened?"

Marhan shook his head. "I don't know for certain. There are tales of something from another war falling onto their world. Who knows? Ah, Lim Talair! That's it. That's the name."

"Oh," Jim said, "That rings a bell, now you say it."

"They travel in groups, hiring themselves out. They take work as they find it, not asking questions. They cut corners. When challenged, they protest their victimhood."

"They sound difficult to deal with."

Marhan put his long face next to Jim's. "They are ill-used by fate but have a bad attitude. No one likes them."

Jim offered his bandaged arm and said, "You know how I would vote."

"We should go back to the ship," Marhan said.

"We haven't seen the Security folks, yet."

"I worry about the others. Were they also followed?"

"Shit! The kids should be back. Let's check in with the others. Try that Group Voice thing."

Anne replied. Davey did not.

. . .

As they hurried back, Marhan said, "I have been thinking of your quest to find this Katrigg person. I don't think anyone here will help you."

"And?"

"You should ask Schpurr."

"Who, or what, is Schpurr?"

"He is often on Station Stacco Ila 32. He's a Mallan who arranges things. He might even know Katrigg."

"What sort of...things...does he arrange? I shouldn't ask, should I?"

Marhan snapped his jaws. "Having the plans for an attack ship gains you nothing if you lack the materials to build it. Moving the materials for a thousand ships may be a small problem in itself. But doing it without anyone noticing requires skills Guls do not have. Did you never think to question how we had done it? How we handled the logistics of our enterprise?"

"I—"

"No. You followed the bidding of the Praestans Rapax and questioned nothing. Find Schpurr. Though go carefully. He will not gladly meet with you. He will give nothing away."

"Thanks...I think."

Jim found the outside of his airlock black with smoke and the door slightly open. "I don't like what they've done with the place. Not my colors at all."

Marhan silently opened the door further and slipped inside. Only the emergency lights glowed dimly.

Jim followed, smelling smoke.

Clo and Davey sat on the corridor floor, shoulder to shoulder, their backs up against the end of the wall.

Marhan walked past them to inspect the body.

"You guys hurt?" asked Jim.

Clo shook her head.

"How many of them?"

Clo whispered, "Just one."

Jim reached down and unhooked the blaster from Davey's fingers. He put his hand under the boy's chin to look him in the eye. "Hi, Davey, you in there?"

"Oh, hi, Uncle Jim..."

"Looks like you need a drink. Clo? Can you go to the galley and make some of the strongest, sweetest coffee you've ever made, please?"

"Sure..." She got up slowly, perhaps at first not remembering which way to go.

"Marhan?" Jim asked.

"Dead Limarc. Battle suit. They were expecting resistance?"

"Raeda! Put the lights up."

The ship did not reply.

"Raeda? Acknowledge."

Marhan said, "There is some damage in here."

Jim stepped past him, glanced at the Limarc, and examined the pilot chair and what he could see of the damaged controls.

He went to a storage locker under the right observation window and brought out two flashlights. One he threw to Marhan; the other he shone above the windows until he found a panel. It popped open when he pressed it to reveal the controls for the voice activation system.

"Still on! Raeda, why aren't you talking?"

Jim switched off the flashlight and listened. All was quiet except for Clo dropping something in the galley.

"Ah!" Jim said suddenly. "Raeda! Resume voice commands."

The ship replied, "Voice commands reinstated by Jim."

"Got you, you bastard!"

"Please restate query."

"Raeda, why were voice commands suspended?"

"Shutdown protocols are in force. All command functions are suspended due to unauthorized access during an absence of command personnel."

"Okay. Well done! Resume all suspended functions."

"Acknowledged."

As the lights came back on, Jim was standing next to the body. Tella and Anne raced down the corridor.

Tella asked quietly, "Is anyone hurt?"

Jim shook his head and took Anne to one side.

She saw a light in his eyes she had never seen before. It unsettled her.

"You and Marhan strip the suit for anything useful. Prep the remains for dumping in space."

She nodded. "Sure."

"And...We really need to talk, but—"

"I know. We'll get to it."

"No, I mean, yes...but I have to bring Davey down carefully. It's his first kill."

"Oh, shit. I thought you'd—"

"No. The kids were on their own."

"Looks like they did good!"

"I know. But he doesn't know it yet. I'm sorry. It may take a while—and like I say—I really need to tell you something."

"Sure, Jim. Sure. We'll get on it. Be with your nephew."

Jim turned to Tella and said, "Boss, I need you to work with the ship. Assess the damage. See what repairs we need. Can we get underway before making them?"

Tella nodded thoughtfully. "Understood. I will ask our hosts if they can help with the door."

"Great idea!" To the ship he said, "Raeda, acknowledge Tella for all command functions."

"Tella is acknowledged."

Jim took Davey down to the galley and sat opposite him across the table. Clo sat quietly on the stool by the coffeemaker.

"Davey?"

"Uncle Jim? Am I in trouble?"

"Maybe. Let's find out before we tell anyone else."

Davey sipped his drink and coughed. "Whoa!"

Clo asked, "Is it okay?"

"Umm...Sure..."

"What happened, Davey? Starting when you got back."

"We got back on time, like you said. Everything was quiet. Umm, there was a noise. An explosion. I looked down the corridor, and this mech-suit was walking in."

"Where were you. Down or up?"

"Up. I leaned over the rail, sort of halfway down, to look."

"Okay."

"I had an idea..."

"Go on."

"We'd been talking about your Chin-Chin. It's...thing...has a wire in it."

"Okay..."

"So I went back up, and we came down the other side."

"With the Chin-Chin."

"Right. And I uncoiled it across the corridor."

Jim sat back in his chair and sighed. "Let's take a moment." He placed his hands flat on the table. "You were on the ramp. You saw the danger. You went back up. Instead of going straight to your module and sealing yourselves in, you came back down to confront the intruder."

Davey frowned. "I guess so..."

"Hmm. So, you have a wire across the end of the corridor. Then what?"

"There was firing. I think that's when it happened. I mean, I think that's when he shot up the controls. I'm really sorry—"

"Don't worry about that. That's in no way your fault. What did *you* do next?"

"We waited until he reached the wire and pulled it up. But it didn't work! It ripped right out of my hand..."

"Of course. It was a mech-suit. They're externally powered. It's not just a man—or whatever. There are power units enhancing each muscle group."

"Right..."

"Then what?"

"He sort of tripped up anyway. Maybe the wire got caught somehow. I don't really know."

Jim nodded.

Clo prompted, "His head hit your chair."

Jim continued to look at Davey's face. "Good. The seat doesn't move for anything. And?"

"The helmet came off. He rolled on his back. I guess he was stunned."

Jim placed the Limarc's gun on the table between them.

"Did you get this off him while he was lying there?"

Davey nodded.

Jim continued, "Then you did what everyone does. You checked how this alien weapon is triggered. And in this case, it's just like one of ours. Then you looked for the safety catch and flipped it to firing mode. Right?"

Davey frowned again. "I guess...I don't really remember that part."

"No." Jim looked from Davey to the gun and back. "Pick it up!"

Davey reluctantly reached out to hold the gun again. He turned it over and over. "I don't see a safety."

"No. What does that tell you?"

Davey's face fell in confusion.

Jim said, "All civilized planets have safety modes on their weapons. Otherwise, anyone could pick one up and start shooting unintentionally—animals, children, the insane. It's a minimal precaution. What the construction of this one tells you, Davey, is that *this*, therefore, was not made on a civilized planet. Right?"

"I...I guess not."

Jim pointed his thumb to the upper level. "That guy was a jerk from a planet of jerks. Point one. Got it?"

Davey's eyes widened a little. "Got it."

"Tell me the last part. How you came to fire."

Davey looked away and shivered. "I-I aimed at his head. It was the only vulnerable spot 'cause of the helmet. But he was waking up. His arm came up, and I heard the onboard weapon warming up."

"You heard that?"

Davey nodded. "Sure."

"And?"

"I dunno. I guess I fired. I really don't remember. It all happened kinda fast, you know?"

Jim nodded. "Yeah, I do. I know."

Jim looked from Davey to Clo and back again. "Here's what I think. You've shown great courage—both of you. Call that point two. You, sir, have shown some natural ability. Listen, the sound you heard, the weapon in his arm warming up? That was the aim confirmation, the 'target acquisition signal.' From that point, how long do you think it would have taken the operator to confirm the weapon should fire?" Without waiting, he continued. "My guess? Much less than a second. And yet you, young man, fired first; if you hadn't, you wouldn't be sitting here. You had no time to consciously think that through; you were acting on instinct. So that's point three. And you acted correctly."

Jim watched Davey's face as the teen's mind worked.

Jim continued, "To sum up then. Point one: You were attacked by a jerk with bad intent. Point two: You both showed courage. Point three: Your instincts are good. You did well."

Davey's frown disappeared. "So...I'm not in trouble?"

"Not with any of us. Far from it."

Jim returned to the flight room. Immediately, Marhan stood in his path.

"How is the small monkey?"

"Davey will be fine."

"I will no longer call him a fool."

Jim nodded. "We'll both appreciate that."

Before Jim could move, Marhan held an extended claw to Jim's chest. "And you. After Sea left us, you collapsed. It was not from the wound to your arm. You look now to be back with us. Am I correct?"

Jim sighed and looked up into Marhan's eyes. "My daughter freaked me out from the first time I met her. At least now I understand why. I felt the connection...almost as if I recognized her. No, I'm not back. I still have no idea how to deal with her. Nor how to deal with her mother." He glanced across to Anne, still working on disassembled parts of the mech-suit.

"Are you saying she will be the mother?" Marhan whispered.

Jim nodded. "Best guess."

"How well do you know her? How will she react to this news from the future?"

"No idea."

"Perhaps you should not tell her."

"What? How can I not?"

Marhan stepped back and muttered, "I am an engineer. What do I know of such things?"

Jim reached out and held the canid's arm. "Listen, I know you came to get your ship and go on your way. Stick around, please. I could use your support. I see you're a friend now, and I'm not letting you go easily."

Marhan snapped his jaws. "It was not so when we first met!" He looked at Jim, at Anne, and at Davey and Clo emerging from below. "Perhaps. But there is business I must attend to. I will meet you again at EBMS, if your officious sibling grants me permission."

Jim nodded and whispered, "Thanks."

Tella came down the corridor to say, "The docking crew has patched up the door. Those Black Tickets were well worth the price you paid."

Jim laughed. Few could deadpan a joke as well as Tella, whose face so rarely showed emotion.

"Also, the ship says there are enough working systems to return us to EBMS. Repairs will be necessary once there."

"That's a relief. Thanks!"

They all gathered round the pile of suit parts Marhan and Anne had made.

Davey was relieved to see no sign of the body.

Jim asked, "Anything useful we can salvage?"

Anne said, "Piece of crap. The suit was as much of a danger to the wearer as to us."

Davey frowned. "Looked scary enough!"

Tella answered, "Perhaps the point was to intimidate. To provoke surrender rather than battle."

Marhan nodded. "Much like the thugs who attacked us. I think they had hoped for less resistance than we gave them."

Anne asked, "What happened? You haven't said how you got hurt, Jim."

"It got...complicated. In the Tuanomena sense."

Anne frowned in puzzlement.

Marhan looked from Jim to Anne but said nothing.

14 RETURN TO EBMS

As Jim prepared the ship to leave Hen Flereat, he noticed Marhan and Tella standing in earnest conversation down the corridor towards the airlock.

He tried to remember the moment when Marhan had become more than the drinking buddy he spent a lost week with. The image came to his mind of one of the Limarc attackers being tossed through the air as Marhan went all out to deal with another. Jim's previous drinking buddies would have been running the other way. Marhan was different.

Jim felt it gave him at least one foot on solid ground in the insane world where dead fathers appeared and not-yet-born daughters popped out of nowhere, where relationships with lovers became complicated before they got going.

"Jim!" called Tella.

"Tella? You ready to go?"

"Yes, but to Tanna Gul, not yet to EBMS. I shall accompany Marhan on this leg of the journey."

"Really?" Jim said. "I thought he didn't like you."

"Neither me nor you. Yet you appear to have changed your minds about each other. I shall try and keep up."

Jim laughed and said, "Sure, but aren't you in a hurry to do something about TMV-One?"

"The government there is, as I understand it, not allowing any further contact. I must be careful in how I approach a return to their system. 'Hurry' is not a word I can use."

"Understood. See you when you get to EBMS."

Tella bowed and left.

Jim sat with Clo and Davey over breakfast in the galley.

He asked, "So what will you tell your Dad?"

Davey shrugged. "Dunno."

Clo asked, "Do we have to tell him anything?"

Jim answered, "Up to you."

Davey sighed.

"Just don't look guilty," Jim said, smiling. "It's a dead giveaway!"

Davey laughed. "Right..."

The ship waited in a line to leave Flereat space. Ahead of them, Jim noticed a sleek black Praestans Rapax craft.

He swore under his breath.

"What's the matter?" Davey asked.

"That's Marhan's ship."

"Oh, cool!"

"Yeah. I should have guessed; it's one of the ones I didn't get to blow up."

Davey looked sideways at his uncle. "What do you mean?"

"It's a long and bloody story, Davey. Another day."

A stern-faced Matt Able met them as they docked at EBMS.

"Hi, Matt!" Jim said, as cheerily as he could fake.

Matt glowered back. To Davey he said, "To your room. I'll talk to you later." To Clo he said, "Your parents are waiting for you. I doubt you'll be seeing Davey for a while."

Both teens hung their heads and walked away, hand in hand.

Jim said, "Mother says hello and hopes you'll visit soon."

"I'm sure she does. Were you off on a bender? Is that why you disappeared?"

"No, not this time. In fact, I haven't had a drop since I got back here with Marhan. I was kidnapped. So was Mom." Matt's face registered his surprise, but he said nothing. "I was grateful for my friends and for Davey and Clo's help in coming to find me."

Matt raised a finger and pointed at Jim's chest. "This is exactly why I didn't want you having anything to do with my boys. You are a bad influence. Your life, your troubles, your friends...I want my family to have nothing to do with any of it!"

"They'll grow up one day, Matt. They'll find out what life out there is like. It's up to you how much of a shock that will be for them."

"Right! That's exactly right. It's up to me! Get back in your ship and get out of here."

Jim shook his head and smiled. "Sorry, no can do. We only just limped here. I need major repairs. It'll be a while before I go anywhere."

Matt's eyes narrowed. "No contact." He nodded to the airlock. "Seal it up."

"Nice to see you again too, brother."

Matt walked away.

15 TO TANNA GUL

In Marhan's ship, Tella sat in silence next to him in the narrow cabin.

Navigating the route out of Hen Flereat's traffic kept Marhan focused for nearly an hour.

"They are quick to bring their customers in and slow to let them leave," he growled.

"Priorities change when we finish spending," Tella said simply.

"Ha! True."

Eventually, Marhan announced, "Our course is now set for Tanna Gul. We may now relax for the journey."

Tella nodded.

"How much do you know of human mating?" Marhan asked.

"That...is an unexpected question. Some. Though I am not sure Jim Able's life is the best source of information for the curious."

"Generally."

"When I first began to work with humans, it was something that bewildered me," Tella replied. "I realized I would have to make a serious study. When Neraffans meet a mate, the pheromones they exchange play a crucial role. So it is with humans also."

Marhan nodded. "Of course."

"You can smell them too?"

Marhan nodded again. "Human smells are...complex. but I am beginning to distinguish the important shifts."

"Would it surprise you to learn that they do not consciously smell their own pheromones?"

"What?"

"Indeed. They are quite unaware of them."

Marhan threw his head back and laughed. "Then how...how do they ever...?"

"It is a wonder. The effect is entirely subconscious, mysterious even, to them. While it is obvious to such as us."

The Gul laughed long and hard again.

Tella stated, rather than asked, "Jim and Anne are mated. As are Davey and Clo."

Marhan nodded. "Yes, of course. And there lies Jim's most urgent problem."

"The mating doesn't go well?"

"All too well, apparently. Through her use of the time device, we have seen the offspring, a daughter. The one called Sea."

Tella's face, usually white from picking up the color of its hood and cloak, turned grayer. "Ah! She met Jim at the temple and she has appeared again?"

"On Flereat. As Limarcs attacked Jim and me, she came with soldiers to kill them all. She announced her intention—to save Jim from injury—and then she returned to her future time."

Tella hunched over in his seat. "So, we know her plan—or at least one part of it. And she wishes Jim no harm. That is great news!"

"She wishes Jim to be present to her as she grows. It seems as she looks back on her younger life, he was unable to be the father she wished him to be."

"And this attack by Limarcs you both suffered was a part of that?"

"Perhaps the whole of it."

"I would ask that question—if another appearance should make it possible. Let us examine the possibility that this was the 'whole of it.' Does that mean all is now changed for her?"

Marhan grinned, rippled his claws on the console, and said, "I am an engineer, Neraffan. You tell me."

"Is this why you have asked me along?"

Marhan's head dropped. "No. But before we address that matter, there is another question I have about Jim."

"Go on."

"The fallout from his mission to Tanna Gul continues. Has he mentioned to you what the Praestans Rapax monk did to him?"

Tella paused before answering. "No."

"Jim has some sort of implant in his back. The monk put it there."

"He speaks highly of Tamric. The monk was young, but I was impressed by what I saw of his skill and attitude."

Marhan scoffed. "Jim knows about it but has done nothing to investigate or have it removed. He talks vaguely of finding a doctor but...it puzzles me."

Tella nodded. "Jim will often prioritize things in a way I would not. I have had cause to address this before with him."

Marhan turned his head but kept his eye on the Neraffan. "You could address it again. You may have more sway than I."

Tella nodded. "And now, why have you asked me along?" Tella watched the Gul. Since no further reply came, it sat back and waited.

Marhan began, choosing his words more carefully than usual. "I was impressed by your use of logic when we sat together at Jim's mother's. You showed aptitude for understanding this...time travel business."

"Thank you."

"But you will well remember our first meeting. I have little time for your people and the uses others make of your abilities."

"You made your feelings clear."

"I value honesty and despise deception. Those who practice spying either by machines or through agents, I believe, lack integrity; if not when they begin, it soon follows."

Tella resisted the urge to argue, leaving Marhan space to speak further.

He continued, "I have business on Tanna Gul. This much I told you. I wish to visit a relative of mine, an aunt."

"Yes, you said."

"She is a Luminant, a religious devotee. It is not easy to gain access. One does not simply 'visit.'"

"Will she welcome you?"

"I think so. Those around her will not. But something has now happened that has changed my plan. I no longer wish merely to talk with her. I wish to...extract her. After that meeting at Jim's mother's...We must bring her to Jim Able."

Tella's impassive face held a thin smile. "My abilities may be of service to you."

Marhan growled. "As much as I hate to admit it."

"What does she have? Or what does she know that Jim needs?"

"History. She has expertise we lack. I will say no more."

"Very well. Is it just her person, then? Or do we need to carry out equipment, books, and so on?"

Marhan's long tongue licked the side of his snout. He said, "Just her."

Tella nodded. "Very good."

16 ANNE

Jim closed the airlock and slowly made his way down the corridor to the flight room.

Anne was waiting for him. "How did it go?"

Jim shrugged. "Matt doesn't change. People don't, do they?"

Anne looked away. "No...they don't."

Jim sat in the seat, which wobbled slightly. "I'd better start the list of repairs. Damn! I hope I can afford all this."

She sat next to him and asked, "What about the Limarcs? Are you going after them?"

Jim shook his head. "I'm sure they only appeared because I was asking about Katrigg."

"And Sea?"

Jim glanced at Anne and looked away. "Sea is the real problem."

"Go on."

"She's from the future."

"And you're sure of that?"

"Our future."

Anne laughed.

Jim persisted. "Really. She says I'm her father."

"And?"

"She didn't say specifically, but she does look a lot like you."

Anne shook her head. "No."

"I didn't know whether to tell you or not."

Anne frowned but said nothing.

Jim continued, "Knowing that—suspecting that—complicates things for us right now, doesn't it? And I really want to say sorry."

Anne straightened in her seat. "No. Not actually complicated at all."

"You sound a bit sure."

"Jim...I like you. Have since we first met. But in terms of a father to children of mine—a life partner? Sorry, no way."

Jim sank back in the seat.

Anne said, "Probably wasn't the best trip to try and make into a romantic weekend anyway, was it?" She stood up. "Well, there never is a way to break it gently, is there? I'll get a commercial flight home. Oh, and if I end up expecting a kid, be sure I'll be cursing your name—but it won't be in person."

She picked up her kitbag from the ramp, walked steadily to the airlock, and let herself out.

Again, Jim sat alone in his ship. All was quiet.

Again.

He remembered the way Tuanomena's thought had hung in his mind.

Yeah, again. That didn't last long, did it?

17 FATE

Jim told the ship to hold all messages and then spent several hours arranging repairs and cringing at the cost. Praestans Rapax customers have few options when choosing services.

Later, when he checked for messages, he found four communications waiting.

━━

From: Department of Extra-Solar Activities, Payments Dept., Account Supervisor Bhattacharjee
To: James Able
Re: FC01 January 12, 2200

Mr. Able, payment has been made in regard to your first contact claim lodged with the Office of External Affairs and the Office of Expansion Services. The reward amount current at the time of your claim has been deposited to your bank account on file.
It is customary for the department, when making payments

of this kind, to recommend payees consult a financial
advisor as to the best long-term disposition of such funds.

Yours,
B.A. Bhattacharjee
Account Supervisor
Payments
Department of Extra-Solar Activities

———

From: Dr. M. Able, EBMS
To Jim Able
Re:

Jim, what is Davey talking about? I can make no sense of
any of it. He's insisting something happened with a Limarc
and a mech-suit.
He's also wanting someone to teach him about weapons.
What the hell happened out there?
Matt

———

From: External Intelligence Agency, Human Resources,
Supervisor Jones
To: Agent James Able
Re: R546

Mr. Able, our records show you are assigned to work under
the supervision of Agent R546. This assignment contra-
venes the current reporting norms for employees at this
office.
We are conducting an internal review. Please make yourself
available for immediate interview at your Unity City
location.

All missions, deployments, vacation, training, and/or other
activities must cease pending the outcome of this review.
If you have any knowledge of the whereabouts of Agent
R546, please notify us at once.

Jones, C.

From: External Intelligence Agency, Agent Ulrich Emerson
To: Agent James Able
Re: Agent Alice Brown

Mr. Able, I have been assigned to follow up with you, as you
are the last known person to see Agent Brown alive.
Please confirm you were with her in the agency flier as it
approached Earth-controlled space as per the attached
record.
Please provide any and all documents pertaining to your
reported abduction by Meoenan operatives.
Please provide dates and times you are available for interview over the next month.
Thank you for your cooperation in this investigation.

Ulrich Emerson

Jim laughed, cursed, shook his head, and made a call.

"Matt! Good to see you again."
    "Hi, Jim. So, what happened out there?"
    "Well, I can't help, I'm afraid. You know your son better than I
do. If he tells you there was something about a Limarc in a mech-
suit, don't you believe him?"

"He's making no sense."

"Hmm. What about the weapons training? Do you have anyone who can do that? I know you're supposed to be a science station."

"We have a couple of retired military working security. They could do it. But why the sudden interest? I'll ask again. What the hell happened when he was with you?"

Jim shook his head. "Well...I didn't see anything...But a bit of training would be good for him, don't you think? Get him out from behind his computer for a bit."

Matt almost laughed. "True."

"He's a good kid, Matt. You've got reason to be proud of him."

"Hmm. Thanks, Jim."

"Oh, Matt, one thing. Very important."

"What?"

"Where do you get your coffee from?"

"What do you mean?"

"You get the real thing, right? Not the stuff Earth exports."

Matt shifted uncomfortably in his seat. "Yeah..."

"I want to order some. A lot. I want to stock up."

"It's not so easy, Jim."

"Didn't think it would be. Listen, I'm going to put in an order with your store. They'll flag it up to you. You just okay it. Alright?"

"Why don't you just go to Earth and get it?"

"Why don't you?"

Matt was silent.

"It means you'll get the real stuff every time you come and visit me."

Matt nodded. "I wasn't intending to. Okay, put the order in. But tell no one where you got it."

"Understood! The secret is safe with me."

Jim wrote two replies.

From: Agent James Able
To: External Intelligence Agency, Human Resources, Supervisor Jones
Re: R546

Dear Jones, C.,
Thanks for your recent communication.
I wish to inform you of my decision to resign my post as agent with the EIA I don't currently have access to the manual about the correct exit procedure. Please pass this note on to those who need to see it.
I know nothing of any irregularities with my position.
If there were any irregularities with the setup of my position, such matters are not my concern as, by definition, they predate my involvement.
Since I can add no further information in an interview setting, I will not attend.
I do not know where Agent R546 is currently. However, I wish you all good luck finding it.
I have some agency items to return to you, which I will do the next time I am on Earth.
James Able

From: Agent James Able
To: External Intelligence Agency, Agent Ulrich Emerson
Re: Agent Alice Brown

Dear Ulrich,
I'm sorry to inform you I have resigned my post as agent with the EIA
I realize this may slow your investigation, but I doubt I have anything substantial to offer that will help.
The Meoenan authorities have all the details of my abduction and imprisonment. I urge you to contact Sonloi-AC's

human administrator, Jayde Duke, first if you haven't
done so.
I will not be on Earth for a while and so will be unavailable
for in-person interviews.

James Able

Then Jim made another call, to his scientist friend Madhar Nect on
the largest moon of Turcanis Major Five. Jim wondered what name
her home would use once it was formally introduced to the galaxy.

"Madhar? What happened?"
"Jim? Is that you?"
"It is. Something has happened and recently; I don't know what.
Has TMV-One finally agreed to make proper contact with Earth?"
"You are amazing, my friend! We have indeed made official—
and secret—contact. I am under strict instructions to tell no one the
details!"
"That's okay, Madhar, I don't need to know anything more.
Remember, way back when, I told you we give out rewards to
people who make introductions to new planets—for first contacts?"
"Yes, I remember. You had competing claims from people who'd
spoken to Sopha Luca. That was why you first visited, wasn't it?"
"Yeah, well, we didn't pay either of them. So I applied, and I
just got paid!"
"Great! And justly so. You did the work. Congratulations."
"Thanks. They've been sitting on my application; I guess until
there was some indication you guys would actually pursue contact."
"Jim, we are so close. The formal channels are being set up.
Things are so delicate still. But we're close."
"I know. It's tricky. But I wanted to say good luck. And person-
ally say thank you."
"For what?"

"You guys just made me rich."

"Really?"

"We use the phrase 'stinking rich.' Does that translate right?"

"Close enough. Oh, so you'll retire and become a person of leisure?"

"I already quit my job."

"Congratulations again. So, come and visit once it's permissible."

"I certainly will!"

"You know, Jim..."

"What?"

"Well, you have a bank account here. Do you remember?"

"No..."

"I created it for you when I registered the designs of the toys based on your spaceship. They've sold well—just like I told you they would!"

"Oh, that's nice."

"Listen. There's no exchange rate set up yet between our currency and yours. That's one of the things that scares us. Your economy could overwhelm us if we don't get it right. And then, beyond that, the galactic economy could really blow us away. We're small, and you guys are...well, you know."

"It's a delicate negotiation. I hope your economists are tough bargainers."

"Sure. They understand what's at stake. But they don't know what they don't know. And, of course, there's a lot of suspicion they're giving away too much. Getting the math right is one thing; confidence in the outcome is another."

"Oh yeah, I know what you mean."

"So, when it's all agreed, how about you invest some of your money here? Put it in your bank account. It'd be a sign that the deal is a fair one."

Jim gagged. "I-I haven't even thought about where to put it yet..."

"I'm sorry, have I spoken out of turn?"

"No...You're right, in a way. I'm suddenly in a position to make a difference in that sort of thing, aren't I. Not used to that. Madhar, let me get some advice. I'm no expert, but I guess I can afford to hire one. I'll get back to you. I'll do anything I can to help. You know that. Glad to!"

"Thanks, Jim! Sorry to spring it on you. I'm no expert either, but I've had to sit through endless meetings where other people have agonized over this stuff. It's horrible to watch."

Jim laughed. "How are the Regdenir?"

Madhar was silent.

"Madhar?" Jim prompted.

"Well, you know I said our negotiators know what they're doing?"

"Yeah..."

"Guess who?"

"Oh..."

"So, I guess we're okay from that point of view."

"You've unleashed the Regdenir on Earth's representatives?"

"Oh yes."

Jim laughed. "Madhar, how could you? We don't stand a chance!"

"When will you visit next?"

"Oh, I don't know. With things in the 'delicate' stage, it won't be for a while. You remember Tella?"

"Of course! He's not someone one forgets."

"It has something going on with an ancient carving at the moment. It suspects there are more of its kind on Mainworld."

Madhar gasped. "Oh...Oh, he—it—had better keep quiet about that! I doubt it's true, but let's not stir up the Regdenir with that sort of talk. Their views on 'Beauty' haven't moderated."

"I know. They're touchy about it. But, I guess, no one will take any action until everything else is settled."

"I hope not, Jim, I really hope not!" Madhar laughed. "Anyway, Jim, what are you up to at the moment? Apart from counting your money?"

Jim's heart sank. How much did he want to say about his father?

His daughter? Her mother? What could he say about Marhan? What could he say about the EIA and Tella?

"Well...you know, I'm pursuing an old investigation. There's someone I need to track down."

"How is it going? Do you have any good leads?"

Jim looked up at the navigation display where he had identified the Stacco system, Station Stacco Ila 32, and prepared a route plan.

"Maybe."

After the call ended, in the silence of his ship, Jim reread the EIA messages.

...Please make yourself available for interview immediately at your Unity City location...

...If you have any knowledge of the whereabouts of Agent R546 please notify us at once...

...Please provide dates and times you are available for interview over the next month...

Oh shit. Tella, just how deep a pit have you dug for us?

JIM ABLE OFFWORLD

SHOCK

13

ED CHARLTON

AUTHOR OF "THE ALERONDE TRILOGY"

Jim toured his newly repaired ship; the Praestans Rapax techs had done a good job. *Of course they did,* he thought, *it's a religious thing with them—doing a good job.*

Jim was lingering in the skeletal structure of the Praestans Rapax docking cradle before setting off. He wasn't sure whether his brother would let him dock at EBMS again. He should go to Earth. Once more, he read through the two summonses to appear before the EIA review board investigating his and Tella's activities.

Well, I'm not going.

Marhan had mentioned someone who might help Jim find mass murderer Jack Katrigg, and the route was loaded into the navigation system.

Though I really should go to Earth and sort out the EIA. Jim sighed and said, "Raeda! Begin route to Stacco Ila 32."

"Beginning route," the ship replied.

—————

The purpose of some space stations is to declare planetary pride; many exist as grand edifices, more monuments than institutions.

Some, more functional scientific facilities, show disdain for fashion, glitz, or bombast. Others, such as Stacco Ila 32, display only a measured message of order, stability, and comfort.

Stacco Ila 32—neither an anarchic collection of tubes and antennae linked at improbable angles nor the fantasy of kings—grew from sensible design, modesty, and the disciplines of fiscal responsibility.

The station consisted of two almost-semicircular arms reaching from a central structure. Docking bays radiated from the outer curves. Modest windows studded the inner and outer walls.

At the meeting of the arms at the central structure, domed above and below, hotels and offices grew with as much planning as any ground-based city—limited by space, limited by imagination, but still realizing a modicum of civic dignity.

Leaving his ship, Jim walked along the curving corridor toward the central structure, advertised on the signs as "32-Core." The corridor was packed with people both coming and going. He could see no staff giving help or direction.

This is a zoo!

He stopped with tens of others by a set of doors. Next to the doors, a sign read "Down for Lower Bays and 32-Core. Up for Upper Bays and 32-Core."

He pulled a door open, and much of the crowd moved with him. They went up, so he went down.

The Lower Bays were less well lit. Many were closed off. Few of the shops were open. The corridor followed the same long curve but was less crowded.

Jim walked past a public restroom. It, too, was closed and dark. He remembered advice his friend Robin had given him on his first OEA trip away from Earth. "Beware," he'd said. "When the lights are low, some bugger'll inevitably pee against a wall."

Especially if the restrooms are closed.
Jim held his nose and walked on.

A bright light came from a shop door. The shop window was covered with blank paper, but the door held a sign. In Standard characters, written in a large firm hand it read "Speak Standard or fuck off."

Way to go! Alienate those who do, and those who don't will come in anyway. Good business plan!

Three or four doors farther down, a line of tired and dirty people sat and waited. They were not human. Jim wasn't sure where they were from. He read the sign on the office window—"Papers Dealt With. Passage Arrangements. Loans. Marlor Tre, Proprietor."—and walked by.

A party of refugees about to be fleeced.

He swallowed hard and walked toward the corridor's end where it connected to 32-Core.

A pale-skinned figure in a long black coat walked tangentially past and said in a low voice, "What you want? I sell. Anything you want."

"Not today, thank you," Jim said with a sigh.

A strong hand grabbed his shoulder, and sour breath blew in his face.

"What? Human too grand to do business with Kevar, huh?"

Jim stepped back. The Kevar's eyes were fierce, and one was tearing horribly.

"Move on. No business. Not today!" Jim said through gritted teeth.

The Kevar spat.

Jim stepped back and bumped into someone else moving around him.

"Stupid ape, look where you're going!" was all they said—enough for Jim not to apologize.

The Kevar turned and barged his way further down the corridor, muttering in his own language.

Jim put his back against a wall and checked his flight bag and his pockets. Some species are experts at fast finger work and can masterfully rob the unsuspecting in a blur of motion.

Nothing missing. So far, so good.

The corridor opened to broad stairs, a wide plaza, and a disorientating lack of ceiling. The dome, far above, barely blocked the view of distant stars.

A helpful sign read "32-Core Main Administration" with neither arrow nor estimated time to walk there. Jim followed the crowd across the plaza to the nearest buildings and hoped for the best.

Beyond a set of retail outlets, he found another plaza—the Ceremonial Concourse.

The concourse was a wide circle of polished walkways and chrome fittings. Its design spoke of a species trying hard to move itself and its ground-based culture into space.

Jim smiled. *Where else would you put Main Admin?*

Inside the double doors of the Main Administration Office was a wide curving desk with a few significant items spread out on its gleaming surface: a nail file, a miniature color spray, a small packet of tissues, and a large personal firearm. As Jim walked through the door, the nail file was replaced by a small mirror.

He noted the microsecond during which she had glanced up at his silhouette in the doorway and assessed him as no threat but left the firearm where it was, in easy reach.

She was Homalic as far as Jim could tell. She had the characteristic circular eyelids, set in the large loop of upper and lower eyebrows. Her nose was triangular and short. She had kept her facial hair its natural orange tan, but the fur on her arms was dyed pink. If she had smiled, he would have seen the double rows of sharp teeth, but she hadn't. She was dressed in a stiff-looking suit. The material was a patchwork of lizard skin dyed the same alarming yellow as she painted her nails.

"Good day. I'm looking for Schpurr, the Kar Mallan," he said as pleasantly as possible.

"Never 'eard of 'im." she said without looking up or missing a beat in the rhythm of filing her nail.

"No, I didn't imagine you would have. But I hear he's a really nice guy. You'd probably like him."

She snorted and continued to concentrate on her fingers.

"Perhaps," he said, leaning over the desk toward her, "you could suggest where I might begin to look for your regular Kar Mallan visitors?"

"Couldn't say," she said.

She put down the file and picked up the color spray.

"Wait!" he shouted, "Before you do that—"

She looked up, the spray poised over an outstretched finger.

Jim continued still pleasantly, "You were either going to tell me where the Kar Mallans hang out or you were going to let me in to see your boss." He smiled.

She began to spray a miniature jet of color onto her nail. After what she must have thought was a suitably withering pause, she said, "'e's out."

Jim sighed, put his backside to the desk, reached back, and pulled himself up onto it. Turning to bring his feet up onto its polished surface, he lay on his back and folded his arms over his chest. He turned his face to hers and said, "I'll wait."

She had already picked up the gun and was pointing it at his forehead.

"I should warn you," he said to the ceiling, "That a human body's circulatory system contains about five liters of blood under quite a lot of pressure. Bright red. Sticky. Makes a hell of a mess."

Looking at her blaster, he said, "Yeah, that could easily blow my head off. But I really wouldn't recommend it."

She glowered but said nothing.

"Where are the Kar Mallans?"

She shrugged and said, "Who knows? There's a lot of people here. You could try asking at Grotta."

"What's Grotta?"

"Hotel. Up the top."

"Which way?"

"Up. There's a map outside if that's confusing."

He sat up and slid off the desk toward the door. Pausing only to look back briefly, he saw she had put the gun down exactly where it had been and was already spraying another nail.

02 GROTTA

Hotel Grotta. Nice! Kar Mallans must be doing okay.

The lobby's glass walls had a panoramic view across the plazas and the station's open arms.

The desk clerk was not much help until Jim said he was checking in for a few days.

"Now, I was asking about a Kar Mallan called Schpurr. I understand he may be here."

"No, sir. There is no one by that name here."

"Please check the register."

"Yes, sir."

The clerk's arms were smaller in proportion to a human's. From the way he moved behind the desk, Jim got the impression of large and powerful legs. The console he worked at had been designed to accommodate the small span of his digits. His mouth and jaw were large, and his nose was upturned under his eyes. Jim could see his nostrils opening and closing with each long breath.

"It would seem sir is correct. Schpurr of Kar Malla is currently registered. But as I have already told sir, he is not here."

"Then perhaps you would be kind enough to pass a message to him."

"Messages can be left through the communication panel in your room, sir."

"Thank you. Are messages secure?"

"Ah, I'm sorry, sir, we do not offer that as a regular service. One of the vendors in the mall may be able to help you there."

"Great."

"Will that be all, sir?"

"Yeah, that's all."

"Here is your room key. Shall I have someone take your bags to your room, sir?"

"No, thanks. That won't be necessary." He patted his small flight bag and felt the clerk's unspoken criticism of guests who have no luggage.

Jim breathed a sigh of relief as he surveyed his room. For years, what he could pay for accommodations was severely limited by OEA budget restrictions. *For the first time in my life, I have money!* He grinned to himself. He'd been doing that a lot since he got news of his first contact claim payout.

Providing facilities for people from different worlds is challenging for any hotel. The varied demands of anatomy and culture tax the abilities of every architect and designer. Jim thought the Grotta designers had done a good job.

The bed was large and suitable for a human or any species that sleeps on the ground. For those who preferred such arrangements, a substantial hammock hung to one side on a large metal ring and could be drawn up to meet a companion ring on the opposite wall. Otherwise, it merely hung as a wall decoration. For those who slept sitting up, there was a comfortable upholstered couch.

Separating the kitchen area from the main room was a series of long low fish tanks joined by short cascades. This was a nice touch for a human, being both restful and colorful, with its variety of exotic inhabitants. For many others, of course, it was a well-stocked snack bar.

There was an enormous entertainment center, with all the latest gadgets for whiling away the time. Jim ignored it and opened the curtains to look at the view.

The station lay spread out below. Beyond it, at only a few degrees, was the local star—Stacco itself. In its pale red light, the metalwork of 32 glowed. Above it to the left was an intense bright spark of one of Stacco's planets. The nearmost planet, Ila—under whose gravitational and nominal legal jurisdiction the station came —was out of sight.

Jim left a message for Schpurr through the communications console. It was an extremely primitive device.

Why does such a well-equipped hotel downgrade its comms like this? The lowlifes docking at the Lower Bays probably have better stuff than this...Oh, so they don't need to steal it. Nice!

Jim went into the bathroom.

Bathrooms, of course, are the biggest problem for hotel designers—so many species, so many ways to be unhygienic. Grotta's designers had chosen the minimalist approach. The bathroom in its entirety was an enameled chamber with numerous handrails at various heights and angles; numerous nozzles, again at various heights, each with buttons showing standard chemical symbols, including one for water; and a single hole in the floor. The rest was up to the occupant.

On a shelf outside sat a vast array of hygiene products—a serious hazard for the unwary traveler since some species use substances to clean themselves that are toxic to others. Above the shelf was a sign absolving the hotel of any liability should the use of any product cause discomfort, injury, dismemberment, or death.

Jim walked into the hotel bar during entertainment time. A smartly dressed person from the same planet as the desk clerk was playing a complex piece on a three-stringed instrument. He played along to the wailing of a commercial recording. Jim was well versed in the classical tradition of karaoke and this setup removed any instrument or vocal from a recording and let the patrons do their best.

Shame he can't play that thing.

Jim sat at the bar.

The Homalic barman, like the admin receptionist, also had some pink fur.

"Do you have beer?" Jim asked.

"From Earth?" he asked, meaning Jim rather than the beer.

"That's right. Do you get many humans here?"

"They don't stay long. It's a loud place. You humans are always looking for quiet. You don't like the excitement."

"It depends who's making it exciting."

"Yeah, you're picky."

"Picky about drinks too. You got beer?"

"No."

"Anything like it?"

"Yeah. Large or small?"

"Large."

"Coming up."

The drink had a certain amount of gas, and scum—rather than froth—on the top. Jim held it up to the light, noting the weight, the chocolate color, and the phosgene smell.

Can't be worse than that stuff Marhan made me drink!

Jim had gone through three before realizing how strong they were.

The song going through Jim's head, an irritating commercial piece, had been all the rage sometime on Sonloi-AC. He lay ignoring the pain in his back, wondering why that particular song should suddenly come to mind. Against his closed eyelids, he could see the lyrics scrolling, just like on a karaoke screen.

It all came back in a sickening rush.

What an idiot! How much did I drink to even consider singing to that infernal backing track?

He opened his eyes, turning his head from side to side.

My room. So far, so good. Bed over there. Fish tank right here. Hello, yellow arthropod. Are you eyeing me?

Jim sat up and quickly lay back down again.

Okay. A day to be approached carefully.

While waiting for breakfast from room service, he checked on his charges so far. Two items: a huge bar bill and a huge room service fee.

When another fellow with small arms brought in breakfast, Jim asked, "Can you tell me what this charge is?"

"Umm...yes, sir. The code there identifies the type of charge— four, dash, four, seven. Yes, that's the charge for returning a guest to his or her room or conveying them to another's room."

"Another's room?"

"It happens, sir. The charge is the same; we don't differentiate."

"Okay, thank you."

Jim tipped him and uncovered the food.

Ugh!

Jim steeled himself to eat it, aware of the distinct possibility that he might spend time gripping the appropriately angled handrails.

It wasn't until lunchtime that Jim decided to get serious about finding Schpurr. No reply had come to the message.

There's no reason he would want to see me.

As he passed the front desk, a clerk called, "Jim Able, Sol Earth? There is a message for you."

It read, "Schpurr Ande Fretsin, Wholesale Transporter, A lifetime of experience in interplanetary trade." On the reverse was written, "Jim Able, Sol Earth, Enterprise Suite 5600, Hour 5."

"When's Hour Five?" Jim asked.

"Usually, it comes after Hour Four, sir." The clerk smiled and cocked his head.

"Thank you. When is it in relation to the current time?"

"Fast approaching, sir. The clock next to the fountain keeps accurate station time."

"And this 'Enterprise Suite?'"

"Our office complex next door, sir. The blue elevators."

"Thank you."

Jim stopped by the fountain in the center of the lobby. An

ornate timepiece sat on a tall pedestal nearby. It had a circular face and only one hand. The numbers read from zero to thirty-five. It was nearer to five than four.

Was last night the day shift or the night shift?

He walked toward the blue elevators. Out of the corner of his eye, he saw an orange flash.

The lobby wall was several stories high, and through the glass, he could see a few shops across the walkway where the stairs and elevators led down to the rest of the station. Beyond the shops rose the protective dome covering 32-Core and beyond that, open space.

Out to his left, an exploding ball of orange flame engulfed the docking arm.

An alarm sounded behind the reception desk, and a recorded voice began repeating "If you are away from your room, please gather in the hotel lobby. If you are in your room, please remain there."

Jim could see blast screens unfurling on the lobby wall and down the outer dome. They cast a gray haze over the scene, but the explosion still visibly expanded. People panicked on the walkway outside, rushing to get in through the lobby doors before they were sealed out by descending screens.

A wave of debris collided with the outer dome. Glowing fragments rained on the outer skin, the larger impacts leaving blackened smudges.

The blast screen rolled back in a few seconds, and the announcement stopped. The faint background music returned, and the murmur of conversations started again.

Jim stood, not moving, watching the maintenance craft swarming out toward the docking bay's ruptured sections.

A voice spoke quietly behind him, "Sir will be late for his appointment."

The clerk walked past without waiting for any acknowledgment. Jim watched as he attended to a guest who had tripped running into the lobby. Then it struck him what had been said.

03 LUMINARY

No one enters the convent of Luminants, the Luminary, without permission.

"There are several doors," Marhan said, showing Tella a map. Moving an extended claw, he continued, "This one is nearest my aunt's room; we shall enter here. But through *this one*, we will leave."

"I assume our leaving will be in haste and under pursuit," Tella commented.

Marhan snapped his jaws. "Fast pursuit. And angry."

Is there ever another kind? Tella wondered.

"The office where the key-keeper will be is by the Luminary main door."

"Am I to steal the key?"

"No. Merely accompany me. When we first met, the rock they kept me in was cold, and I could clearly see the heat from your body as you stood against the wall. Here you will be moving, and the rooms will be warm. While I talk to the key-keeper, you will *take* the master key."

Tella nodded.

Marhan added, "I prefer to do all this without harming any of the Luminants."

Tella sighed. "They are females, and none are soldiers. Yet they will actively resist us, you say. So achieving our end without conflict may not be possible."

Marhan growled. "I know." The canid looked down at the map and shook his head. "Speed is our friend and is the only thing that will save lives."

"Understood."

Marhan stayed in orbit of Tanna Gul for many hours. Tella didn't question him. Eventually, the canid said, "Well, night is approaching our target. The Luminants are done praying and will soon sleep. It is time."

"May I ask a question?"

"Better now than later."

"Why are the Luminants locked in their rooms?"

Marhan smiled and grunted. "Not all are. When you meet my aunt...Well, you will see."

Snow fell on the grounds of the Luminary. Marhan landed on dormant flower beds that surrounded the approach to the building. He oriented the craft to bring the weapons to bear on the historic front doors and fired.

Tella ran after Marhan but had trouble keeping up. He was far faster than the Neraffan expected, and Tella had to step over hot rubble from the explosion to access the office. *Marhan didn't think this part through.*

In the office, a small frightened canid stood behind a desk. Glass and debris from the explosion covered every surface. Marhan towered over the desk. Over the wailing of alarms, he shouted, "Give me the master key!"

"Never!"

Tella was only just in the room but caught the slight twitch of the Luminant's left claw. Conscious of sparkling glass reflecting through the skin of its feet, the Neraffan walked steadily around the desk.

"Who are you?" the Luminant demanded.

"You do not need to know," Marhan replied. "The key...Now!"

"Never! I'll die first!"

Standing next to her, Tella could see a wrist strap hanging loosely from her left claw.

With an easy move of its invisible hand, it had the strap in its fingers. The cord's black color flooded its hand.

"I have it!" it called out.

The Luminant shrieked at the voice suddenly so close to her and pulled away.

Tella extracted a key device from her claws with its other hand.

To Tella's horror, Marhan leaped over the table and threw himself on top of the Luminant, delivering three vicious blows to her head.

She lay still. Marhan leaped back onto the desk and called, "Now, quickly! Second corridor on the right!"

Tella found the corridor outside the office already filling with bewildered students and staff, most in their night clothes.

Marhan fired his blaster into the ceiling, bringing down sparks and more debris, causing the Luminants to cringe and back away.

The pair ran swiftly past one side corridor and skidded left into the second. Marhan shouted, "Betih! M'Tary!"

With a panicked look, he read the room numbers. Tella examined the master key device.

"It's a generic electronic key. Which is her room?" it asked.

Marhan whimpered and said, "They aren't marked as I expected!" He stopped dead. Turning his head from side to side, he bellowed, "Betih! Betih!"

A voice shouted from a room to Tella's left, "N'agh dork? Frot Betih!"

Marhan turned and rolled his eyes. He gestured with his thumb to the door. "That's her."

Tella put the electronic key to the plain panel on the door. The panel lit up, and the door clicked open.

Marhan pushed past and held the door ajar.

An elderly canid stood on her bed, dragging a large bag down from an opening in the ceiling. In Standard she said, "A little help here! And no looking up my nightdress, you youngsters!"

Marhan jumped onto the bed and grabbed the bag. "Be quick, or we won't get out!"

They glanced at each other for a moment by the side of the bed. Marhan shouldered the bag as Betih wrapped a pink robe around herself. She stood at half Marhan's height, and much of her fur was silver. Her eyes, though a little protruding, sparkled with life.

"Failure of a rescue attempt is never the fault of the rescued," she countered as they both left the room.

Marhan fired again at the ceiling at the beginning of the corridor. Shrieks sounded from around the corner.

Betih bumped into Tella. "What was that?"

"That, madam, was Tella of Neraff. Good evening," it replied.

"Oh-ho! I *am* in interesting company. Which way?"

"This door!" shouted Marhan.

Pursuers soon cried out behind them. They ran through the snow along the building's outer wall, unsure of their footing. The elderly Gul glanced back at Tella's legs glowing white, the rest of it hardly visible.

Marhan murmured several things in his own language and his aunt made few replies.

The Luminants were close behind them as they reached their flier. Tella was again surprised by how fast Guls moved when provoked.

Marhan turned and shouted, "Look up, Luminants! Look up!" He held up a remote control and the flier's lights suddenly burned on full. The effect on the chase was immediate. The Luminants stopped in their tracks, covering their eyes, shaking their heads, growling, and cursing.

"Now! In!" Marhan urged the other two.

They were inside and the flier's door safely closed before the Luminants had recovered.

No one spoke until they were in orbit.

Tella had dressed in its white robe once more.

Marhan turned from the controls and said, "Tella, this is Ernot Bard Betwen. Betwen, this is Tella of Neraff."

Betwen bowed slightly. "Tella, I am pleased to meet you."

"And I, you, Betwen. I understand you two are related."

She replied, "I know he is an Ernot. Probably an Ernot Dirl. Which one of them, I'm not sure."

"Marhan, you old fool!" Marhan replied. "Don't you recognize me?"

"No. Why would I? It's years since I've seen any of you!"

"True. But you heard what I said, and you remember me well enough!"

She smiled, looked him up and down, and wrapped her robe tighter around her.

Tella spoke. "May I ask what it was you called out in the corridor?"

Marhan chuckled. "I said, 'Betih M'Tary!'" He gestured to her with his snout. "You tell Tella what it means."

She shook her head and turned to Tella. "He said, 'Betih,' which is what the children used to call me. And 'M'Tary' means 'get your coat.'"

Marhan said to Tella, "When she would visit, she'd never leave. My father had to shout it at her many times before he could take her home."

Tella smiled. "And another question, if I may? Why were you imprisoned?"

She turned to Marhan and asked, "Can he be trusted?"

"Can you?"

"Ha! Less than ever."

Tella said, "I prefer to be referred to as 'it.' I am neither he nor she."

"Yeah, yeah, whatever." She waved a paw at it. "The ways of the Luminancy are strange to outsiders—of course they are. We used to have more liberal living arrangements. But now...a stricter interpretation of the rules is in force. That satisfy your curiosity?"

"Perhaps."

She smiled, squinted at Tella, and said, "Ooh."

Tella continued, "I don't yet know why Marhan, an otherwise sensible creature, decided to risk life, limb, and reputation to rescue you. I doubt it was for nostalgia's sake. But I don't have much to go on. I see your age, which is an argument against your being dangerous. But the lock on your door is an important counterargument. The Guls I have met surprise me at every turn. And so, I look forward to getting to know you better."

She nodded and wagged a claw at Tella. "The lock and my age are *both* arguments in favor of my being dangerous, Tella, as you'll soon enough come to know. But, yes, as to why this—what did you say?—'otherwise sensible creature...'? That's him. That's him. What is he up to? I know no more than you." She smiled at the Neraffan. "It's going to be fun finding out, isn't it?"

Marhan muttered, "Oh, what have I done?"

Betwen announced, "Now, I'm ready for a drink. What celebratory liquids do you have on board? I'll give you a flash of my teats if you've got Lak-weed! Ha-ha-ha-ha!" She doubled over laughing and flapping the front of her robe.

04 TEA

Schpurr's suite had been tailored to Kar Mallan tastes; the institutional paintwork artfully covered by thick woven hangings, the curtains missing, the tables low and crescent-shaped.

A servant escorted Jim to Schpurr, who stood at his window watching the repair and cleanup at the docking bay.

"Jim Able, thank you for coming. A most unfortunate incident." He nodded toward the site of the explosion.

"Any idea what happened?" Jim asked.

"I have ideas, yes. But I, like you, am well-advised not to give voice to those ideas in public."

"I take your point. You don't think it likely to have been an accident then?"

"Are you a mathematician, Jim Able, or a gambler?"

"Neither, really."

"Well, if you take the chance of an accident occurring at any station, let's call it 'x.' And then take the chance of something unfortunate but deliberate happening at this station, let's call that 'y.'"

"Okay."

"'X' is much less than 'y.'"

Jim nodded and watched the maintenance craft, all well practiced at their work.

Compared to some species, Kar Mallans looked humanlike, though with longer arms, so they could comfortably walk on all fours if necessary. They wore no shoes. With thick pads on all four paws, their fingers splayed at odd angles—something only disconcerting when first shaking hands.

Schpurr said, "Please sit with me! I have coffee and tea."

"You have genuine Earth coffee and tea?"

"Of course! I understand how a traveler longs for a taste of home. My trading partners have taught me well what to serve them."

"But tea is becoming rare on Earth now. I'm amazed."

"Let it be tea then."

He clapped his paws, and the servant reappeared, quietly moving from behind a curtain.

"We will have tea."

"Sir," he said and returned to the other room.

In the light from the window, Jim had taken Schpurr for a much younger person. In the light from the lamp at a side table, he could see lines in the face, gray in the hair, and the rheumy eyes.

"You," Schpurr began with a twinkling smile, "are something of a celebrity on this station."

"Uh-oh. What did I do?"

"Your performance in the Administration Office was most extraordinary!"

"What?"

"You must understand that nothing that happens here goes unnoticed. Everyone is watching someone else, and rumors are the lifeblood of this station."

"Oh."

"Now the delectable Corrie Gna, the Homalic receptionist the absurd Goffa Tre keeps as his watchdog, is the object of the attentions of Hunfar, the electronics merchant across the concourse and up one level. He has three cameras trained on her body through all the Hours; you might call it something of an obsession. He recorded your little performance on her desk and showed me a copy."

"Oh, no..."

"No, no, Jim Able, I tell you, you are a celebrity! No one has been able to get information out of Corrie Gna with such speed and efficiency. She once kept an Ila investigator waiting for fifteen hours. She has been known to take potshots at those who dare touch her desk—Hunfar being one of them! But you, you lay upon it! To lie on it and live! Not only that, but you got what you wanted from her. We are all aghast and want to know how you did it."

"I—umm—I appealed to her need for neatness."

"How wonderful! There is more to you than meets the eye. As you see, you interest me enough to meet with you. How could I refuse to speak to someone who bested Corrie Gna?"

Jim smiled and relaxed a little.

"Now, why does James Able, of Sol Earth, of the Office of External Affairs wish to speak to my humble self?"

Not the demeanor of a hard-bitten trader. Much more sense of humor. Jim said, "May I be honest with you, Schpurr?"

"Oh...if we are to be honest with each other, perhaps you must call me Fretsin."

"Okay, and please call me Jim."

"Jim."

"Fretsin, I'm not here to speak to you officially. I no longer work for the OEA. I am here as a private citizen. What brings me here, though, begins firmly in my time doing audits for the Office."

Smiling, Schpurr watched Jim and said nothing.

The servant arrived with the tea. He arranged it on the two curved tables between them. Fretsin sat in the center of one crescent; Jim sat in the center of one opposite. Around them, the servant arranged dishes of various sizes—the larger where the table could accommodate, the smaller toward the narrowing ends. Various Earth foods appeared with the tea, from cookies to small triangular sandwiches.

"How did you find all this stuff, Fretsin? This is amazing!"

"Through my various partners who have contacts all over your world. Once it was decided you would be coming, I asked for items that would be culturally appropriate for you. I trust I was not misled?"

"No, it's great. Thank you for going to so much effort."

Fretsin waved his paw, and the servant poured the tea.

"What do you think of Stacco Ila 32?" he asked.

"It sucks. There's a bunch of people getting badly used around those Lower Bays."

Fretsin laughed and said, "Ah, I had forgotten. We are being honest with each other, aren't we? You're right, but you must forgive it; it's not the station's fault."

"I suppose not. Why do you come here?"

"Well, I have been coming here since the place opened. My friends gather here often to meet and reminisce." He sighed and looked over in the direction of the window. "There were seven of us who were close friends. Only four of us remain. I may not come again."

"Why not?"

"I am ill, Jim. I have a condition that may prohibit much further travel."

"Oh, I'm sorry."

"That is partly why I can still tolerate the ways of this place. It is a place of happy memories, and as for the rest, well...What does it really matter? There is nothing much of great significance that happens here, you know. Ask any of the small fry out there. They'll tell you of big deals going down and how they've joined forces with so-and-so and all that nonsense. They try to hang onto the coattails of people they see as important. It's all a fantasy—a mean fantasy but nonetheless unreal. And, yes, you are correct; people sometimes suffer as a result." He sipped his tea. "I probably don't strike you as a typical Kar Mallan, do I?"

"You're not what I expected, no."

"That's because I am old and tired. I was quite a hustler in my youth. But one can't always paint with a broad brush, Jim. I mean, look at you. You're a bureaucrat, but you get the better of the most notorious female on the station and then go on to entertain a hundred people with your singing."

"Oh God! You know about that too?"

"I was there. I wasn't sure I wanted to meet you then. I only decided when Hunfar showed up with his recording."

"So, I'm not what you expected either?"

"Not at all. Earth people have a reputation, you know. For one thing, you are one of the few planets that actually take all the paperwork seriously. I mean, everyone has it, some even process it, but very, very few do anything with it. Earth, though, takes it all *so* seriously. We have no idea why. You're a mystery to us." Schpurr closed his eyes and continued. "You perhaps think that this station and the many, many like it is full of traders and businesspeople whose working lives are spent pursuing a paycheck or a commission. But, no, a far more varied fauna migrates to and from these places. You need to distinguish the types and kinds."

Jim waited.

Schpurr's eyes were still closed. "Do Earth businesses use slave labor, Jim?"

"No. We don't approve of slavery."

"No, no, of course. But you realize that others have either no opinion on the subject or have come to approve wholeheartedly of the institution."

"I suppose so..."

"So you have two types already: the slavers and the non-slavers. How can they trade between themselves? It becomes tricky as soon as questions are asked. Perhaps trade occurs best when questions are avoided, hmm? But the distinction is not entirely an accurate one, is it? You see, there are planets where slavery is frowned upon only when it is the planet's own inhabitants under consideration. Some think it a fine practice to enslave the peoples of other worlds. And so, there you are dealing with not two but four distinct groups, each with their own assumptions. One will say 'No, we never use slaves' and mean it. Another will say the same when they mean 'We do, but not of our own kind.' Another will say 'Slaves? Of course. How else are these goods made for this price?' While the last will tolerate slaves at home yet frown on their deployment elsewhere."

"I guess so."

"Let us consider further since the matter of slavery is not just one of morality but of law. Do Earth traders always obey the law?"

"Whose law?"

"My point, in truth. Of course, everyone will say they must obey their own laws. But out here, far from the judgmental light of their own stars, perhaps the force of law is felt less strongly? In this, we must also consider the role of laws applied by one's customers. Are they always to be obeyed?"

"They should be."

Fretsin's eyes lit up. "'Should' is such a misused word, isn't it? A structure built entirely of off-ramps and hidden ladders."

Jim laughed.

"And so, how many different types of trader do we have now? They multiply, yes? And we have only just started. One cannot always know, Jim, if a trader is offering goods made by enslaved people or created in some other immoral fashion by local or foreign workers. Nor can one know if the trader is a person of integrity in legal matters. One faces each person with all these possibilities held in mind."

"And where does that get us? That interplanetary trade is always a bit dicey? That we shouldn't do it?"

"Ah, no! We must proceed, of course. My point is to highlight something of inestimable value: a reputation. If a trader comes recommended as someone of integrity from a planet of lawful seriousness, then can we begin to say his business is worth having?"

Jim nodded. "I'd say so."

"And so, by way of example, we drink tea from Earth, supplied by my friend Mr. Sinclair."

"And he is a person of good reputation?" asked Jim, now sipping his tea with suspicion.

"Of course. Though I must confess, this is the first time I have ever tasted anything of the product we have so often traded in."

"You don't normally drink tea? It's not to everyone's taste."

Schpurr smiled. "I'm sure. No, I mean our accounting ledgers are full—have been full for a long time—of trades in tea and other Earth products. We have shown crates of tea and coffee in every audit. But those are presented at audits. What is carried to Mr. Sinclair's ships? What is unloaded from his ships at other times? Of this, I have no idea."

"Wait..." Jim began, putting down his tea. "What do you mean 'no idea'?"

"Mr. Sinclair is a person of high reputation. I need not inquire further."

"You're implying our audits are a waste of time!"

"I tell you this to help you understand the value of a reputation out here, away from the troublesome eyes of watchers. Mr. Sinclair is free to run his business and pass his goods through me and my business as long as no shadow is cast upon me and mine."

Jim sighed. "Fretsin, you are unpicking years of my life here."

Schpurr smiled again. "I'm afraid so. It keeps humans happy to fill spreadsheets with goods in and goods out. It keeps us happy to fill actual ships in and out. Who suffers if, technically, there is not always an exact match on every occasion?"

Jim scratched his head. "Well...It matters when the ship is full of harmful goods. It matters when someone is supplying, for instance, the makings of a thousand attack ships—being built from stolen plans—for one world to wage war upon its neighbor. Interplanetary war makes losers of us all, doesn't it?"

Fretsin was silent, unsmiling, assessing Jim anew.

"A fine reputation," Jim continued, "is a good thing but not if it gives cover to criminal intent. Or actual criminal activity."

"And yet, who are we to judge such things? Under whose law?"

"Some actions are in no one's interest."

Schpurr shrugged. "Out here, things are not so clear."

"Really?"

"I repeat, reputation is everything here. Without it, no goods move. No food, no drink. No medicines, no charity. Neither lawful trade nor lawless."

Jim sighed. "I suppose I do see what you mean."

"I doubt it. Not yet. Take, as an example, my friend Mr. Sinclair. He has supplied so many good things to my customers and my customers' customers. He has enjoyed a solid reputation until just recently."

"What happened?"

"It...it is enough to say, through an indiscreet action, he cast a shadow on me and my reputation."

"And?"

"You could ask him yourself, if they weren't scraping his remains from the docking arm."

Jim looked Schpurr in the eyes and didn't turn to the window. He thought the Kar Mallan was laughing inside, not just at Sinclair, but at Jim also. The aftertaste of the tea turned bitter in his mouth.

"You killed him."

"Not personally."

Jim smiled back and said, "But close enough for your reputation to be enhanced as someone not to mess with."

Schpurr closed his eyes and nodded his head. "More tea?"

"Not just now. Thank you."

"And so, Jim Able, now that we know each other a little better, to the point of our meeting. Why did you ask to meet with me?"

"As someone with much experience in matters of trade, you may have done business with a courier called Jack Katrigg. I want to find him. And I want to do it quietly."

"Jack Katrigg is a person of impeccable reputation."

Jim swore. "You know him!"

Schpurr smiled. "I know many people, Jim. I have done business with many. Jack Katrigg has been known to me for a long, long time."

"Where can I find him?" Jim asked through gritted teeth.

Schpurr laughed. "You must learn, my young friend, that I do not share my philosophy and my analysis lightly. What did I just say about so many different types of traders?"

"I understand that—"

"No, I don't think you do. You imagine I'm warning you—as a watcher and former enforcer—how you should behave."

Jim frowned.

"I have told you the crucial place of reputation. I am teaching you the solution developed for *our* problems, not *yours*!"

Jim frowned again. "Okay," he said steadily. "Imagine I'm a slow learner."

Schpurr placed his paws gently on the table in front of him. "Every so often, each trader is called to account for something going wrong. Perhaps an official discovers the goods are slave-made, to use our former example. Perhaps a manufacturing defect causes death. Perhaps the shipment is short. Institutions employ many people to preempt such occurrences. But nothing is perfect."

"As we say, 'Shit happens.'"

"Indeed. But if one can always deal with a reputable trader, one known to be sound, law-abiding, and ethical, unfortunate occurrences may be few."

"I guess so; you have a better chance your goods will be okay."

"No. I mean, the external scrutiny itself will be much reduced."

Jim was silent.

Schpurr continued, "The appearance of clean trade is far more important than actual clean trade."

"That's...so cynical. What's it got to do with Katrigg?"

"Two things. When there is a conflict...when perhaps the reputation of Jack Katrigg is pitted against the reputation of an accusing authority. We ask who has said the shipment is short? Who performed the inventory? Were they members of a union? Is that, in this particular case, a good thing or a bad? What is the provenance of the paperwork? Was it paper? Was it electronic? How secure? How secure was the chain of handling of the goods? Who could have removed inventory without the shipper's knowledge?" Schpurr smiled. "How many counterindications are necessary? How much doubt does an investigator need before Katrigg walks away with an apology?"

Jim shook his head. "What's the other thing?"

"What other thing?"

"You said, 'the appearance of clean trade is far more important than actual clean trade' and that it had two things to do with Katrigg."

"Jack Katrigg is the courier of preference. He is much in demand. He isn't merely a single, space-born Earthling with a great reputation. He is everyone's space-born Earthling with a great reputation. He is the front behind which many hide. When something needs to be fixed, he is where we go."

"Okay..."

Schpurr waited.

Jim waited.

He's not going to tell me unless I phrase the question just right. As Jim panicked, a horrible thought came to him. *Katrigg isn't singular.* He asked, "If he's so popular, how can he do it all? Have you cloned him?"

Schpurr laughed. "I don't know. I don't ask how it is done. Perhaps it is more like a franchise? So, tell me, why do you pursue him? Did something go wrong with a particular trade?"

"No. He tried to kill me."

Schpurr smile vanished and he frowned. "No. No! That cannot be. In his case, there is nothing to be added to a reputation by killing someone such as yourself. But, of course, even if you catch up with him, know that he will inevitably have proof of being somewhere else at the time."

Jim thought through his two encounters with Katrigg. "First time he did, yes. Second time...well, I haven't been able to find him at all since the attack at Ch'Garratt."

"Oh, Ch'Garratt! Yes, I remember. You were there?"

"That was Jack Katrigg."

"One of them," Schpurr corrected.

"How many are there?"

"Oh, no one knows. And you wouldn't want to meet more than one. How confusing!" Schpurr laughed. "They each have their own areas. How they organize themselves...who knows? No one will ask. He is too valuable."

Jim shook his head. "It's impossible. Someone would see his

name coming up all the time! If there were multiple Katriggs, someone would spot it in the records."

Schpurr shook his head. "Why? The galaxy is big, and trades are many. And when do you need the reputation of a good intermediary to reduce the risk—or burden—of oversight?"

Jim answered quietly, "When you've really got something to hide."

Schpurr smiled.

Jim swore again. "I knew this was big."

Schpurr sighed. "I recommend, at this point, you let it drop. Even I, with a lifetime of business among the stars, cannot tell you how, where, or by whom it is done. I have used Katrigg and his reputation—including his ability to verifiably prove he was somewhere else at any given time—to my great benefit. I have gladly paid for the service. So have many, many others. You will not be able to stop it. You will not expose it. You will be stopped long before you can harm such a useful institution."

Jim sat, staring at his hands.

Schpurr gestured to his servant to clear the table.

Jim said firmly, "I don't care about exposing it. I don't care about the others. I just want the one who tried to kill me and killed many others in the attempt."

"Ah," said Schpurr, drawing himself up to sit tall in his chair, "So you truly look not for the authorities on Sol Earth or Sin Har, but for yourself. This is a personal matter."

"Damn right, it is."

Schpurr put his paws together, rested his chin on them, and looked at Jim with a new regard. "That is different. But I'm not sure how one would go about such a thing. The Katriggs are all the same. Tracking one rather than another is—quite intentionally—not possible since, of course, on the surface there can only be one."

"How do you contact him—them?"

Schpurr shrugged.

Jim waited. He saw the butler standing at the corner of his vision, a shadow against the window.

Schpurr said plainly, "I now have a clearer picture of why you are here. You want revenge on a Jack Katrigg. That is understandable. It's personal. No one would stand in your way. But you have not been entirely honest with me."

"I've been completely honest with you."

"No." Schpurr growled softly. "You have not. Who are you?"

Jim shrugged. "Jim Able, Sol Earth."

"Formerly of the OEA"

"Right. Currently unemployed."

"Then perhaps the better question is *what* are you."

All Jim's nerves tingled. *This sounds dangerous.*

"What do you mean?"

Schpurr stood and his front paws pounded the crescent table, making it knock into Jim's. "You sit there, unarmed! You perform alone in a bar and get so drunk you have to be carried to your room! Who are you that has such...brazen confidence? Only a fool—or someone absolutely sure he is in no danger—would dare act so cavalierly!"

Poker face! Now isn't the time for a joke. Jim forced a smile.

Schpurr shouted on. "On Hon Hen Flereat you slaughtered a gang of Limarc thugs. A Limarc in a fully armed battle suit broke into your ship and was never heard from again. *What* are you?"

"Schpurr..."

"And you come here. You ask simple little questions. But you seek to dig up a cornerstone of the galaxy's business! I was right to have ten armed guards stationed in the next room. I do not understand who you are. I do not trust the evidence of my eyes as to what you are! And why me? What harm have I done you?"

Oh shit! "Please, Schpurr. Sit down. Calm down. You are in no danger." Jim waited while Schpurr reluctantly sat again.

Jim straightened up and said, "I want Jack Katrigg, and I'm going to get him. You are going to tell me how I hire one. That's all. I don't even care about what you did for the Tanna Guls." He continued slowly. "Despicable though it was. I'm not going to tell anyone about that." Jim swallowed hard, his mind racing. "If it will help, I'll give you something to sweeten the deal, okay?"

Schpurr looked at him with deep suspicion.

"You say Hunfar is your friend, and he likes Corrie Gna?"

Schpurr nodded.

"I'll give you the way to Corrie Gna's heart for the details of how to hire Jack Katrigg. Then I'll go away. Your goons can stand down. You can retire in peace, and we'll never see each other again." He hoped Fretsin couldn't hear his heart pounding from across the table.

"You make it all seem so...regular. So ordinary."

Jim nodded. "Think of it as this kind of story: I left my job. I have a friend from Tanna Gul who recommended I see you about setting up in business. We had tea. Very nice, thank you. You gave me a contact. Ordinary? Sure. Why not?"

"Nothing about you is ordinary, Jim Able."

"It seems you have been listening to a different kind of story about me. And I came into this room with something of a reputation already built by other people, didn't I? But what harm can that do to you?" Jim stared back without smiling.

Schpurr nodded. "I am now known to have had dealings with you. I do not know what that will do to me. And that uncertainty..." He scowled at Jim, sighed, and gestured to the butler. "Plain paper for both of us."

On his paper, Schpurr wrote an address.

Jim wrote "Have her life turned into chaos, then be the one to rescue her from it."

They exchanged papers across the tables.

Jim read and nodded.

Schpurr read and laughed. "Oh, that might work! Cruel but possibly effective."

"Thanks again for the tea. I'll be on my way."

Schpurr said quietly, "I will retire, and we will never see each other again. If we do, it will not end amicably."

Jim nodded. "As I said."

"I pity Jack Katrigg when you find him." Schpurr nodded to the butler, and Jim was escorted out.

05 SEA

Jim's heart continued to beat faster than normal all the way back to his room. He packed quickly and went to settle his bill.

"Leaving us so soon, sir?" said the receptionist.

Jim nodded. "A successful visit."

"We hope the first of many, sir."

Jim smiled but said nothing.

In the docking ring, he found that repair crews had closed off the upper corridor, and a long line of travelers snaked from the middle. He went down to the lower level.

His mind was full of how much Schpurr had known about him. How Sea's visit had given him a reputation that had already reached the middle-of-nowhere station Stacco Ila 32.

I don't want to be famous.

Jim failed to notice he was not alone in the corridor.

A hiss alerted him to a shadow ahead.

Where is everyone? Where did the crowds go?

"Human!"

"Who's there?"

Five Kevar stepped out of a maintenance room, weapons drawn.

Oh shit! The blaster's in my bag.

The five lined up across the corridor. Behind them, the air pulsed. No one turned around.

Jim closed his eyes. Sea and her crew had appeared and were firing. The Kevar fell without ever seeing their attackers.

Jim said nothing as Sea trod carefully around the bodies. "Hi, Jim! How are you doing?" she said.

"Hi, Sea. You've done it again," he replied stiffly.

"I just saved your ass. Aren't you going to say thanks?"

"Again? What did I say last time?" he asked.

"What do you mean 'last time'?"

"Flereat. You wiped out the Limarcs who attacked me then. Are you going to do this every time I get into a fight?"

"Flereat? Nothing happened to you at Flereat! This is where you would have been injured."

"And then failed you as a father. I know. You said at Flereat."

Sea shook her head and frowned. "Never been there. You have, I know, but nothing bad happened. Here is where it all went wrong!"

Jim shook his head. "Time travel gets complicated, doesn't it?"

Sea smiled. "Anyway. Mission accomplished. Bye, Dad!"

"Can't we talk?" Jim called. "Sit down for a drink or something?"

Sea cocked her head and said, "Shouldn't need to now. You'll have all my life to talk to me."

Jim smiled. "Humor me. Come back—alone—and talk calmly. I don't think things are working out quite as you imagine. You *were* at Flereat. You *did* save me there. And now, here. We need to talk about this."

Sea nodded slowly. "Okay. Where? When?"

"Sonloi-AC. The café. Two days from now."

Sea nodded again. "Early shift, though, before it gets busy."

"Sure."

She turned to her associates and raised her arm. They formed a circle, each touching a hand to hers.

The air thumped, and they were gone, leaving Jim alone with five formerly unpleasant, but now dead, Kevar.

06 TELLA'S NEWS

Betih was sleeping on the floor of the passenger cabin of Marhan's ship. The walls supported a line of utilitarian lockers. Marhan had moved two benches up against the locker doors to give Betih more room.

Tella asked softly, "Is she alright?"

Marhan sniffed and whispered, "She is old and tired. But at least now she is quiet! Will you sleep?"

"No. If I may, I will access my messages. I have a project on Earth that I fear is slipping out of control."

Marhan nodded and waved the Neraffan into the cockpit again. With a sigh, the Gul stretched out on the benches.

To: Tella
From: Pritas

In Quavvour's name, greetings.
Your construction in Unity city is secure. The Neraffan

government has lodged Freedom of Access requests with
both the Earth government and the city authorities.
I am on my way to see it as I write.
What would you like me to do first? I can record my reading
of the carvings. Will a full reading take a while? I can
contact the government of TMV-I, though I think, since you
have been there before, that is more your role.
Let me know.

▭

To: Tella
From Pritas

In Quavvour's name, greetings. I hope all is well. I worry
that you have not replied.
I saw enough of the carving to understand both the urgency
and the importance of your discovery.
Do you recommend I contact the government on TMV-I or
go straight to TMV?
I hope you can reply before I arrive in the system.

▭

No, Pritas, Tella thought, *I cannot reply because I do not know what to tell you. Whatever we do will be wrong in someone's eyes.*
Tella turned to its news feeds.
It read and reread two items. Transparent tears ran down its transparent face.
No one will understand.

General Briefing
203044

The **Turcanis Major** system is currently under
Early Contact Quarantine.

All ship captains, colony heads,
base commanders, and station managers
are hereby henceforth required to

NOT APPROACH the TURCNAIS MAJOR system
or allow any other vessel with whom you have
contact to do so.

REPORT all sightings and contacts with craft on
approach to the **Turcanis Major system**.

This requirement is mandatory for all vessels
and crew under Sol Earth authority

This order is enforced upon the authority of
Elizabeth Curacao
Assistant to the Secretary
Office of External Affairs
Department of Extra-Solar Activities

Memo from External Intelligence Agency

From: Section Chief Maxwell

To: Internal Distribution

Re: O.E.A. General Briefing 203044

The O.E.A. has Turcanis Major under Early Contact Quarantine.

Local reports state a craft of Earth design has approached and landed on TMV.

Any and all information on this craft and its occupants are to be submitted to my office ASAP.

Please use any and all local contacts to gather intelligence, but do so discretly according to the ECQ.

A grade 2 reward is offered for any information linking this incident with former agent R546.

Maxwell

07 THE RETURN OF SEA

On Sonloi-AC, Jim set himself up at a table in the café—his mother being under strict instructions to remain elsewhere.

Having no night or day, Sonloi-AC worked on shifts that were of equal length. Sea had specified "early," but that was a relative term. Jim connected his tablet to his ship to continue researching the address Schpurr had given him.

"Great view!" Sea said as she sat down across the table from him.

He nodded. "Best seat in the house."

He looked at her face, slightly flushed and smiling. He noted her hair, still cut short yet somehow managing to be unruly. So much like his own. Her eyes shone.

"Glad to be here with you," she said.

"What will you have?"

"Water, please."

"Only that?"

She nodded. "Best when...traveling."

"Okay." Jim waved at the Meoenan waiter, who came over and nodded deliberately at the pair.

"Black coffee for me and a water for the lady."

"Certainly," the waiter replied.

Once he had gone, Sea asked, "You wanted to talk. About anything in particular?"

"You, mainly. And what you're doing."

"Not doing much. Have you ever seen this? I brought it as a way of letting you know something about me."

She pulled a book from her backpack and slid it across the table.

"*The Galaxy's Top Twenty Unsolved Robberies*," Jim read as he picked it up. He put it down again and said, "I hate stuff like this. Who says these are the 'Top'? Who decides?"

Sea shrugged. "The author has done his homework. It's incredibly detailed. Well researched."

"That's something, I suppose." He picked it up again and, with half of his attention on her, started to glance at the contents.

Well thumbed. She dog-ears pages! Shame on her parents. "It's a disrespectful thing to do to a book, turning down the corners."

"Yeah, whatever. I thought you'd at least be impressed I have a printed book!"

"I am. Shame about the subject matter."

"You'd rather I studied Earth trade regulation manuals?"

"God no! I'd save anyone from reading those things!"

Near the middle of the book, his eyes landed on the diagram of a house. "Wow...You're right. This is detailed; thickness of walls, light fittings, wiring for security cameras. Who is this author?"

"Don't know anything more than what it says on the cover. Love the book though."

"Hmm. Why? What attracts you to it?"

"Income is good."

"What do you mean?"

"They're unsolved. Some of them seem impossible. As if the thief just appeared and disappeared again."

Jim sat up straight. "And..."

"For a girl with the right equipment, this is a script. It's not a whodunit or a how'd-they-do-it; it's a how-I-will-do-it."

Jim swallowed. "That would be illegal, immoral...You can't be serious!"

Their drinks arrived, and the conversation stopped. When the waiter had left, Sea smiled. "I'm not altering anything that happened."

"Sure. Until you go into one of these properties and find the actual thief already about his business."

She shook her head. "Not a problem; I'd just go back a little further and get the goods before he arrives."

Jim began to laugh. "Unbelievable!"

Her face became solemn. "The only thing I'm changing is your life. I'm fixing it for both of us."

"Like at Flereat."

"I don't know why you keep saying that! Nothing happened to you at Flereat. Absolutely nothing! Stacco was the problem, and I've fixed it."

"You fixed it at Flereat so that nothing happened to me. Why you don't remember, I don't know."

"Didn't happen."

"Didn't happen to you. But it happened to me."

Sea frowned. "I'll have to think about that. I lived and studied at the temple for eleven years—it was a big investment—so I hope they know what they're talking about. This Flereat business doesn't jive with what I learned. They've got a good handle on time travel there."

"You have to stop."

"Oh, here we go...No thanks. Not until I've worked my way through the book. And not until I remember you being there as I grew up."

Jim fell silent and looked out at Sonloi in full sunlight.

How much do I tell her? What did Anne tell her? "It's not right," he said softly.

"Yeah, I suppose that's the sort of thing a dad would say. Be there to say it to me as a kid and I might listen. Until then, what you see is what you get."

"A time-traveling thief with a gang of trigger-happy goons."

"Ouch! Judgmental much?" She smiled and sipped her water.

"This isn't funny."

"It is what it is. But I can change it. I may be able to change our lives sufficiently to make none of this necessary. I might not need to study at the temple. I may never see the T-switch. But I still find it incredible that you two—the smartest men I know—couldn't see the potential in Tuanomena's gift. You couldn't see the good that can be done."

Jim drank more coffee, smiled, and said, "In what way do you *know* your grandfather?"

Sea picked up the book and avoided Jim's eyes. "I met him at the temple. You were there."

"He followed you."

Sea smiled.

Jim nodded and said, "Somehow, he ended up with you in the future. He didn't die here after all, did he?"

"I'm not supposed to tell you. He said it might cause unnecessary hurt. He doesn't want that."

"Too late."

"Sorry. But he's really happy. He loves it!"

"Doesn't help."

"Sorry."

"And now you will want me to not tell Alfie, I suppose."

"Would she care?"

Jim sat back in his seat. "Of course she would!"

Sea shrugged. "Not the impression I get."

"That's a surprising gap in your knowledge. I suspect there are others."

"Yeah, well, thanks for the drink. Thanks for the talk. I'll be going now."

"Sea...you have to stop. You have to give the damned machine back to Tuanomena."

"I don't see why."

"Because things will go wrong! You'll make a mistake. You'll destroy something, get someone killed who isn't supposed to die. And, as you say, you'll just go back and fix it. You'll spend more and more of your life trying to fix what you broke. And—I suspect—you're doing all this on faulty evidence. You can't know the past in the detail you need for this sort of operation. No one can."

She held up the book and slid it into her backpack. "You're wrong. Totally wrong about me. Like this guy, I'm a great researcher. I plan carefully. It's something I'm good at. You should have more confidence in me."

"Sea..."

"Bye!"

Jim asked loudly, "Who the hell named you 'Sea'?"

"I did." She stood but didn't leave. "It's my initials. Sasha Epsilon Able."

"Ah, Able. Not Brewer?"

"I chose Able. 'Able by name, able by nature.' Isn't that what you used to say?"

"When I was young and dumb."

"Well, pardon me for inheriting something from you."

"Sea...Sasha..." Jim chuckled. "Oh, wait, that makes sense! That's why Tuanomena called us that!"

"What?"

"Tuanomena always called Dad 'Lem-Jim-Sea,' but Dad didn't understand the 'Sea' part until he met you." Jim stopped. "Hold on, though...That's what we're called, not what we're named. Why doesn't Tuanomena think of us as Lemuel-James-Sasha?"

Sea sat down again as she thought. "That is odd. Beyond the question of how he knows who we are in the first place. Why would he know what other people call us?"

Jim shook his head, then stiffened his back for his next question, hoping it would keep her talking. "So, why hasn't your grandfather gone back in time and rescued Mazette? How has he been able to resist that temptation?"

Her eyes flashed up to his.

He thought he saw more than just a glimpse of contempt. *Shit!*

"I've read a lot in the temple. There's one guy, Gror Gute. Strange stuff, a lot of it. He wrote this thing that's more like a cookery book than a theological treatise."

"The original potghor recipe?"

Jim saw the fun coming back to her face, but she shook her head. "Lost to history. I wouldn't know where to start looking for that! No, this book is about time and the universe and Tuanomena. Gute says space-time is like a soup. We're the ingredients."

"Sounds uncomfortable."

"He says there's no plot, no story, no advancement, no retreat—just the changing flavors. You can't—you shouldn't, he says—take out an ingredient. I read into that, that you *can* change how we interact with each other, make certain flavors stronger *here* rather than *there, then* rather than *now.* But killing someone—removing them from the soup—alters the recipe too much. Once someone has died, going back and changing the fact would cause the same problem in reverse. You go and read up on it. I'm a student, not a teacher." She shrugged.

"You're doing fine. But...it opens up a whole new set of questions."

"Not ones I'm prepared to answer."

"Like the Limarcs you killed. Like the Kevar you killed."

"Bye, Dad. It's been real."

"I want to understand! And, so far, I don't."

"You can't see it all the way I do. You might, later, once I'm sure I've done what I need to."

"What if I don't want you to do anything?"

"Again, your perspective is limited by your place in time."

"So is yours! You don't remember us meeting on Flereat. I do."

Again, he saw the coldness in her eyes as she said, "I'm doing the right thing. I'm doing it for the right reasons. You're in no position to judge me!"

She stood quickly, and Jim watched her walk away across the café and through the doors.

He sat staring at the table, his head buzzing with possibilities, until Alfie sat down with him.

"It didn't go as well as you'd hoped, I take it," she said gently.

"You saw her?"

"Oh yes. Clearly a relative. Got the family's features. And, unfortunately, she also has the flinty eye."

"What do you mean?"

"I saw the same in your father's face often enough. It's an iciness that bodes badly for anyone close."

"You're crazy."

"Yes, dear, I am. But I'm not wrong. You get it, too, if anyone mentions your drinking. And Matt, whenever anyone crosses him about anything. You Able boys don't realize what a frightening lot you are when you want to be."

They locked eyes until she said, "Come on, son, let me buy you cake."

"Sure, Mom. But then I have to get back to EBMS. Marhan and Tella are due back there."

Alfie nodded. "Glad for your visit. Come more often. And make sure you visit the doctor again. Make sure that wound on your arm is healing properly." She signaled the waiter.

"Mom, there's something I want to ask you."

"Go ahead. Don't be shy."

"Mazette. Dad had the time machine for several years, but he didn't..."

"Go back and repair the hovercar?"

"What?"

"He talked about it—when we could bear to talk at all. 'If only I could go back, I'd save her. I could find that damned car and fix it!' That sort of thing. We'd call it 'painting over.' Like going back to a bad painting and putting it right." She sighed.

"I wanted to go back too. I seriously thought about it."

Alfie nodded, sadly. "I know. You're a good man. I'm sure you'd help where you could."

"That's the point, isn't it? Choosing where to help and where not to? You can't save everyone. You can't make it so no one dies...no one suffers."

"You're right. He may have kept it secret for years before he decided to find you. But how do we know he didn't make other changes, Jim?"

"Shit! I hadn't thought of that."

"It's what's keeping *me* up at night. How bad was our life? What did that past look like if your sister's death wasn't the worst thing?" Alfie sniffed. "How bad did things get, that...that you'd leave such a senseless thing the way we remember it, and you'd still be making this version of life somehow better?"

The cake arrived, but Jim ate it without any sensation of doing so.

He continued, "It's all way more complicated than I thought. We can't know what he did—if anything. We can't know what she might yet do. But...that's the same thing, isn't it? If you're in the future and then do something in the past..."

"Yes, dear."

"You know,"—Jim's eyes fixed on the distance—"Sea doesn't remember rescuing me on Flereat. How is that possible? She came back to fix something. Fixed it. And then...she didn't need to fix it? There was nothing to fix? Then"—he shook his head—"God, words like 'then' and 'again' don't mean what they used to mean."

Alfie smiled and watched his face.

"What, Mom?"

"You and your father. Always the ones to work out how things work. You, more than him, in a way. You'd disappear into a completely other world while you looked at a problem. And you always came back with the answer. He'd take longer, with more swearing and hammering and banging. You have a mind like no one else's I know."

"Thanks, I think..."

"And more than likely, any progeny you've created will inherit at least some of that talent."

"Hmm. Without the right data, I'm no better than anyone else. With the wrong information, I could probably be quite dangerous. She'll be the same."

Alfie nodded. "I'd like to say you can leave it to her. She's perhaps in a better position to know what's best to do. In fact, she may already have done it. As you say, how would we know?"

"You'd *like* to say..."

"But, now...no." She looked away, through the window of the café, across to Sonloi. "Now that I've seen her—seen that look in her eye—I don't trust her. I'm reluctantly more inclined to trust Lem. So where is he?"

"What do you mean?"

"He disappeared, Jim. Vanished. Before I heard you tell everyone about the T-switch, I had to believe what they told me about a power fault in the thrusters on his suit. But they never could trace him. Never found him. Then you came along with this story of a device where he could make himself vanish. I'm a painter; I can connect dots."

"He could never get anything over on you, could he?"

"Apart from the temple thing. That I didn't know."

"She said he's there, with her, in the future."

Alfie blinked. "Well. Best we can hope is he has a moderating influence on her."

Jim shook his head. "Yeah, he's at the right end of all this— looking back. While we have no way of knowing what's going to happen."

"Same as always, Jim. I just paint the next picture and hope it's a good one. You have to do the same."

08 THE CLOUD

Matt Able argued with Jim for half an hour before letting him dock again at EBMS.

Matt argued with Marhan for a full hour before letting him dock next to Jim's ship.

Jim opened the airlock door, and Marhan steamed in muttering, "I shall roast your brother over an open pit with an *orgra* in both his mouth and his ass!"

"And good morning to you too," Jim replied, smiling. "I hope he's tasty."

Tella stepped through the doorway. Betwen followed smiling. She said nothing, but her eyes quickly took in the ship and Jim.

Tella said, "Jim! It is good to see you."

"Hi, Tella. Been busy?"

"This is Betwen, Marhan's aunt."

"Pleased to meet you."

"You are Jim Able?" she replied. "You are bigger in Marhan's stories of you."

Jim raised one eyebrow and said, "I hope that's a compliment."

She laughed and snapped her jaws at him. "Take it how you like. How well stocked is your kitchen?"

Jim looked her in the eye and said, "Best food on the ship. You won't be getting a better breakfast anywhere else."

She licked the side of her snout and replied, "Oh well, I'll make do. You learn to do that by the time you get to my age."

"Glad to hear it. I've prepared Module Three for you. Up the ramp, second on the right. The galley is down the ramp on the left. Welcome aboard."

"Thank you. You're from Sol Earth, he tells me."

"I am."

"I won't hold it against you."

Jim stood with Tella and watched her walk down the corridor. "We've both been to Tanna Gul. Isn't it funny how the insulting manner doesn't work anymore?"

"Indeed," Tella replied. "Being with Marhan has been a useful education."

Tella followed her down the corridor and up the ramp to her module.

Jim sat in the command seat. Marhan sat nearby, still in a foul mood.

"So, tell me about her," Jim said.

Marhan growled. "My aunt. She's old."

Jim bowed his head and watched the canid from under his eyebrows. "Yeah. Got that bit. Why is she here?"

"I'm not sure. Now. It may be a mistake."

Jim shook his head. "Not like you. Your instincts are good."

Marhan stared at Jim as if both brothers were about to be roasted. "When she has eaten, let us meet in the galley."

"Sure."

"Tell me, is it safe to use your device—the one that stops all electronics, all surveillance—is it safe to use it on board the ship?"

Jim frowned. "Oh. Better not, if I don't have to. It'll reset all sorts of systems. But then, we're not underway. It probably won't affect EMBS. Sure,"—he nodded—"We can do that."

Marhan nodded. "Bring it then. Seal the airlock. Let us not be disturbed."

Jim watched him climb the ramp to the upper level. *No bounce in your step, Marhan. Something is seriously up with you.*

Jim whispered to Tella, as they stood by a refrigerator in the galley, "She has a prodigious appetite for an elderly canid."

"I doubt she feasted like this in the Luminary. I sense that 'austerity' was the byword there."

"Lucky us."

"So, Jim Able," Betwen called, "What do you do? How can a monkey like you afford a Praestans Rapax custom ship?"

Jim replied, "You noticed, huh? Didn't Marhan tell you all about me?"

"You tell me your own story. He's biased."

Marhan got up from his seat at the table and stood by Tella.

Jim sat opposite her and began. "My story is fairly simple. I was born on Earth, grew up on a station. I used to work for Earth's Office of External Affairs."

"What's that?"

"It deals with legal matters having to do with trade while looking for news of new peoples and chances for first contacts. It's Earth's official face to the galaxy."

"Ugh! Sounds terribly dull."

Jim smiled and went on. "And then, more recently, I've been working for Tella." He paused to glance in the Neraffan's direction. "At the External Intelligence Agency."

"Which does what?"

"The darker side of what the OEA does. The investigations of criminal activity, security, intelligence, protection of Earth's assets. You might think it less 'dull.'"

"Hmm. Sounds better. And that's your future?"

"No. I recently got paid for a first contact introduction. I'm suddenly wealthy—if I don't waste it. I hear I may soon be a father. Time to work out where I go from here."

Marhan prompted, "Tell her of the courier."

Betwen tilted her head to one side.

"I had...a bad experience with someone. He tried to kill me. Instead, he killed a hundred innocents, injured as many others. I hope to find him."

"And kill him," she added.

Jim sighed. "I don't want him out there doing the same thing, elsewhere, to other people."

She nodded.

Marhan spoke again. "And what of "Daum Robertus Graffen?"

Jim's face colored. "I don't want to talk about him."

Betwen laughed. "Ooh, this sounds good! Go on! You're amongst friends here. By the look on your face this fellow did worse than try to kill you. Tell us *all* about it!"

Marhan waved his arm at Jim. "Tell her! Hold nothing back."

Jim got up, poured another drink, and sat down again. "Okay. He gave me this ship."

"That's nice. Lovely gift." Betwen smiled, her ears erect.

Jim continued, "I was on a mission with a PR monk. Graffen is —was—his superior. Tamric was killed on the mission."

"Hmm."

"Marhan has told me—convinced me—that Tamric was ordered to do something to me. We don't know what yet. Maybe an implant of some sort, I don't know. But I guess it's all part of the same thing as giving me the ship. The PR are up to something. A plan within a plan, within a plan."

"Hmm. Tell me," she asked quietly, "which bothers you most, that they used this Tamric, or that they try to use you?"

Jim looked her in the eye, smiled, and said, "Yes."

"Ha-ha-ha! Well answered! And will you answer as before about this Graffen? You don't want him out there doing the same thing to other people?"

"Not if it's in my power to stop him."

Betwen laughed again. She looked over at Marhan and nodded. "Okay, Marhan, I begin to see."

Jim's face colored up again. "Okay, you two. What's going on? Betwen, who are you? Why are you here?"

"Simple enough, youngster. I'm a Luminant from Tanna Gul. I should have gone off to die in the wilderness long ago, but they haven't let me. So you see me, shrunken and senile, a shadow of my former gorgeous self."

Jim snorted. "A front that is minute by minute less credible."

Marhan sat down next to Jim with a sigh. "Betwen is the most senior professor of ethics at the Luminary. She is the author of the definitive books on the subject. Her critique of the recent Raeff and his actions forced her superiors to lock her up for her own protection."

"I see," said Jim, nodding.

"Bring out the device, Jim."

"Oh, right! Should we have activated it before?"

"No. No need. Just put it on the table."

Jim fished the silver globe from his pocket and placed it between himself and Betwen. She looked from Marhan to the globe and back again.

"How do you come to have this?" she asked in a whisper. Her ears flattened to her skull, and she swallowed.

"An EIA agent had it. He...mislaid it. Now I have it."

She looked at Jim for a long time. "Have you read the inscriptions on it?"

"No, I can't read them...Wait! You know this thing?"

"I've seen something like it before, yes."

"Do you know where it comes from?" Jim said, while he thought, *You are old but not as old as this thing.*

"Hold it in your left hand and roll up your sleeve."

"What?"

"Go on. It won't bite."

Marhan countered. "It might."

Jim looked to Marhan for advice, but he was getting up again.

Taking the sphere in his left hand, Jim rolled his sleeve back. He waited with his bare arm resting on the table.

"Hmm. I see."

"See what?

"Tella? Bring something with a fine sharp point."

"Betih!" said Marhan.

"Quiet boy!" Betwen snapped back.

"What's going on?" Jim asked. *Who do I trust here?*

Marhan said, "I asked you to tell us! That's all!"

It does something. What is Marhan scared of?

Betwen shrugged. "Tella?"

While Tella searched, she asked Jim, "Do you see anything that looks like this, written on it?" Using ketchup, she drew three letters on the tabletop.

Jim brought the sphere close to his eye and searched. "Oh, yeah! There they are, at the end of these other marks... What does it mean?"

"Those are my initials," Betwen said.

"Oh! So this is yours? How did you lose it?"

Marhan walked from one side of the galley to the other saying, "The Luminants are sloppy. They kept Betih's treasures locked up but not truly secure. The key-keeper knew, I'm sure. They are responsible for so much!"

"Yes," she agreed. "It was stolen, but it had passed from my use by then. It was time it went to another."

Tella delivered a pointed, thin-bladed knife to Betwen.

Jim thought, *Okay, it passes down a chain of owners, that's why it's so much older than her.*

"So, Jim. Take this. Carve your initials as close to mine as you can, as small as you can."

Jim took the knife and squinted as he worked.

What am I joining? It's a cool device for an investigator. Marhan's worried, but there she sits—ancient but with her full faculties. I could do worse.

Marhan walked with increasing distress until he burst out, "You cannot do this! Not without warning him!"

"He already told me! I have heard enough."

"Okay!" Jim said, "I've signed it. So tell me!"

"It is now yours."

"Thanks! What are Marhan's misgivings—" Jim turned over his hand to put the sphere back down on the table. He could not let go. Rainbow patterns began to show on the sphere's surface and then spread to Jim's fingers and hand. "Tella? What's happening? My hand's going like yours!"

Both Tella and Marhan stood at the table beside him. Betwen sat back and watched in silence.

The rainbow patterns spread up Jim's arm.

Tella asked, "What have you done to Jim?"

Betwen simply said, "Bring paper and something to draw with."

Shit! It never did this before. What has she done to me?

They watched as Betwen drew two circles, one within the other.

"This is the outer perimeter."

She drew several looping lines, like a cloud, at nine o'clock on the outer circle.

"The security guards will be watching. What do they see? Their screens flicker for a moment as this device passes. Then all is restored. Do they report the matter? Perhaps. They might write it in a log. They might discuss it amongst themselves."

She continued drawing the lines of the cloud across the inner circle. Her voice held all the calm authority of a teacher. "Here is the internal perimeter and access to the inner sanctum. The guards will see what? The same. A brief interruption. Are they alert? Yes, but where do they look? Outward. They are trained to expect threats from without. But the holder of that device has already passed through and is within.

"Here at the center is the target who thought herself safe. All alarms are silent. All attempts to call for help fail. And here,"—she continued the lines of the cloud across the other side of the diagram —"the device opens the way to retreat unobserved."

Jim looked again at the device and the colors flickering around his arm.

This isn't sounding so much like a club for detectives.

Marhan added, "The device has a name. It is called The Assassin's Cloud."

Betwen continued, "Before I heard the call to the Luminancy, I lived the assassin's life. Even as a teacher, my superiors understood and let me disappear on missions as I had need. Then things changed on Gul, and I could no longer leave. Soon my tools were taken from me and were then lost to a thief. I have since led a reduced life. I am happy The Cloud has found you, Jim Able."

"But I-I am no assassin!"

She nodded. "Yet you tell me—a stranger—of two people you will kill. Two people who should not be allowed to repeat their crimes. Two people for whom there will otherwise be no justice."

"I..."

Marhan spoke quietly. "To be an assassin is to hold a noble position, delivering punishment where none can be brought, justice when it cannot be found."

Jim turned his hand again, and the sphere dropped to the table and switched off. A faint rainbow streak remained on the outside of his forearm, like an old, faded tattoo.

Betwen rolled up her left sleeve and pinched back her fur to reveal similar faint colors in the skin of her arm. "Only a fellow assassin will know this mark."

Jim stared across the table at her and asked, "Were you ever paid? Did you kill for hire?"

"Never."

"How do you know? How do you know the people you killed were the right ones, the guilty ones?"

"I was careful—as, I hear, you are careful. I never forgot that the lives I held in my paws could well be innocent. I made sure I knew." She smiled. "Isn't that how you would normally behave?"

Tella sighed. "I see."

Jim turned to it and said, "What?"

"I was going to protest and demand she undo what she has done. But I see now. She is right. You are, sometimes and in your own peculiar ways, meticulous. You hold high innocent life and justice. When necessary, you are not afraid to bring punishment upon the guilty."

"Tella...?"

"Jim," interrupted Marhan, "I know the details of when the Raeff was killed. You and Tella were in the room when the boy killed his father. If Larc had not acted, would you have stayed your hand?"

Jim groaned. "Marhan! I..."

"You were there? Both of you?" Betwen sat back in surprise. "How did I not know this? Explain it to me, Marhan! How did someone from the jungles of Sol Earth witness the death of our Raeff?"

"How does he have your Cloud, Betih? Was it not the spirit who brought him? Is it not the spirit who will guide him forward?"

She gasped.

As they talked, Jim was thinking. *She's right. I hadn't pictured the details of killing Katrigg. But what other outcome is there? What legal system won't he wriggle away from? And the PR are way above the law. But an assassin who isn't just a killer-for-hire? Who kills for the right reasons? She's been an* ethical assassin*! Could I do that?*

Silence descended on the galley until Betwen said, "Jim Able, I will teach you what you need to know. I hope that you never need to put into practice anything you learn from me. Yet, if you find it is necessary, you will be prepared."

Jim nodded slowly and said, "Okay." To Marhan and Tella, he said, "You two sit in on it all."

"No," she said. "They cannot."

Marhan stood over Jim and said, "I was never supposed to know Betih's secret, but I was a quiet and inquisitive youth. It was good that we liked each other so well. And now I am to share the same secret with you, Jim. I'm sorry. You see now why I thought I may have made a mistake. She has thrown you into this the way we teach our pups to swim! I had hoped you would have longer to consider the matter. I trust no harm will come to you from what I have done."

"I think this is good, Jim," Tella said. "Have no fear. This is a job for which you already have all the necessary qualifications, and you require no one else's permission."

"Sure. Thanks. I think..."

09 FRIENDS

Tella stood in front of Marhan as they came back up to the flight room. "I hope I was of use to you on Tanna Gul and in acquiring your aunt. I now understand both your reasoning and your inability to explain in advance."

Marhan nodded.

Tella continued, "I, now, must ask a favor of you."

Marhan paused to look Tella closely in the face. "I begin to see fragments of emotion in your face, colorless though it is. And I see reluctance to ask me, which is good; we are not friends."

"True. However, we share a friend in common. Let us work together for Jim's sake."

Marhan nodded and waited.

Tella turned and sat in Jim's seat. "I have left my employment at the External Intelligence Agency. I suspect Jim, if he has not yet, will do the same. My departure has not been as clean or orderly as I would have wished."

Marhan snorted. "You're in trouble."

"I am. Specifically, I wish to return my rented flier, but to do so will make me vulnerable to my former employer's attentions."

"And?"

"I noticed the controls for stealth flight on your craft."

Marhan walked over to the ramp to the upper floor and sat down, just at the edge of Tella's vision. "To Earth?"

"Yes."

"In stealth mode?"

"Yes. There and back. I don't want them to know you are there. I would prefer to create a mystery about how I left."

"Earth is a busy planet. Orbital approach is carefully controlled. Beyond the approach, there are atmospheric craft by the thousands! Stealth flight under such circumstances is outlawed for good reason."

"That is the favor I am asking."

Marhan sighed. "Following you in your rental? I would have to fly close behind you. And for an extended period."

Tella waited.

"The consequences of being caught..."

"Are far greater for me than for you."

Marhan laughed and replied, "Trouble is too small a word."

Tella said nothing.

"Tell me," the canid continued, "why return the flier at all? If you are in such a large mess, what is a small theft amongst it all?"

Tella shook its head. "I have no love for the EIA or its human employees, but I have no quarrel with the rental agency."

"Then abandon it and tell them where they can find it!"

"Perhaps."

"Even better, can you not devise a way to send it back unmanned?"

Tella turned to look directly at Marhan. "An intriguing idea."

Marhan laughed again. "It would not put me in danger or involve me in your problems."

Tella turned away and said quietly, "You complimented me on my analysis of the issues around time travel. Let me return the sentiment. You approach problems in a way I do not. You have superior tactical skills."

Marhan replied, "I'm an engineer, pale monkey. We can work on your flier together. Later, we can work on being friends. But I warn you, that will take some time."

"Good things always do."

10 HERE

After Marhan and Tella left, Jim felt the presence of the Praestans Rapax monk, Tamric. Jim remembered him trying to explain the word *nirrorvar* after having impressed Jim with a display of technical prowess involving a helmet and infrared sights. Jim never understood the word beyond a vague idea of skills, tools, attitude, and the universe coming together to produce superior results. Tella had just told him he already had *nirrorvar*.

No one ever said that to me before. Though maybe Mom did, in her way, talking about me solving problems even better than Dad did.

Jim remembered what she had said in the café about a painter connecting dots. Here were some big ones: the OEA, Tella, Tamric, TMV-I. And now this scary canid in her pink robe.

Alone in the galley with the ancient former assassin, Jim said, "I should never have told you I needed to work out where I go next, should I?"

She gave a soft bark and said, "You were already here."

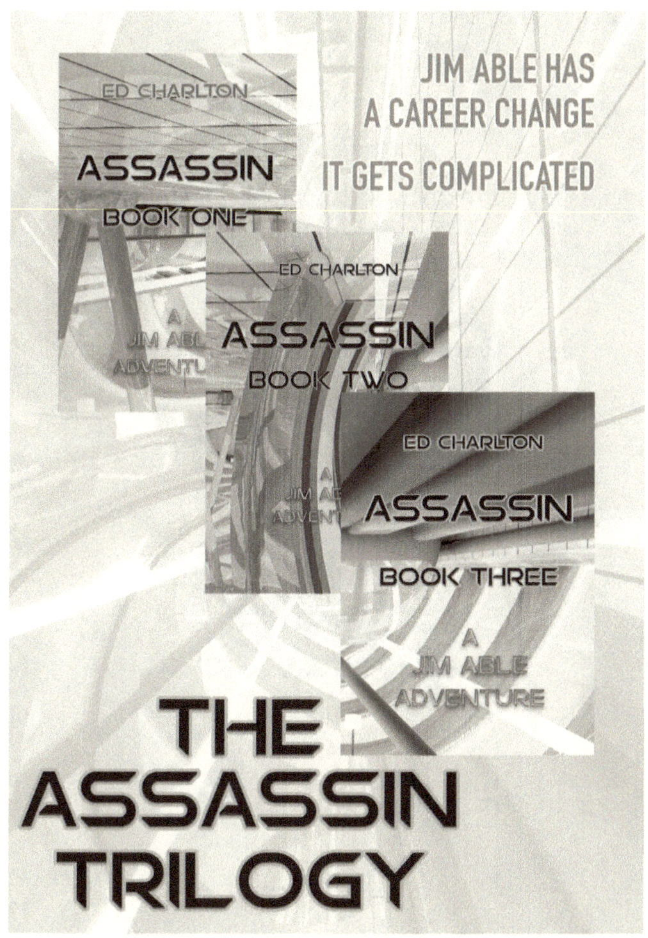

More tales of quirky aliens, flawed humans, and heroes who work in outer space. Jim Able takes action against the hidden schemes of criminals, governments, and interplanetary corporations.

Book One

Jim's Target: Jack Katrigg, the courier who destroyed Ch'Garratt Spaceport Terminal Two with Jim in it.

Can Jim find an ethical solution to the problem of justice denied?

Book Two

Jim's Target: The power couple who have caused so many of Jim's problems.

Is learning the truth more important than life or death?

Book Three

Jim's Target: Is it the Praestans Rapax monk, Daum Robertus Graffen, or his entire organization?

Welcome to the network.

Available at edcharlton.com

In *Aleronde the Great*, the significance of Uncle Teddy's memoir and the Ambulatory are revealed, and one small act of kindness unleashes trouble of galactic proportions.

The Aleronde Trilogy at edcharlton.com

How to murder someone on a space station

and get away with it

Hoyle Station is a murder mystery with a cast of thousands, some of them human.

And there are many questions. How has a member of Earth's Historical
Guild so completely vanished? Are the Recorders who run the business of
the station as helpful as they seem? Who are the aliens watching from the
dark of space?

Hoyle Station